Scoring

THE

PLAYER

CAMPUS *Wallflowers*

BOOK THREE

REBECCA JENSHAK

This one is for the sporty girls.

Chapter
ONE

Dahlia

"T HESE SHOES WERE A BAD IDEA," I SHOUT OVER the music as Jane, Violet, and I push our way through a crowd of people in the backyard of the off-campus house party.

I nearly twist an ankle when someone knocks into me and throws off my balance on these four-inch heels. Then someone else bangs into me from the other side, steadying me somewhat but also making me feel like I'm in a human pinball machine.

It's the first week of a new school year, and the parties have been amazing. It's only Wednesday night and I've lost track of how many different off-campus houses and frats we've been to this week.

Jane comes to a stop on one side of the yard and turns her head to look at me and Vi, excitement sparkling in her eyes. "I had no idea there'd be so many people here tonight. The football guys know how to throw a party."

She's right. It seems like the entire student body is here. It isn't a huge house or outdoor space, which makes it feel even more crowded.

"Have you seen him?" Violet asks, while she cranes her neck to look around the party.

"Who?" I'm careful not to meet her gaze. "Your boyfriend?"

"No. Gavin is coming later. He had a basketball thing." When I give in and look at her, she arches a dark brow and tips her chin so that her long, black hair falls over one shoulder. "You know who."

I do know, but I stay quiet anyway.

"Felix Walters," she says pointedly, amidst my silence. "The cute QB who is totally crushing on you."

My own laugh catches me off guard because her words are so ludicrous. "He does not have a crush on me."

Felix Walters is the most popular jock on campus. He's the face of the university's nationally-ranked football team, rumored to definitely be going to the NFL, and he hooks up with only the most beautiful girls. A lot of them.

"I think Vi's right," Jane says. "He always makes a point to come talk to you when we see him out. Sunday night at The Hideout and then again at the hockey guys' apartment, Monday night at Phi Kappa Theta, Tuesday at Sigma."

My face is on fire. He's so far out of my league that even thinking about talking to Felix makes me hot and sweaty. I've never had a boyfriend. I've dated so infrequently; I can count them all on one hand. I'm not the kind of girl guys clamor to be with. Let alone guys like Felix. I'm too shy. Too awkward. Too average. I'm not at all like the girls he dates.

Instead of responding to their ridiculous claim that Felix has a crush on me (ha!), I focus on the party and finding Daisy. She left before us to meet up with her boyfriend Jordan. I finally spot them across the yard, hanging with a group of guys, hockey players, I think. I don't spend a lot of time scoping out the people in their circle.

Jane and Violet are the outgoing half of our foursome. Jane is enthusiastic and fun at every turn. So fun that she often convinces me to live outside my comfort zone. The four-inch heels, for example. And Violet is confident and stunning, and so head-over-heels in love with her boyfriend Gavin that she wants everyone to be as happy as she is.

I love them, but right now, I need a dose of reality that I know Daisy will provide. Felix is not into me. He's a nice guy, that's all. But still, my skin is buzzing with adrenaline at the thought.

Earlier tonight, the four of us (Jane, Violet, Daisy, and I) wrote wishes for the new school year on paper and then burned them. When Jane suggested we 'put our desires out into the universe,' I thought it was kind of silly. But as I held the paper in one hand and the lighter in the other, I felt a flutter of something. Nerves mixed with anticipation and…hope.

I've made lots of wishes in my twenty years—on birthday candles, shooting stars, fallen eyelashes, fountains, wishbones, dandelions, pennies, and on clocks that read 11:11. I don't remember all the things I've wished for, but I know the big things have never come true.

I'm still me. Dahlia Brady, shy and awkward, destined to never have a boyfriend.

There are worse things, I know. And it isn't that I hate who I am or anything. I am a great friend. I'm athletic and kind, and am generally optimistic and happy.

It's just that being shy and awkward makes it hard to do things like date, or even talk to guys. I like my life, but I'd also like to make out with a hot boy (or many hot boys) on the regular.

"I see Daisy," I say, nodding my head in her direction and then taking off that way.

Relief washes over me as we get a foot away from our friend. A smile spreads across her face and she opens her stance to greet us.

Only, when she does, I get a good look at one of the guys standing with her. *Felix.*

I avoid staring directly at him, while I hug Daisy. Jordan says hello and the group quiets as the circle opens to let us join.

My skin pricks and I know Felix is looking at me. It's always like this. I don't know what it is about him, but I'm extra awkward around him. We aren't exactly friends, but Felix is friends with Daisy and Violet's jock boyfriends, so we seem to keep running into each other.

Summoning every ounce of courage possible, I glance up. His eyes are a gray blue that is a stark contrast to his jet black hair. He's tall enough that, even in these heels, he still towers over me, and his chest is broad, biceps straining against the white T-shirt.

Here's the thing about Felix. He's *suuuper* hot. No question about that. But it isn't just that he's a hot guy that throws me so off balance when he's nearby. He remembers things, asks me personal questions, gives me the type of attention that most guys, hot or not, don't really give me. I like his voice and the way he smiles at me like he's happy I'm around. And I admire that he's this successful football player with big dreams but still likes to kick back and have a good time.

He's definitely not trying to get me naked, but he likes me well enough to carry a conversation (usually a one-sided one). It's unnerving.

He isn't the first guy to do this, though. It's part of my curse, I'm afraid. Guys that can get past my whole shy and awkwardness, want to be my friend. I'm sporty and safe, and they get a sense right away that I'm not about the drama. Because I'm not.

Here's the thing about all guys. They say they don't like

drama, but in the end, they always choose the girls that are all about the drama.

"Hey, Dahlia." Felix's deep voice wraps me up in a warm caress. "I'm glad you came."

I open my mouth to reply. My lips form the word, but no sound comes out. I manage a small wave with an inaudible "hi," which only makes my face flame hotter.

I tend to have two responses to uncomfortable situations: I freeze or I blurt out something embarrassing. I guess all things considered, freezing is the less horrifying option. If I told him all the things I'm thinking, I'd never be able to show my face again.

He smiles at me, despite my awkward silence. "Did you just get here?"

My chin dips in a nod.

"Do you need a drink?" he asks. His dark gaze does a slow sweep over my tank and shorts that show a lot of leg, and finally down to the very tall heels I'm precariously balancing on. When I still don't respond, he looks to Jane and Vi, extending his drink invitation. "We've got beer, seltzer, and there was still some vodka and Wild Turkey last time I checked."

"She'll have a White Claw. Black cherry, if you have it. It's her favorite," Jane answers for me, and the way her voice emphasizes every word makes me wish the ground would swallow me up.

"All right. And you two?" He flicks his gaze quickly to my friends.

"Same," Vi adds.

Jane nods.

"You got it." Felix backs away from the group, still pointing that panty-melting smile at me. He returns before I can even relax without his presence. He hands a can to Violet and Jane then to me. The tips of his fingers brush against mine during the hand-off and I nearly drop the can.

"Oops. Fumble." I laugh at my own joke. Then cringe. Felix's smile just gets bigger.

I let out a shaky breath as he takes a half step away from me. He's still too close. The seltzer can is cold, and if he weren't watching, I'd love to press it to the back of my neck. It's the closest thing to a cold shower available right now.

"Oh, I love this song," Jane says as the music changes. She starts to move to the beat.

"Let's dance," I suggest.

"Really?" she asks, surprise clear on her face. I'm not usually one for hitting the dance floor this early in the night, but I'm all about putting some distance between me and the hottie QB.

"Really." I try to communicate with my eyes that I need to get the hell out of here.

One side of her mouth quirks up like she's totally onto me, but she agrees and then so does Violet. Daisy doesn't look like she's going to budge from her spot nuzzled up next to Jordan.

"Come dance with us. One dance?" Jane asks her and sticks out her bottom lip.

Daisy and Violet are both in serious relationships, which means we've seen a lot less of them lately. Last year, we attended all the first week parties together. This year, it's mostly been me and Jane going to the parties together and hanging out with our friends and their boyfriends. Things are different, but one look at how happy they both are stops me from feeling too melancholy for old times.

The four of us head to the middle of the yard, where a small group of mostly girls are dancing. I pull my long hair over one shoulder and then do exactly what I wanted to do a few minutes ago—press the cold can to the back of my neck.

Daisy leans closer to me so I can hear her. "You look amazing. New shoes? I could have sworn you were wearing white sneakers when I left."

"They're Jane's," I reply.

"Ah." She nods her understanding. Jane's closet is like nothing I've ever seen before. Even as a fashion designer, I can say with zero hesitation that her wardrobe is a dream. Top designers mixed with cheaper fun pieces. She has a great eye, and everything looks good on her. I appreciate all types of fashion, but I'm more casual—shorts, skirts, tanks, t-shirts, and sneakers.

We dance long enough that my body relaxes, and I mostly forget about Felix being here. I finish the seltzer at the same time that Jane says she needs to find the bathroom.

Daisy heads back to Jordan and Vi disappears to find Gavin, who texted that he was here. I go with Jane.

"Dahlia!" My name is yelled in a chorus of voices. It takes me a second to find the source. Some of my golf teammates are waving at me from where they're congregated next to the keg.

"I should go say hi."

Jane gives me a pleading look. "I really gotta pee."

"Go. I'll catch up with you."

She nods and hurries inside in search of the bathroom, while I start back across the yard to say hello to my teammates. Before I get to them, I spot Felix. I don't mean to. I always just seem to find him in a crowd. Like my brain is searching for him even when I don't realize it.

He's standing with Bethany. His ex-girlfriend. She's universally acknowledged as the hottest girl on campus. Long legs that go for miles, shiny blonde hair, and these big, brown eyes. They look great together.

They dated last year, before I ever met him, but I've stalked his social media enough to see the pictures of them together. She's beautiful. One of those girls that never has a bad hair day. I had a lit class with her one semester. She showed up to every single class dressed like she was ready for paparazzi to take photos of her. I admire her dedication to looking flawless.

Felix and Bethany are in my direct path to get to my teammates. I either have to walk by them or circle around. I'm seriously considering the latter, but I decide to suck it up. *This year is going to be different.* That was my wish for the year. I want to stop waiting for life to happen and put myself out there more. I figured asking the universe for a boyfriend was a little cliché.

When I'm a foot away, Felix looks up and directly at me. I freeze, like I've been caught doing something terrible, instead of existing and breathing the same air as him. He seems surprised at first and then a slow smile spreads across his face. Bethany notices his attention has drifted from her, and she whips her head around to see why.

Her pretty glossy lips pull into a scowl when she finds him looking at me. I wave and try to keep moving, but the crowd is making it difficult. A group of guys, definitely drunk, start pushing and shoving each other. I think it's friendly fighting, but I have to quickly sidestep to avoid being stepped on.

Felix moves in front of me and claps the guy, who almost squished me, on the shoulder. "Watch where you're going, Brogan."

Brogan turns and a lazy smile tugs at the corners of his mouth. "Sorry about that."

"It's okay."

Felix crosses his arms over his impressive chest. "It's not okay. You could have hurt Dahlia."

"It's fine. Really," I say at the same time Bethany says, "What am I, invisible?"

"He wasn't even close to you, Bethany," Felix clips and his features harden. "Besides, you were just leaving."

"Whatever." She spins on her heel, making her blonde hair flip around her shoulders like she's practiced that move a million times.

His expression softens again when Bethany is gone. "Did you lose your friends?"

"No, I saw some of my teammates and thought I'd go say

hello." My voice shakes as I speak. I point in the general direction I last saw them. "I should have just texted."

He chuckles. "Want me to clear a path?"

"No. I'm okay. Thank you."

Someone yells his name. His gaze moves from me long enough to jut his chin in acknowledgment to the person, but then his attention is back, focused solely on me. "Are you sure? I don't mind."

I think about my wish, about how this year is going to be different. Maybe it already is. After all, I just spoke to Felix Walters. Go me. Baby steps.

"No, really. I'm good. Thanks." I duck my head and continue around him.

It takes a few minutes, but I finally push my way through the party crowd. My teammates started drinking early and are so beyond drunk that it's hard to even talk to them. I promise them I'll go out with them tomorrow night and then I fight the crowd back toward the house to find Jane.

I'm curious about the inside of this off-campus house. Felix lives here with some of his teammates. The house is small, or maybe it just seems that way with so many people crammed inside it. There aren't a lot of personal details. It looks like your average college digs.

At the dining room table, people are playing cards. In the living room, there are guys playing video games and girls standing around stealing glances at the guys while chatting.

I find Jane still in line for the bathroom. I lean against the wall next to her. The girls behind us glare at me for cutting.

"I'm not in line," I tell them and give them my back.

"I would kill for your hair," Jane says as she runs a hand over my blonde waves.

"I will happily trade you." I lift the strands off my neck again. My hair is thick and heavy. I let it grow long because the shorter it is, the more it looks like a giant mushroom on top of my head.

Jane's hair is a shade lighter than mine, but thinner and straight. She added a few extensions tonight to make it longer and the effect is stunning.

Across the hall from where we're standing is a bedroom. The door is open, but the room is dark, and I can't make out enough of it to decide if it's Felix's room.

"You're all flushed." Jane's stare gets more scrutinizing. "Did you meet a cute boy?"

"No. I just ran into Felix again."

"Oh yeah?" Her eyes sparkle as she smiles.

"It was nothing," I say, and then tell her exactly what happened.

"He looks especially good tonight," she says. "He really pulls off jeans and a white tee."

Heat climbs up my neck.

"What? You don't think so?" She elbows me lightly.

"No, of course I do. He's…" I search for words, "indescribably hot."

A big smile takes over her face. "And totally into you. I was standing next to you batting my lashes and he never even noticed. Can you imagine? Not noticing all this." She waves a hand down her body.

"The nerve," I say, meaning it. Jane and Bethany have the always-looking-amazing thing in common. But the thought of Felix hitting on Jane makes my stomach twist.

"You should go back out there and ask him to give you a tour of his bedroom."

"No way. I always freeze up around him."

Her head bobs in agreement. "Good point. We better get you a couple shots first."

Laughing lightly, I shake my head. "There is not enough alcohol in the world."

"Why not? You're gorgeous—inside and out. He would be so lucky to make out with you."

"Make out with Felix Walters?" A frantic giggle escapes. "Felix is in a completely different league. He makes genuinely hot girls look meh by comparison. Those arms and that hair." I sigh.

She laughs again and it eggs me on.

"He just looks at me and I start sweating and my mind goes blank. He's stupid hot. As in he makes me totally stupid. I lose brain cells every time he speaks to me. I would probably die of sensory overload if he kissed me. Or if I saw him shirtless. Forget about it." I groan. "I'd like to lick every inch of his body and climb him like a freaking tree. Of course, I'd have to duct tape his mouth because when he says my name, 'Dahlia,'" I mimic his deep voice, and then fan my face, "I'm two seconds away from orgasming."

Jane bursts into hysterical laughter and I join her because it's a funny thought. Me and Felix Walters? No freaking way.

Chapter
TWO

Felix

THE CLANG OF METAL FIRST THING IN THE MORNING IS usually the perfect way to wake up, but I grimace as someone drops a barbell across the room and the heavy thud echoes in the gym.

"You look rough." Teddy gives me a once-over with one brow arched.

"Feel rougher."

"What happened to taking it easy last night?" He sits on the bench and wipes his sweaty forehead with the hem of his T-shirt.

We had a big party at our place and while the goal was to have a good time, I had not planned on getting shitfaced. We're gearing up for the start of the season and it could be a very big year for us. We have five returning seniors and we're all hungry to win a national championship.

"Bethany happened," I say, and Teddy's mouth forms an "o."

Theo Radford, aka Teddy. My best friend, teammate, and

roommate. He's about the nicest guy I've ever known. Loyal and hardworking, an absolute beast on the field. He only has one flaw—he's dating my sister. But I try not to think about it too much, keeps me from wanting to hit him.

Teddy lies back, and I help him unrack the bar, then spot him as he benches the heavy weight. The way he's throwing up the iron today, he obviously didn't drink as much as I did last night.

Only when he's done and sits back up, does he ask, "What's the evil ex-girlfriend up to now?"

A small chuckle escapes my lips. Not because the situation with Bethany is funny—it most definitely is not—but hearing Teddy talk smack about anyone is so out of character for him that it catches me off guard.

"She tried to corner me last night. She misses me, blah blah."

"It's been how long? Girl is persistent."

It's been six months since we broke up. The worst part is, she doesn't even want me back. Not really. She wants to say she's my girlfriend, but she doesn't actually want *me*. "It's all bullshit. She's hooking up with Armstrong. I walked in on them last night. In my damn bed."

"Fuuuuck." Teddy stands, and together, we adjust the weight on the barbell. "Seriously?"

I nod, and then take a seat on the bench. "She's hell-bent on pissing me off."

And she knows using my teammates is the easiest way to do that. I don't know what I ever saw in her. No, that's a lie. I saw what she wanted me to see—a gorgeous girl who told me I was awesome and wanted to hook up with me. It was only after my dumb ass fell in love with her that I realized she was full of shit.

"What did you do when you walked in on them?" my buddy asks.

"Nothing." I wish I could say I was shocked, but nothing Bethany does surprises me at this point. "She wants to get a rise out of me. The worst thing I can do is let her know it's working."

"So instead, you got trashed and then slept in the freshman's sex sheets?" He shudders.

"Definitely not. I slept on the couch." I roll my neck to work out a kink. That lumpy couch is only slightly more comfortable than sleeping on the floor.

Laughter across the room catches our attention and we both glance in that direction in time to see Armstrong, all smiles, standing on top of a chair dancing to the music pumping through the workout room.

"He seems energetic." Teddy's jaw works back and forth.

I hum my annoyance. Carson Armstrong is a freshman. He's a quarterback, just like me. Second-string, so he still has a lot to prove, but he's a talented kid. Talented, but naïve. Bethany is going to eat him alive.

I make it through the rest of weightlifting without throwing up and my headache has lessened. I shower and get dressed for class, but before I head out to breakfast, I corner Carson in the locker room.

"Hey." I step closer to give us some semblance of privacy. Even so, guys are glancing our way. Bethany made sure that everyone saw her hooking up with my backup last night, and they're all waiting to see how I'm going to react.

"Walters," he says in his thick southern accent. His green eyes flick to me and then quickly dart away. "Some party last night, huh?"

"Yeah, it sure was."

He chances another look at me and I catch the hint of nervousness before he can mask it.

"What time's your first class?" I ask him, leaning casually against the locker next to his.

"Uhh." His brows furrow. He was expecting me to go off on him, and now he doesn't know what I want. "Nine. Why?"

"Good. That'll give you time to wash my bedding."

He swallows, Adam's apple bobbing, but his lips twist into a smirk. "I'm sorry, man. She pulled me in there. I was drunk…"

"Bethany's real convincing when she wants something," I say. It's the only hint of understanding I'll give him. Whether it was her idea or not, he knew it was shitty to fuck on my bed. And he might be new, but he knows the history between Bethany and me. Everyone does.

I push off the locker. "I expect my sheets to be cleaned and bed remade by lunch. And if you fucking pull something like that again, with me or any of the guys on the team, you'll wish you stayed in Alabama."

I leave without waiting for a response. A good breakfast, and maybe a twenty-minute power nap between morning and afternoon classes, and I'll be good as new by practice.

In the cafeteria, I grab a tray and get in line for food. It's busy in here today. First week of classes and people are still getting up early enough to have breakfast, instead of waking up five minutes before class and downing a granola bar on the way. That isn't an option I have with football, but I've noticed a routine over the years.

I get more than a few looks from groups of girls while I load up my plate. Being the face of the team gets me attention from chicks, that's nothing new, but there's something in their glances today that has me on edge. I shake it off and head to my usual table.

Teddy and Lucas are already here. These guys are my closest friends. The three of us have been at Valley together since we were freshmen. If Teddy is the nice, quiet one, then Lucas is his polar opposite. Lucas Moore is loud and goofy. His mom is a stand-up comedian and his dad is a car salesman. And yes, there is a joke in there somewhere, but I'm too tired at the moment to find it.

I take a seat and twist open the top of my Gatorade. After a long gulp, I set the drink down and meet their gazes.

"What's up?" I ask. They're looking at me weird too. "Do I have something on my face?"

A giggle behind me makes me turn. A curvy brunette waves her fingers around a can of Diet Coke.

I nod and force a smile, then start to turn, but before I do, she mutters, "I'd like to climb you like a tree, too."

"That was weird," I say. I have a sudden fear that I did something stupid last night that I don't remember. I do a quick replay of the night as I remember it, but nothing jumps to mind.

"You haven't seen it?" Lucas asks me, then turns to Teddy. "He hasn't seen it? How have you not seen it?"

"Seen what?" I ask.

Brogan Six, a sophomore wide receiver, drops onto the seat next to me. A deep chuckle rumbles in his chest as he gives me a side glance. "Walters, my man, you are a legend."

His buddy, Archer Holland, sits across from him and Brogan makes sure to give him enough of his face, so he can read the words. Archer is a tight end, also a sophomore. He's deaf, lost his hearing when he was a kid. He wears hearing aids and he can read lips really, scarily well. Thanks to him, the entire football team knows how to sign a lot of really inappropriate things. He and Brogan are always together. The latter is a cocky, troublemaking shit, but he's good at making sure Archer doesn't feel left out of any conversation when the rest of us forget to be as considerate as he is.

"Tell me something I don't know," I mumble, then I pause and say it more carefully for Archer. While I'm repeating it, I realize I can't remember the last time Brogan gave me a compliment. "Wait. I know I'm a god among men, but why are you suddenly a prophet?"

One of his brows quirks up.

"He hasn't seen it," Lucas tells him.

"What the fuck is going on?" My gaze bounces around the table. Seriously, we were all just together fifteen minutes ago. What could I have possibly missed in that time that is this important?

It's silent for far too long.

"You are all over social media this morning," Teddy says with a smile that's more like a grimace.

"I left my phone at the house." Coach has a strict no-phone rule in all practices, workouts, and meetings. "What is it?" I ask, scanning the room again and noting that a lot of people are looking my way now. *What the hell did I do?*

Lucas unlocks his phone and then taps on the screen a couple of times before turning it toward me. I don't know what I expected, but it wasn't to see Dahlia on the screen.

I take the phone from him, watching as the video begins. She's standing with her friend Jane in our house, wearing the white tank, cutoff jean shorts, and sexy heels she had on last night. She's holding her thick blonde hair in one hand and fanning her face. Fuck she's pretty.

"*Felix is in a completely different league. He makes genuinely hot girls look meh by comparison. Those arms and that hair.*" She laughs—a sound I've never heard out of her, but instantly want to hear again. "*He just looks at me and I start sweating and my mind goes blank. He's stupid hot. As in he makes me totally stupid. I lose brain cells every time he speaks to me. I would probably die of sensory overload if he kissed me. Or if I saw him shirtless. Forget about it. I'd like to lick every inch of his body and climb him like a freaking tree.*"

At first, I'm flattered. I met Dahlia last year through a buddy, Gavin. Dahlia is his girlfriend's roommate. She seems cool, but every time I try to talk to her, she shuts down, and barely says two words to me. She's shy, I know that. My sister, Holly, is a lot like that.

But after she sprinted away from me last night, I was finally prepared to accept that her disinterest in me isn't because she's shy. So it's a welcome surprise to hear that I was wrong and she is into me. But the longer I watch and the more she goes on and on, I realize that she has no idea she's being recorded.

"Who posted this?" I ask. My stomach twists with anger. Not for me. I don't give a shit what people post about me. For Dahlia.

"No clue," Lucas says. "It's been reshared so many times it's hard to tell where it started."

"Fucking Bethany." I slam my fist on the table.

"You think?" Teddy asks. "Between fighting with you and screwing Armstrong on your bed, when would she have had the time?"

"And why?" Lucas adds. "It isn't like you're hooking up with this chick and she's jealous or some shit."

They're good questions that I don't have answers to, but it still reeks of something my manipulative ex would do.

"I think it's awesome." Archer smirks. "She's hot. If you're not gonna let her climb you, then mind if I text her?"

I think my blood actually starts to boil under my skin. I like Archer and that's the only reason I don't tell him to fuck right the hell off. Or sign it, because it's one of the few signs he taught us that I've perfected.

"Ooooh shit." Teddy chuckles. "You're poking the bear, Holland."

"Wait." Brogan swipes Lucas's phone from me. "Now I recognize this girl. She's the one you were talking to last night."

Saying that we were talking might be a stretch. More like I was trying to ditch Bethany, so I could finally speak to Dahlia alone without her friends, and she was trying to flee as fast as she could.

"The one you almost trampled, you mean?"

"I didn't see her. Besides, you were all too happy to swoop in and save the day." He takes a bite of food. "I have never seen a chick run from you so fast. Which makes this video extra curious. Did you screw it up before or after she said she wanted to lick every inch of your torso?"

I grunt.

Brogan keeps on grinning at me.

Chapter
THREE

Dahlia

> *Unknown Number: Hey, Dahl. It's Eddie Dillon.*
>
> *Unknown Number: Penelope gave me your number. Hope you don't mind me texting you. Hit me back. I want to talk to you about some designs for the tour. X*

I STARE AT THE TEXT AS MY BUSINESS COMMUNICATION professor begins the lecture. I can't properly freak out that a rockstar just texted me and asked if we could chat about me designing something for him because I have a nagging feeling that people are watching me. Also, it's possible that it's a prank. I'm certainly the butt of many jokes today, thanks to the video of me talking about Felix.

I want to lay my head down on the desk and disappear.

The video didn't out me by name, probably because they didn't know it, but it'll only be a matter of time before someone reveals my identity. What's worse: going viral and no one on campus being able to identify me *or* the things I said in that video?

I wish I could blame it on the alcohol, but I was still perfectly sober when I went on and on (and on and on) about Felix.

Pushing my humiliation aside for the moment, I focus on Eddie's text. He's a musician I met while designing a dress for pop star Penelope Hart. Saying that sentence still gives me butterflies. It sounds so surreal. It was a school project. We came up with designs and then she picked her favorite (mine, eeeep!). All of that was crazy enough, but I got to go see her in concert this summer. She was so sweet. Even brought me backstage after the show, which is where I met Eddie. He was opening for her. When he asked if I'd ever consider doing menswear, I thought he was kidding. If this isn't a prank, it could be a huge break for me.

When class is over, I still haven't figured out how to respond to his text. I slide out of my seat in the back of the giant lecture hall quickly, so I can get out of here before anyone sees me. I was lucky this morning, managing to get across campus without anyone noticing me. Or as lucky as a girl who had her most intimate and embarrassing thoughts shared on social media can be.

Two years I've walked this campus practically invisible, while wishing someone would notice me, and today, the first week of junior year, I'm wishing for some of that freshman and sophomore-level invisibility.

I'm the first one from class out in the hallway, but other classes in the building let out at the same time and the sight of so many people around me makes me instinctively drop my head and shuffle toward the front doors. I have an hour break until my next class, and I have every intention of hightailing it back to the house and hiding until then.

As I'm trying to escape without being seen, I think I hear someone call my name. Oh god. Did they finally figure out who the girl is rambling on for five minutes about how she wants to climb Felix Walters? Freaking hell, what was I thinking?

Most people take the stairs—we're only on the third floor, but I make a last-minute decision to take the elevator to avoid the crowd of people already moving up and down between floors.

I hit the down button and the doors open immediately. As the metal doors close me in, I breathe a sigh of relief.

Very short-lived relief. A hand shoots between the doors with only a few inches of space, and long, strong fingers push the doors apart. I gasp when I spot Felix.

"Hey," he says softly.

My face immediately heats, and I squeak my surprise at running into him. I swear I must have done something really awful in a past life. I take back all my other wishes. All I want is to rewind last night and erase everything I said about the guy standing in front of me.

"Can we talk?" he asks, not coming any closer.

"Umm..." I glance around, nod, and then step out of the elevator.

Standing before him, my gaze drops to his arms, which are hanging at his sides, hands clenched. He's wound tight. The space between us suddenly feels way too small. I take one step to my right.

"I saw the video," he says.

"You and half of campus," I mutter. Who am I kidding? I'm sure everyone on campus has seen it by now. Probably even the professors.

He says something, but there's a ringing in my ears as humiliation washes over me all over again. I hear the words from the video replaying in my head and now knowing he's heard them too... groan.

"I'm sorry," I say, not quite meeting his eyes.

He inches closer. He's always doing that when we talk—moving closer like he wants to make sure he catches every word. "Why are you sorry?"

I flick my gaze up to his face, which now hovers above me,

only inches away. His dark hair is covered by a black hat that's pulled low over his eyes. Eyes that look more gray today than blue.

His backpack is slung over one shoulder and long fingers wrap around the strap. Felix has really nice hands. They're athlete hands, strong and calloused. More than once, I've thought about what it'd feel like to have those hands on me. Which, in turn, always makes me a little lightheaded. But it's not just me that fantasizes about Felix, going by how many times that video has been shared. He's every girl's fantasy.

A flash, and the distinct sound of someone taking a picture, draws me back to our surroundings. Great. I can't wait to see what they say next. *Desperate Girl Stalks QB*. I mean, he walked up to me. I was planning on avoiding him until the end of time, but no one would believe that now after that stupid, stupid video.

He shields me from a girl quite clearly taking photos of us with her phone. He must have hit the button for the elevator too, because it opens and he puts a hand at the center of my back to guide me inside. I'm sure he means it to be comforting, but it sends about a million jolts of electricity up my spine. His palm is warm, and his fingers stretch out, spanning almost my entire back. It isn't the exact scenario I had in mind, since there's a layer of cotton between his hand and my skin. On instinct, I stiffen, and he removes his hand in a flash, and even though my brain was seconds from short-circuiting, I miss his touch instantly.

I hurry into the elevator and hide in the corner, out of sight from the girl trying to photograph us. Felix steps in with me. Someone calls to hold the elevator, but he ignores them and hits the close door button repeatedly until it shuts us inside. Alone.

"Where to?" he asks.

"First floor."

Once we're moving, he angles his body to face me. "I'm gonna go out on a limb and assume you didn't post that video?"

"Me?" My voice is a screech. "Of course not. I didn't even know I was being recorded."

"I didn't think so." He mutters something else under his breath that I can't make out. "Are you okay?"

"I'm…fine." I'm obviously not fine. "Nothing hair dye and transferring to another school won't fix."

"Most likely it'll blow over by lunch."

"Yeah, probably so." I don't believe that—I'm not that lucky—but I hold on to his words with hope anyway.

The elevator stops and I position myself for a hasty exit. I was only half-kidding about dying my hair. I always wanted to try red.

I tap my thumb against my thigh, equal parts anxious to get away from Felix and nervous about what awaits me as I trek across campus. Except the doors don't open. The lights flicker and the elevator dings, but nothing else happens.

Felix hits the open-door button. When that doesn't work, he tries pressing the two, to take us back up. Nothing. "I think we're stuck."

"No," I say, then proceed to push every button in rapid-fire succession. "No, this isn't happening."

I am a good person. My karma can't be this bad. The alarm goes off and I jump back. Felix's hand returns to my lower back. I jump again when a voice booms from the speaker. "Valley Emergency Services. What's your emergency?"

Felix's voice is calm and steady as he responds. "We're stuck in an elevator in Monroe Hall."

"How many people are in the elevator?"

"Two." His gaze flits over to me.

"Is everyone okay?" the voice asks through the speaker.

Felix nods. "Yeah. We're good."

We are so *not* good. He might be, but I'm living my worst nightmare. I'm stuck in a confined space with a guy that knows I have a mega crush on him. Seriously, this day cannot get any worse. I feel like I want to cry or scream, maybe both.

Felix continues to talk with the emergency responder,

providing details like what floor we were on and if the doors opened at all. I happily let him do the talking.

We're assured help is on the way and they'll be here in the next thirty minutes.

Thirty minutes?! I'm not sure I can make it thirty more seconds.

"Well, shit," Felix says finally. He sets his backpack on the floor and then slides to sit beside it.

The full weight of the situation hits me, and I drop down to the floor across from him. We're as far apart as we can get in the small space, but it's still way too close.

"We're stuck in an elevator." I bring my knees up and rest my hands on top of them, tapping my thumbs in an erratic rhythm. I'm not sure if it's adrenaline or nerves, but my arms and legs feel tingly. "Me and you. Me and Felix Walters."

"That's me," he says in a playful tone.

"People will probably say I planned this. Because you know, I'm such a psycho stalker and all."

"Well, you haven't tried to climb me like a tree yet, so…" He cocks his head to the side. I know he's teasing, but I still want to die as he repeats my words from the video.

I cover my face with my hands.

"Ah shit, I'm sorry. That was a bad joke." His voice is closer, and I can feel him next to me, even though I don't look up.

My throat is thick with emotion. Tears prick my eyes and then I start to laugh. It's quiet at first, but I've officially reached hysteria levels of stress, and soon, it's one of those awful laughs where you alternate between no noise coming out and loud, awful outbursts that you can't control.

Between gulping for air, I glance up and look directly at Felix. He's even closer, still facing me, now only a foot away. I can see that it's been a day or two since he's shaved. Dark stubble dots his jaw.

I look away from him again. It's the only way I can get out the apology I owe him. "I'm sorry I said all those things. I got carried away. I'd just run into you and, for the millionth time, couldn't say anything because that's what happens when I try to speak to guys. I totally freeze up. Even worse around you because, well, you're hot." The words tumble out and I wave a hand in front of him. "Really, really hot. Not that you need me to tell you that. Girls line up to date you or hook up, or just stare at you. I saw a girl swipe one of those posters of you hanging up around campus. The one where you're staring out all intensely from your helmet with dirt and black paint on your face. She probably has it hung up over her bed. That's where I'd put it." Falling asleep lying under Felix Walters? Yeah, that might be worth a potential theft charge.

"I hope I didn't make things too weird for you or like objectify you. Who am I kidding? Of course, I objectified you. I stand by the stupid-hot comment, but you also seem like a pretty decent guy." I finally take a breath. "The point is I know that you don't see me like that and it's fine. So, if you came here to let me down easy or whatever, you don't need to worry."

I meet his steel-colored eyes and find it even harder to form words. Also, he doesn't look worried. He looks amused. Probably because I'm word vomiting all over him, and I can't seem to stop.

"It's actually pretty funny. Me and you." I point between us. "You're the hottest guy on campus and I've never had a boyfriend."

Both of his brows lift. Oops. Didn't mean to share that little tidbit. Not like he's ever going to want to date me anyway.

"I'm sorry. I'm going to stop talking now."

And continue to pray for the ground to swallow me up.

Chapter
FOUR

Felix

"**Y**ou think I came here because I'm pissed about what you said on the video?" I ask, staring at her small form hunched over, hugging her legs.

"Umm…yes." After her outburst, Dahlia looks like she's going to retreat back into the quiet girl who hardly speaks to me. And I want to hear more. So much more.

"No. I'm not pissed. Not at you, anyway."

She continues to look at me, confusion marring her face.

"I'm pissed at the person who took and posted that video. It was a shitty thing to do."

"Yeah, they're on my shitlist for sure." Her posture loosens and her hands drop to her lap. "You're really not mad about the things I said about you? It was…"

"Flattering?"

"Not the word I had in mind. Did you actually watch the

video? All of it? The part where I said I wanted to lick every inch of your torso?" Her face is bright red as she finishes the sentence.

Nodding, I can't help but smile. She really has no idea how much I dig her.

"And you tracked me down, just to make sure *I'm* okay? The girl who said she wanted to climb you like a tree." Her face scrunches up adorably. "Not my classiest moment."

"You could have said I was ugly, and you'd rather ride a cactus than me, and I'd still have been hanging on your every word. It's the most I've ever heard you talk. Until now. You have a nice voice."

She holds my stare, a slight smile on her lips. She has really nice lips. Her top lip is as full as her bottom one and makes a perfect heart shape.

I'm still just staring at her, trying to figure out how to proceed in a way that doesn't scare her off, when the emergency responders announce their presence.

Dahlia and I both scramble to our feet. It's only a minute or two until they have the doors open and are helping us out. It all feels very anticlimactic as we exit the building. The break between classes is long over and very few people are walking around campus.

"Do you have a class you need to get to?" I ask, squinting in the sunlight.

"Not until ten," she says. "I was going to go home and hide until then."

"I'm really sorry. Let me walk you." I should head straight to my econ class, but I'm already late, so there's no use in hurrying now. Besides, this way if anyone so much as smiles in her direction, I can kick their ass. I need to find Bethany later. The damage is done, but at the very least, I want her to know this is the worst possible way to get my attention and win me back.

Even if I wanted to get back with Bethany, which I absolutely don't, I'm not into this petty shit.

"You don't need to keep apologizing." Dahlia lifts her shoulder in a small shrug, but then comes to a stop in the middle of the sidewalk. Her voice lowers as she continues, "I wanted this year to be different and I guess it is. I should have been more specific in my wish."

"Wish?"

She blushes and looks away. "Last night before we went out, my roommates and I did this thing where you write down a wish on a piece of paper and then light it on fire. Burning it is supposed to represent giving it to the universe, or something like that. Obviously, the universe has a sense of humor."

"And you wished for this year to be different? Different how?"

She's quiet for a few beats. A breeze blows her long hair into her face. "I wanted to go to parties and not feel awkward, talk to guys without freezing up, be wild and spontaneous and all the other things everyone else seems to do without any problem. I don't expect you to understand."

I do understand, or at least I'm trying to. She's pretty and sweet. She's a talented designer. I know because she won some design competition last year. And I've met her friends. They all seem fun and nice, so all signs point to her being a cool chick.

She seems so different from the girls I usually date. Or mess around with, since I have zero interest in anything beyond hooking up. Not since Bethany and not until after graduation. Football is my focus this year. It's my final chance to prove my worth to NFL teams, and I'm not screwing it up. I've worked too damn hard. Still, I find myself wanting to know more about Dahlia and to spend more time with her.

"Are you going to The White House tonight?" I ask, looking for a safe topic and, okay, yeah, an excuse to see her again.

"I was planning on it, but I don't think that's such a good idea anymore."

"You should go. Don't let a few jerks stop you from doing what you want. And I'll be there. We can hang. No one will say anything. I promise." I might need to enforce some sort of gag clause on my teammates. They wouldn't mean to be assholes (or most of them wouldn't anyway), but tearing each other down is ninety-percent of our daily conversations.

"Thanks, but I don't think so." She lifts one hand in a small wave and then leaves me staring at her back as she walks away. Well, shit. Fuck me very much, I think she just blew me off.

When I get home from practice, I go straight to the fridge for a beer. The day did not improve after I saw Dahlia. Classes were boring and practice was brutal. This week, Coach has us divided up into groups, working with the assistant coaches on role-specific drills. Which means I had to spend two hours with Armstrong. I can't see him without thinking of Bethany, and well…two hours later, I'm ready to drink.

"Grab me one of those," Lucas calls as he steps into the living room, pulling on a clean T-shirt. He has to duck under the archway that leads from his bedroom to the main living and dining area.

It's a small, older house with low ceilings, small closets, and a smell in the kitchen that none of us have been able to identify. It wasn't designed for three big dudes, but it's close to campus and only a block away from the practice field. We've been living here together since sophomore year.

I toss him a cold one at the same time Teddy comes from the opposite side of the house, my sister trailing behind him.

"You look like crap," Holly says as we all move into the living room.

"Aww, thanks, little sis." My tone is dry as I ruffle her hair and plop down onto the couch with my beer.

"I'm sorry."

It's such a Holly response. I have two sisters, Holly and Stella.

They're twins, two years younger than me, and their favorite pastime is ganging up on me. Holly is shy, quiet, and considerate. She doesn't have a mean bone in her body. Stella is her opposite. Instead of apologizing, she'd be piling on if she were here.

"I heard about the video." She makes a face. "A girl in class tried to show it to me. Like I want to hear some chick say how much she wants to get with my brother."

Dahlia's not just some chick, but I don't correct Holly.

Lucas, on the other hand, is happy to spill all the details. Including my many failed attempts to talk to her.

Holly leans forward, taking in every word. When he's finished, she turns to me with a shit-eating grin. "Wait, let me see the video again. I didn't realize this was *the* Dahlia. The infamous girl who runs away from you. She's practically a legend in my book."

I shoot Teddy a look. I've never mentioned Dahlia to my sister, which means he has. He's the only one I've confided in over my many failed attempts at talking her up.

My longtime buddy just shrugs. "She was worried there weren't any girls left that didn't find you charming and irresistible." A smile tugs at his lips. "I was happy to correct her."

I flip him off while draining the rest of my beer. Lucas and Holly are huddled up rewatching the video. I squeeze my eyes shut like that is going to drown out Dahlia's words. Normally I'd be fucking delighted to hear anyone talk about me like that, but knowing it's just surface-level has me thinking back to Bethany and all the things she said when we were together.

Holly interrupts before my mind goes too far down that black hole. "I can't watch anymore. If she's as shy as you say she is, then I feel awful for her. I would have died if something like this happened to me before Teddy knew how I felt."

"Are you saying you had conversations like this about me?" Teddy slides a hand onto her thigh. Holly blushes and leans into his touch.

That's my cue to kick Teddy in the shin. He grimaces, but he also doesn't move his hand.

"I wasn't quite that eloquent." Holly motions toward the phone. "But yeah."

My leg bounces. "I talked to her. She's embarrassed, but she's okay."

"She said those words?" Holly doesn't look convinced. I'm not sure I am either, but I don't know what else I'm supposed to do.

"More or less." I shrug. "She doesn't like me, not like you're thinking."

My roommates and sister share a look like they're all in on some joke together. Holly laughs first, then the other two join her.

When she finishes laughing at my expense, my sister says, "She may have said that she doesn't like you to save face, but she absolutely does."

"No, really. I asked her to come out tonight and she blew me off again." Fuck it. I'm ready to party. Standing, I glance at Lucas. "Ready to head to The White House?"

"Already?" He checks the time on his phone. "It's early yet."

When I head for the door, he slowly gets to his feet. "Yeah, all right."

Teddy and Holly stay behind. I already know from talking to Teddy at practice that they're staying in tonight.

"Hey, Felix?" Holly stops me before I can slip out of the house. "I don't know Dahlia, but I'd be willing to bet that the reason she blows you off has more to do with her than you."

"Meaning?"

"If you're really into her, then you're going to have to try harder than you usually do."

Chapter
FIVE

Dahlia

I TAKE MY GIANT BOWL OF POPCORN AND SODA TO THE living room, ready for a night in by myself, but when I see my roommates spread out on the furniture in comfy clothes I pause. "You do not need to stay home just because I am."

"Oh, please, we're not leaving you alone tonight." Violet looks offended that I'd think otherwise. She scoots over to make room for me on the couch between her and Daisy. It's early still, but they should be upstairs, trying on outfits and fixing their hair and makeup. I know the routine. Two to three hours before going out is prime get-ready time.

"I'm fine," I say for what feels like the millionth time today.

"If that's true, then you are way tougher than me," Daisy says. "I would die. A viral video and then getting trapped in an elevator?"

"Same." Vi wraps her arms around my shoulders and squeezes lightly.

"What? No way." Jane is sitting in the chair all curled up

with her feet tucked underneath her legs. "Own it. Felix is HOT. Everyone on campus knows it. Half the female population has already slept with him and the other half wishes they had. You have nothing to be embarrassed about."

"It's true," Vi says. "Most of the comments on the video were agreeing with you."

"And the others were calling me a slut." My stomach sours at the memory. I knew better than to read the comments, but I was in the mood for a little self-harm after my run-in with Felix.

I cannot believe I told him I've never had a boyfriend. He must think I'm totally pathetic. And then he invited me to come hang out with him tonight, like everyone wouldn't be staring at me. No way. If I'm lucky, someone will make a fool of themselves tonight at the party next door and I will become a distant memory.

"I know it will suck, but you should go to the party and show everyone you don't care. That's the fastest way to shut them up." Violet gives me a reassuring smile.

Is that true? If I were sure that would be the end of it, then I might consider it. But I'm doubtful. "I just want to lay low for tonight."

The four of us watch a movie, eat several bags of popcorn, paint our nails, and generally avoid mentioning the loud music and noise next door. The party is picking up by the sound of it. I love that they are willing to drop everything to be there for me, but I don't want my friends to miss out because I'm too chicken to show my face.

"Jordan is on his way over from The White House," Daisy says, and shoots me a nervous look. "He's just stopping by for a bit."

"You guys should go back to the party with him," I say, trying to assure her that I don't care that her boyfriend is coming over. They don't need to tiptoe around me. "I'm just going to crawl into bed anyway. Seriously. I appreciate that you want to make sure I'm okay, but we've been looking forward to this party all week."

It's the easiest drunk walk home compared to the other frats and off-campus jock houses.

"You should come too," Daisy says pointedly. "We said it was going to be the best year ever, remember?"

"A much more optimistic version of me said that."

"Are you sure?" Violet asks. "Gavin will kick out anyone that's shitty to you."

Violet's boyfriend, Gavin, lives next door at The White House, with three other basketball players. Their party tonight will be one of the biggest of the year. They absolutely can't miss it. But the thought of walking around while people stare at me and talk behind my back…I just can't do it.

"I'm positive. Eddie texted me earlier today and I still haven't figured out how to respond, but I need to before I go to bed."

"Ooooh." Vi smiles big. "That's so exciting. Pretty soon, Dahlia Brady is going to be a household name with pop stars and musicians. I think you've found your niche."

"He didn't say he was hiring me, just that he wanted to talk about designs." I read his texts to them word for word. "What do I say back?"

They toss out some ideas, none of which I send. I know I'm overthinking it, but this could be a huge deal. Violet's right. I've found a niche and I don't want to screw it up with my awkwardness. He's handsome and charming and I have no idea how I'll ever be able to work with him and not fumble all over myself. I finally decide on a short reply that hopefully sounds excited but not too eager.

Me: Hey! Good to hear from you. I'd love to chat about designs. What did you have in mind?

"Ahh, this is so exciting." Daisy bumps my shoulder with hers. "Eddie Dillon is texting you! He might be even hotter than Felix."

The front door opens as Daisy is speaking and her boyfriend

steps inside. Followed by Felix. His brows rise at his name. Yep, he definitely heard that. The universe really hates me.

"Not you too," Jordan says, taking the few steps to the couch and dropping a kiss on his girlfriend's lips. We all squeeze together to make room for him, but it isn't really necessary since he pulls her onto his lap. "Everyone at the party is all, 'Felix this and Felix that.' He's batting chicks away with a stick."

"No one is as hot as you," she tells him, and I feel a little pang of jealousy at how easy it is between them. Daisy and I used to be so much alike when it came to guys, quiet and shy, always sitting on the sidelines, wishing they'd come to us or that we were brave enough to approach them. And now she's in this crazy romantic relationship with a guy that none of us ever would have seen her with. Jordan is so into her and it gives me hope, on top of that jealousy, that maybe I'll find a guy who adores me that much someday.

Felix stands awkwardly just inside the door. "Hey. Sorry for dropping in unexpectedly. Jordan mentioned he was coming over and I wanted to see if you'd changed your mind about going to the party."

Everyone turns to stare at me and my face flushes. It was a nice gesture by him, but completely wrecks my never-see-Felix-again plan.

"I'm gonna go get ready." Vi stands quickly.

"Me too." Jane follows.

Jordan and Daisy aren't quite as smooth, but a second later, they're excusing themselves to check on something in Daisy's room upstairs, and I'm alone with Felix.

"Eddie Dillon, huh?"

I don't hate the surprise on Felix's face.

"It's not like that. He maybe wants me to design something for him."

"That's cool." He takes a step farther into the room but doesn't make a move to sit. The genuine smile on his face reminds me how excited he was for me when he found out I was designing for Penelope Hart.

"It might not happen. I've never done…" I trail off as my phone vibrates in my hand. The name flashing across the screen makes me gasp. "Oh my gosh, it's him."

I can't sit still, so I stand. Felix moves closer. "Are you going to answer it?"

"Definitely not. It has to be a butt dial." I didn't expect him to reply tonight. I definitely didn't expect him to video call me! "What kind of rock star is sitting by his phone on a Thursday night? He should be hooking up with girls or still sleeping off last night's hangover."

Eddie doesn't really strike me as that cliché, but he's hot and famous so who knows.

"You should answer it. It isn't a butt dial."

"I'm wearing a T-shirt and my hair is still sweaty from practice." Saying it out loud makes me realize just how much I can't answer, but if I don't, then am I going to lose this opportunity to work with him?

"Help," I plead to Felix. "What do I do?"

"Hit ignore."

I do it without questioning him, then sit back down. Felix takes a seat next to me.

"I just ignored a call from Eddie Dillon." I whisper the words.

Felix's short, gruff laugh is so close. Hottie QB is sitting on my couch and a hot rock star is calling me. What in the world is happening?

"Now what?" I set my phone down on my lap and shake out my hands. "I'm so nervous, my fingers are trembling."

"May I?" He reaches for my phone.

I nod and he picks it up, then taps something out. Before he sends it, he hands it to me for approval.

Me: *I'm at a party and it's too loud to answer. Can I call you tomorrow?*

"Not bad." Some of my nerves relax as I hit send. "Thank you."

When Eddie replies a second later, Felix leans in to read the text and my nerves ramp right back up.

Eddie: *Sounds great. I'm in rehearsals all day, but I'll give you a call as soon as I'm done. Can't wait to work with you.*

"Success," he says, jaw tight and voice a little deeper than it was a minute ago.

"I just lied to a rock star."

"It doesn't have to be a lie. You could still come to the party."

"I can't."

"Sure, you can. Put on some shoes, maybe some deodorant, and we'll walk next door."

"I don't stink," I say, but it was grossly hot out at practice so that might be a lie. "Okay, I might, but I can't go either way."

"Wild and spontaneous, remember?" He lets his body lean against mine for a second. "You can't hide forever. Or maybe you can, but you shouldn't."

"Not forever. Just a week or two."

"No." He shakes his head. "No, I'm sorry, but I can't let you do that."

"Why not?" I arch a brow at him.

"Because I'll be worrying about you and won't be able to properly enjoy myself, and the parties this weekend promise to be next level."

"So, it's about you?"

His playful, cocky smile returns. "Always."

Butterflies flap around in my stomach, and I'm almost tempted. Almost. "I can't."

He considers me for a minute, and I think he's going to continue to protest, but then my roommates are coming back downstairs, and Felix stands to join them by the door. They all say their goodbyes and file out. Disappointment almost has me changing my mind, but the second I think about all the looks and whispers I got on campus today, I stay firmly seated on the couch.

Felix is the last out the door. "If you change your mind, you know where to find me."

"Thanks, Felix."

"You're not going to change your mind. Are you?"

I slowly shake my head. I squeeze my hand around my phone and lift it. "Thanks for your help."

He bites down on his bottom lip and nods. "You're welcome. I'll see you around, Dahlia."

Chapter
SIX

Dahlia

"NICE JOB TODAY. No practice tomorrow while they do some maintenance on the course. See you Monday." Coach Jones drops his hands from his waist and gives us a tight smile. It's his first year at Valley U, so we're all getting to know each other. He's loads better than the last two coaches. I've had a different one every year since I was a freshman. As a result, our team numbers are down.

"Hey, Dahlia," my teammate Harper calls as I head off the practice green. I pause for her to catch up. She's the only other member of the golf team that's stayed through the change in coaching staff. "Emmy and I are having people over to our apartment tonight."

"That sounds fun," I say. "But I promised my roommate Jane that I'd go watch her sing at The Hideout."

Harper's eyes light up. "I've heard she's amazing. Maybe we'll stop by. I'll text you."

"Sounds good." I wave with the hand around my golf bag.

I'm walking past Ray Fieldhouse, the main athletic facility, when I spot the football team. The coach barks orders from the sidelines as they scrimmage. Felix is easy to spot, since he's the only one on the field in the red practice jersey the quarterbacks' wear. He shuffles back, scanning the field, and then sends a beautiful spiral twenty yards away, to who, I have no idea because I can't tear my eyes off him.

It's been two weeks since the viral video. Things around campus have not died down. If anything, it's worse. There are at least a dozen remixed versions of the original video. Oh, and they definitely figured out my name. Desperate Dahlia. Yeah, that's what they're calling me. Most people are nice enough not to say it to my face, but not a day goes by without someone recognizing me around campus. I haven't run into Felix again (small mercies), but Violet said he asked about me at a party last weekend.

I haven't gone out at all. School, practice, home, sleep. That is my existence.

I know, I know. This year was going to be different. Which is why I'm forcing myself to go out tonight. That, and I'd do just about anything for Jane. Even risk public humiliation.

The action stops on the field. Felix bumps wrists with another guy and then walks toward the sideline, where someone hands him a cup of water. I'm still staring and walking at a snail's pace when his gaze turns in my direction. With his helmet covering most of his face, I can't be sure his eyes are on me, but I feel them.

I have regretted not going to the party with him that night only about a million times. Would he really have kept people from saying anything dickish? Would it have been better to face it instead of hide? Maybe that would have been the end of it. I guess I'll never know.

The Hideout is a local restaurant. It's close to campus and has a nice bar area with lots of tables that Valley U students take over on weeknights and weekends. Tonight, Jane is singing with her friend Eric and his band. They do a lot of nineties and early two-thousands covers, even though I know Jane writes original songs. She only sings in public occasionally, when she's filling in for their main lead singer, and never any of her own stuff.

I ride over with Jane, but she goes straight to help set up. Daisy and Violet are meeting us here. It's early, so there's not a lot of people yet. It's mostly families and couples having dinner, a few guys at the bar are watching the various sports playing on the TVs.

After grabbing a soda from the bartender, I claim a table not far from the small stage area. We want to be close enough she can hear us cheering, but not so close that we can't talk over the music.

Violet and Gavin are the first to show up. He orders a pitcher of beer, and Vi and I get an appetizer sampler. By the time Daisy and Jordan arrive, the band has started playing.

"I'm so glad you came out tonight." Daisy leans her head on my shoulder and sways us to the beat of "Crazy" by Gnarls Barkley. "I've missed you."

"Mhmm. I bet it was just terrible without me," I say dryly and glance toward Jordan's hand. It hasn't moved from her thigh since they sat down, and they kiss every few minutes.

She smiles. "Not terrible, but I did miss you."

"Same." And I did miss hanging out with them. Even being the fifth wheel isn't so bad. I like both Jordan and Gavin, and I'm getting more comfortable around them. When Jordan first started coming over to our house, I couldn't talk to him. Sadly, my ability to talk to guys isn't that much better when I'm not interested in them. Though it's certainly not as bad as trying to talk to someone like Felix, who makes me feel…everything.

By the time Jane takes her first break, The Hideout is packed like I expected it would be.

"You were incredible," Violet tells her as Jane slumps into a seat at the end of our table.

She gulps down an entire glass of water before speaking. Her blonde hair is pulled up into a tight, high ponytail that makes all her sharp, angular features look amazing. "Thank you. Any more water? I'm dying. I should have hydrated better today."

"Jane!" Eric motions for her to come over to where he's standing next to their bassist.

She looks longingly toward her empty glass.

"I'll get it. Go be a rock star." I shoo her away and then stand to head for the bar.

"Thank you, groupie." She kisses the air and turns on her very high, very expensive Jimmy Choo heels.

I momentarily forgot what a feat it'll be to get to the bar now that more people are crammed into the space. Good thing I love her.

I push through the crowd to the far side of the bar. It's quieter and darker and there's an open spot just big enough that I can slide up to the front.

"Another Dr. Pepper?" The bartender looks up at me as he pours a row of shots.

I shake my head and then lean forward so he can hear me over the crowd. "Water, please."

He nods and continues pouring his shots. I stand back to wait.

Then I notice a guy sitting at the bar a couple seats down is staring at me, I fidget and keep my gaze down, but it's too late.

"Hey." He juts his chin toward me. I want to ignore him, but then he waves his hand and makes it impossible to do so, without looking like I'm purposely snubbing him. Plus, the people between us are now looking at me too.

I glance up and smile timidly. He's cute. Nice smile, light brown hair that has that whole styled-but-slightly-messy look. I can't tell if he's a Valley U student. He looks like he's right at that graduate student age.

"Hi." My voice wavers slightly, but I'm proud of myself for getting any sound out. Go me. I'm out of the house and I'm talking to a cute guy. Next up: world domination.

His handsome smile turns sly, and he glides his tongue over his bottom lip in what I think is supposed to be a seductive move, but I'm instantly grossed out. "I'm no Felix Walters, but I'd have sex with you."

People nearby snicker. My whole body warms and I'm frozen in place. For a few seconds, I forgot about that stupid video, but this is exactly why I've avoided going out. Stupid guys who think I'm easy because of what I said to my friend in a private conversation (or what I thought was private). I want to run away, but I can't make my legs work. The back of my eyes sting with the threat of tears. I cannot let this asshat see me cry.

Before I can force my stupid frozen body to turn away, another voice cuts through the laughter and chatter around us. "Hey, asshole. That's my girlfriend you're making a pass at, and trust me, you'd be so lucky."

Felix steps so he's in front of me, partially blocking me from the guy still smirking in my direction. A gray T-shirt stretches across his broad back, and he smells like soap and mint.

"Sorry, man. I didn't know you two were a thing." The guy clearly woke up today with a death wish because he cocks his head to the side and adds, "Can't blame me for trying. I love a desperate chick. They're the most giving in bed. Guess I don't need to tell you."

Felix lunges, and on instinct, I reach out and grab his bicep to stop him. Heat radiates off him. The muscles in his arms flex as he tightens his hands into fists.

My touch distracts him enough that he pauses and glances down to where my fingers are wrapped around his warm skin.

"Here's that water," the bartender says and sets the glass down in front of me. He eyes Felix and then the mouthy guy carefully, like he's trying to communicate with his stern gaze to calm down or take it outside.

The idiot that was mouthing off is already standing and walking away. Maybe he doesn't have a death wish after all.

"I should kick his ass," Felix grumbles, watching the guy disappear into the crowd with his beer.

"No, you shouldn't." I finally peel my hand off of him. "He's not worth getting kicked out."

"It would absolutely be worth it." He finally faces me and slowly takes me in. A slow perusal that starts at my lips and scans my basic white tank and Levi cut-off jean shorts then finally settles on the Jordans on my feet.

"Nice shoes." His lips quirk up into a smile. All traces of the anger radiating off him a second ago are gone.

"Thank you." I click my heels together. Because of-freaking-course I do. I lift the glass. "And thanks for saving me back there. You didn't need to do that, but I appreciate it."

"Anyone gives you any trouble, just tell them you're my girlfriend."

A slightly psychotic sounding laugh slips from my lips. Yeah, sure, that's what I'll do. I lift the glass of water in my hand. "I need to get this to Jane."

"I'm gonna grab a beer," he says. "Maybe I'll see you later."

With a stiff smile, I turn and head back to the table.

"Was that Felix I saw you talking to?" Jane asks as soon as I hand her the glass.

"Yes." My face still feels warm. "He walked up right as some guy propositioned me."

"Oh, honey, no. Where is he?" Jane stands to her full height and cranes her neck like she's going to be able to pick him out without any identifying details. She's already tall, but her shoes add a few inches, making her close to six feet. She's not as muscular as Felix, but she's scary when she wants to be. And right now, she wants to be.

"He probably left," I say, so she'll relax. "Felix was five seconds from kicking his ass, and I doubt anyone here's dumb enough to fight him with the rest of the football team here to have Felix's back."

I spot his teammates easy enough, in direct eyeline from my seat, sitting at a table behind us. They're big, loud, and the majority of them wear some sort of clothing that identifies them as members of the team—shirts, hats, sweats. College guys have it so easy. Wake up, toss on a hat, some clean-ish jeans, and a T-shirt, and they're good to go. I'm not gonna lie though, I'm not any more immune to the messy, sporty look than the rest of my peers.

Jane heads back to the microphone and the band starts back up. The Hideout gets more and more packed. It's standing-room only, which makes me super thankful we snagged a table.

The later it gets, the handsier the couples get. Jordan is telling a story about how his mom almost walked in on him and Daisy having sex in the kitchen of his parents' house over the summer. Daisy covers her face, but Jordan leans in and pries her hands away so he can kiss her. "Nothing to be embarrassed about, sweet Daisy. Everyone knows I'm irresistible."

A familiar pang of longing for that kind of intimacy and understanding hits me. Jordan brings Daisy out of her shell in a way no one ever has, without even trying. She trusts him enough to be herself. And to have sex in his parents' kitchen, apparently. I'm not adding that to my bucket list, but finding someone that I'd be willing to risk it with definitely is.

I'm laughing along with the others when a shadow falls over

the table. I look up in time to see Felix pull a chair up to the end of the table and take a seat between me and Violet.

"What's up, Walters?" Gavin asks as he extends a hand for Felix to slap.

Felix gives his head a small shake and a few dark strands of hair fall onto his forehead. "Not much. We're heading out soon. Early morning conditioning tomorrow. Thought I'd come say hey first."

He isn't even talking to me, and my throat goes dry.

The band finishes a song and I focus way too hard on clapping for Jane. She smiles back at me with a devilish glint when she spots Felix.

"This one is for the coolest, hottest chick I know. She'd kill me if I said her name up here in front of a busy bar, but if you know her, then you know it's true. Love you, babe." Jane leans into the mic stand and winks at me before the guitar and drums start in on "Blank Space" by Taylor Swift. I know the song immediately, even before she starts singing. It's our go-to song to blast in the car.

I'm sure I'm blushing at her singling me out, but the bar is too packed for anyone, but the five other people at our table, to realize she's talking about me.

Felix swivels around to listen to Jane as she croons out the first verse, then he turns to me with a playful grin. "She's good."

"She's amazing."

"Why this song? Are you a Swiftie?"

"Who isn't?"

He nods. "True, I guess. Speaking of, how'd things work out with the musician?"

"Eddie?" I ask, as if there are a slew of musicians I'm friendly with.

"Yeah. Did you two talk?"

"We've been playing a lot of phone tag. He's busy on tour."

There's some commotion as his teammates get up to leave. Felix nods his head to them and inches back in his seat.

"My ride's leaving," he says. "I'll catch you guys later."

He says his goodbyes and then Felix lowers his voice so only I can hear. "What are you doing tomorrow night?"

I hesitate. "I'm not sure."

"There's a party at Phi Kappa Theta. Go with me."

"Go *with* you?" I repeat, trying to make sense of his words. "Like a date?"

He chuckles softly. Oh god. Of course, that's not what he meant.

"I don't usually take girls to frat houses on dates, but sure, something like that. A casual hang at a party with half the school."

I'd love to ask where he *does* take girls on dates, but somehow, I'm able to keep the question from blurting out of my mouth. Instead, I ask the more important question. "Why?"

"I like talking to you. I want to do more of it."

I'm speechless, not that that's unusual for me.

Felix must take my hesitation for uncertainty because he continues, "I've been thinking about all those things you said in the elevator."

Groan. The humiliation never ends. He thinks I'm an easy lay now too. I guess I can't blame him. The things I said about him did indicate that I was DTF.

His face twists up. "That sounded super cringey. I didn't mean it like that." He takes a breath. I'm glad this conversation is as painful for him as it is for me. "You're a cool chick. I hate that you've been avoiding parties since that video."

"I'm not avoiding parties."

He cocks a brow.

"Fine. I am. Can you blame me?"

"No, which is why you should say yes. We both get what we want. Let me be your tour guide. If you're with me, people won't be able to say shit."

Now it's my turn to raise a brow.

"And if they do, I'll kick their ass."

A small laugh breaks free.

"Say yes, Dahlia."

Oh god, he said my name. I wonder if he did that on purpose? It doesn't matter. Of course, I want to say yes. Only an idiot would turn down Felix Walters and I should know because this idiot turned him down the last time he invited me out.

"Yes." It comes out in a breathy whisper. This is a terrible idea, but I can't wait.

Chapter
SEVEN

Felix

THE NEXT NIGHT I'M STANDING AROUND THE KEG outside of Phi Kappa Theta with Lucas, Brogan, and Archer. My friends are well on their way to being wasted and it's only ten. This morning's conditioning and then practice this afternoon has us all happy for the week's end. We have tomorrow morning off and we're ready to kick back.

I, however, am completely sober. Mostly sober. I'm three beers in. I don't want to be drunk when Dahlia gets here, but I'm fucking nervous.

"Yo, Walters?" Brogan says my name louder than necessary and in an amused tone like it's not the first time he's tried to get my attention.

"What's up?" I ask, while taking a sip of my beer (fine, it's number four) and tearing my gaze away from the back door where people continue to step outside to the party.

The guys chuckle. Okay, so I'm a little distracted. Did I

mention I'm nervous? I'm never nervous about hanging out with girls, but it's taken a lot of tries to get Dahlia to agree to go out with me.

"What time is your *date* supposed to be here?" Brogan's lips curve into a smug smile as he asks the question.

"It's not a date," I say, trying to play it cool. Dahlia said she and her friends were planning to get here around thirty minutes ago. I'm feeling all kinds of out of sorts as I wait for her to do just that.

What does it say about my chances with her that I had to basically offer myself up as a friendly bodyguard to get her to agree to spend time with me? I promised to keep people from saying shit, so I'm on edge, wondering who I'm going to have to hit first. I've already had a few people mention the video tonight. They're just joking around, but if Dahlia had heard them, she would have jetted out of here so fast. Why can't they all let it lie? The things she said weren't that shocking. Trust me, chicks have said worse straight to my face.

I take a deep breath. This isn't me. I don't freak out over spending time with a girl. Truth be told, I'm still not positive she'll even show up. And maybe that's partly why I'm such a mess. Though she hasn't texted to cancel, and she doesn't strike me as the kind of person to be a no-show.

"I've never seen you sweat a girl so hard," Lucas says. "You must be really into her."

"Or really wanting to give into some hardcore hero worship fantasy." Brogan's joking, I think, but it annoys me that he and others might be thinking that.

"It's not like that." The truth is I was into Dahlia before I saw that video. Maybe not so into her that I was watching the door for her to show up to every party, and looking for her on campus between every class, but when I did run into her, I was always pumped. Maybe that's not something out of Shakespeare or a Taylor Swift song, but I've never had to try all that hard to hookup.

I don't give them any answers and Archer changes the subject.

"Did you confront Bethany about the video? It had to be her, right?"

"She says she didn't post it."

"And you believe her?" Lucas scoffs. "The girl will say anything to get you back."

"I'm not sure, but it doesn't matter now anyway. It's out there."

"Bethany is straight crazy. Hot, but crazy." Brogan's eyes widen. "And she just walked in with Armstrong. Twelve o'clock. Damn, could that shirt get any smaller? Not that I'm complaining."

I don't want to look, but I do, then grind my back molars. Armstrong's smile is all teeth, arm slung around Bethany's shoulders, gaze locked on her tits. He's dick over cleats and has no idea she's using him. She'll drop him as soon as she realizes that sleeping with my teammate isn't going to get me back. I almost feel sorry for him. Then I remember he had sex with her in my bed.

They stop near a group of freshmen football players playing beer pong on the patio. Bethany turns her head and leans closer to Armstrong to say something. He hangs on her every word, then nods and removes his arm. He joins the guys, and she continues moving into the party, right in my direction. Fuck. I know what comes next. She does it at every party.

Bethany doesn't make eye contact until she's only a step away. Then, her big, brown eyes look up from thick lashes and widen in fake surprise. "Felix, hey."

"Bethany." I give her a tight-lipped smile. I've learned that showing any emotion eggs her on and flat-out ignoring her just makes her try harder to get my attention.

She stops and stands directly in front of me. Her gaze rakes over me and her hand reaches out like she's going to touch my arm. I take a step back.

"You look good tonight," she says, then inches her face closer. "Are you wearing cologne?"

When I don't respond, she says, "Come on, don't be like that."

"Like what? We broke up months ago, and you're sleeping with my teammate. We're nothing. Less than nothing."

"Armstrong? We're just having a little fun. Don't tell me you're jealous? You hook up all the time." There's a bite in her tone as she says the last part.

"I'm not jealous," I say honestly. "It's none of my business. But he's a decent guy. Don't screw with his head to get to me because it won't work, and it just makes you look petty as hell."

As I give her my back, I hear her annoyed huff.

"Damn, she's persistent," Lucas says when she's gone.

"And so, so hot. Why in the world did you ever break up with her?" Brogan stares after her.

Because she was vicious and cruel, and I didn't see it until she was under my skin so deep that she left scars.

Archer elbows him.

"What?" Brogan gives me a sheepish smile. "I know, I know. She's the worst. But wow."

As he says the last word, I turn my attention back to the door. This time, the girl I'm waiting for steps through it. "You're right. Fucking wow."

Chapter
EIGHT

Dahlia

"I DON'T THINK I CAN DO THIS," I say as I pull on the hem of the short spandex dress that rides up with every step I take. "I haven't worn this much makeup since prom my senior year and that night did not end well. Let's just say, I shared a hotel suite with a group of people, and somehow, I'm the one that ended up sleeping in a bed with my crush and best friend while they had sex."

"I thought I was your best friend," Jane says, ignoring the rest of my rambling.

The four of us step out into the party at Phi Kappa Theta. It's early and not crazy packed yet, and somehow that makes me feel more visible.

We're running thirty minutes later than planned because I changed my outfit about a dozen times.

"Why didn't you sleep somewhere else?" Daisy asks me and then Violet adds, "Or tell them to leave?"

"They thought I was asleep when they started making out. Then I felt weird about moving because they'd know I was awake. It was awful." I stick out my tongue at the horrible memory.

Jane clears her throat.

"My former best friend," I clarify for her.

"Much better." Her smile makes the knot in my chest loosen a fraction.

"I'm freaking out."

"We noticed." Vi bites the corner of her lip to keep from grinning too big.

"You look incredible," Daisy tries to reassure me, but it has the opposite effect.

It isn't every day (or any day in the last twenty years of my life) that you get a chance to go to a party and hang out with the hottest guy on campus. I wanted to look the part for this once-in-a-lifetime experience, but now I'm afraid I overdid it. I look like I'm trying too hard. I *am* trying too hard. A Herculean-level effort is the only way I'm going to survive an entire night talking to Felix.

I really hope that this is what it takes to stop all the knowing looks and whispered comments around campus. If it isn't, I don't know what I'll do.

I stop. "What am I going to say to him?"

My friends turn back to look at me. They've been so supportive. Jane and Violet spent hours picking out different dress and shoe options; Daisy helped me do my makeup and curl my hair. And when I thought I was going to puke, seconds before we walked out the door, the three of them lied and said everything was going to be fine. The thing is…I don't feel fine.

"We're not going anywhere." Daisy steps back and takes my hand. "If you need anything, we've got your back."

"Okay." I let out a shaky breath. "But what do I say? I *need* to know what to say."

She laughs lightly. "You'll figure it out."

"But say something," Violet pipes in, taking my other hand. "Rambling is better than silence."

"Are we sure about that?" Jane asks.

"Rambling is what got her this date." Violet adjusts one strap of the bright orange dress. It's some cheap brand that I've never heard of, but it hugs my curves in all the right places. One of Jane's, obviously. The amount of confidence required to buy an orange dress is not something I possess.

"It isn't a date."

"It's kind of a date, though." Daisy pulls me toward the center of the party.

My nerves ramp up as the four of us weave through the backyard, where music pumps and people stand all around in small groups talking and drinking. I spot some of Felix's teammates playing beer pong and I stop breathing while I look for his dark head. When I don't see him, I relax.

"I see Gavin and Jordan." Vi tips her head toward the far right.

"Is Felix with them?" I ask, suddenly afraid to look.

"I don't think so." She stands taller and cranes her neck.

I fidget with my hair, moving it off one shoulder and then pulling it back so I can partially hide my face behind it. I'm not ready to face him. This was such a bad idea. He's going to take one look at how overdressed I am and say—

"Wow." Felix's voice freezes my movements from head to toe. He steps through the crowd, eyes locked on me.

"Dahlia, you look…wow." He clears his throat. "I've forgotten all other adjectives."

My friends break into a chorus of "aww" and then giggles.

"Thank you." There's a one-hundred-percent chance I'm blushing all over. He's in his standard jeans and T-shirt, this one navy blue. The way it stretches across his chest and matches his dark hair is…well, he looks phenomenal. "You too."

"Do you want to get something to drink?" he asks, nodding his head toward the keg.

Daisy nudges me forward.

"Okay," I tell him, and then say to my friends, "I'll see you guys later."

They're all smiling so big and nodding their heads like I'm the kid sister going on her very first date.

Felix walks slowly, allowing me to keep up with him. I notice he doesn't have to push through the crowd the same way others do. When people see him coming, they move. That's the power of Felix Walters.

At the keg, he pours me a beer and then refills his cup. I take a tentative sip. His gaze is on me, which does not help my nerves.

"You really look great," he says. "I kind of feel like I swallowed my tongue."

Even if he's just messing with me to make me feel more comfortable, it works.

"Thank you. I'm sorry we're later than I said."

"Are you?" he asks and takes a drink. "I didn't even notice."

Of course, he didn't. *This isn't a date*, I remind myself. When the keg is kicked, I'll go back to my life, and he'll go back to his. But for the next few hours, I'm going to do my best to stop freaking out and just enjoy this weird yet sort of amazing situation. I'm hanging out with the hottest guy at Valley U.

"Walters!" A guy calls as he emerges from the crowd to stand in front of us. He and Felix both jut their chins to the other. "How've you been? Haven't seen you since..."

"Last weekend," Felix fills in for him. "You were about eight shots in, so I won't take offense that you don't remember talking to me."

The guy huffs a laugh. "You aren't the only part of that night that I don't remember. I woke up with two girls and a guy I'd never seen before."

Felix laughs and then, as if he just remembered I'm standing here, covers it with a cough. "Bobby, have you met Dahlia?" He glances at me. "Bobby and I lived on the same floor freshman year."

I lift a hand and wave. "Hi."

"Hey," he says. "You look familiar. Are you on the cheerleading squad?"

"Umm…no." I shake my head. "I don't think we've met."

"What year are you?" he asks, still staring hard to figure out how he knows me.

"I'm a junior."

"Huh." His gaze continues to assess me as he fills three cups with beer from the keg, and I can tell the second he realizes where he's seen me before. "You're the girl from that video. Oh man, that was hysterical."

His smile is wide and disbelieving.

"That's me. I'm Felix Walters' number one fan. If there weren't so many people around, I'd be climbing him like a tree or licking him from head to toe."

Oh my god, what am I saying? *Shut up, shut up, shut up.*

Bobby chuckles, but nothing about his reaction feels mean or malicious. I've basically put him in the position to laugh or cringe at my weirdness.

"I'm kidding. Consent is important." The more I talk, the more flustered I feel. I should have prepared a standard response for the many times I expect to be recognized tonight.

Felix takes a step closer until his arm rests against mine. It's a small amount of contact, but it does the trick of shutting me up. It isn't exactly reassuring; it's more like a jolt, but I revel in it.

Bobby laughs, taking in our body language. "I love it. I thought it was a joke, but you two are hooking up for real?"

I expect Felix to correct him, but instead, he glances over at me with a smirk that I bet has gotten him laid every single time he's used it. "You saw the video. Who else would she be hooking up with?"

My body tingles from head to toe.

"All right. Well, I gotta deliver these." Bobby lifts the cups filled with beer in his big hands. "See ya around, Walters." Then he nods to me.

Felix stares at him, only long enough to say bye, and then his attention is back on me.

I think this dress is too tight because I'm struggling to breathe. Did I misread him completely? Is Felix expecting me to sleep with him tonight? A large part of me says, hell yes, but there's this tiny, annoying part that doesn't want to be a funny story he tells his friends for years to come. *"This one time at college, a girl told the entire school how much she wanted to have sex with me, so I asked her out and we did it in the bathroom of a frat house. She was spectacular. Best sex of my life."*

All right, that last part is unlikely, but a girl can dream.

Chapter
NINE

Felix

"LISTEN," DAHLIA SAYS, LOOKING AT THE GROUND WITH those big, royal blue eyes lined in black. I've never seen her wear so much makeup. It's all dark and sexy, and it's such a contrast to her sweet and shy personality.

"I need to get something out of the way."

"What's up?" I ask.

She takes an audible breath and then looks me dead in the eye as she says, "I'm not going to sleep with you tonight."

I nearly spit out my beer. Her cheeks turn red.

"Come again?"

"It's just…I know that because of the video, you're probably expecting me to tear off your clothes and make good on all the things I said. So, if you invited me here because of that, then you should know now that isn't going to happen."

"That thing with Bobby, I was just trying to shut him up. I didn't invite you out to have sex with you." I bounce my head from side to side, trying to decide how honest to be with her. Something about her rambling makes me want to open up more than usual. "Okay, I might have been hoping that we'd end the night partially naked, but even if we don't, I still want to hang out with you and get to know you better."

"Why? I'm not that interesting."

"Sure, you are. And for the record, I've been trying to get to know you better since last semester. Long before that video."

"You have?"

"Is that really surprising?"

She nods, biting the corner of her lip. "What do you want to know?"

So many things, but none of my current questions feel appropriate now that she's taken sex off the table for tonight.

"Do you like beer pong?"

"Sure."

"Well, that's not very enthusiastic, so I'll take that as a no. What about cards?"

This time she shakes her head.

"Flip cup?"

"Yes!" she screams, a little too eager and with a whole lot of sarcasm.

Laughing, I motion toward the table where a group is playing. "Let's see what you got."

Brogan glances up as we approach. They're just finishing a game and people are leaving. We step up across from Brogan and Archer as the teams re-form.

"Are you sure you want to be on that side of the table?" Brogan asks her. He points at me. "That guy might be better at throwing a football, but drinking is my specialty."

"That's Brogan," I say as I fill our cups with beer. "Brogan meet Dahlia."

"Heard lots about you," he says.

I lean closer to Dahlia. "He's shit at flip cup. Don't let him psych you out."

"We'll see." Brogan grins.

"Nice to meet you." Her voice is barely audible over the music.

"On three," Archer says, glancing up and down the table. He counts down and then Dahlia and Brogan start us off.

If I expected her to be as hesitant in her flip cup skills as she is in everything else, I was wrong. So wrong. She's slower to drain the cup than Brogan, but she slams the cup down and then flips it lightly with one finger. It lands perfectly. I wasn't expecting it and I'm slow to pick up my own cup. Luckily, Brogan is still struggling. I chug and then flip, getting it on the first try too, just not quite as perfectly as Dahlia.

The guy next to me goes, but I turn to Dahlia, instead of watching him.

"You're pretty good at that."

"Did you expect me to be bad?" Her brows rise.

"Maybe."

"Because I'm a girl?"

"No, because you usually seem so timid."

"I'm good with competition. It gets me out of my head."

Speaking of, the cheers at the end of the table draw our attention and we glance over in time to see Lucas lifting both arms up in victory.

"We won!" I lift my hand up for her to high-five.

With a smile that spreads her pink lips wide, she smacks my hand. Her touch is warm, palm soft. I can't resist closing my fingers around hers to prolong the contact.

Our gazes are locked when Archer says, "Can we trade Brogan for Dahlia?"

"Hey," Brogan scoffs at his buddy.

She pulls away. Her chin drops slightly, letting her hair fall into her face. "The more I drink, the worse I get. And I'm a lightweight. So basically, I have one or two more good games in me and then you'll be kicking my ass."

The table laughs. Everyone except Archer. I repeat what she said and then say to her, "Archer's mostly deaf. He reads lips."

"Oh. I'm sorry." She signs something, hands moving with an efficiency I've only ever seen in Brogan.

Archer's lips curve and he responds. He typically just signs when he and Brogan don't want us to know what they're saying. Fuckers. I'd love to know what he and Dahlia are saying now, but I've only mastered, 'fuck you' and 'eat a dick.'

They continue signing at a rapid pace as all eyes at the table watch them. When Dahlia realizes the attention they've gathered, her chin drops.

"Do I want to know what you two were talking about?" I ask them.

"I asked him if he signs and then I was telling him that my dad is hard of hearing," she says. "He doesn't sign that often, but my mom and I took classes with him when I was in middle school. I'm rusty."

"You did great," Archer says with a wink.

"All right, are we doing this again?" Brogan asks. "I need redemption."

I'm still staring at Dahlia. Every piece of information she gives, I want more.

"Can we join?" Bethany squeezes into the space between me and the next guy at the table. He takes one look at her and is all too happy to make room.

Fucking hell. I don't want to be an asshole to make my point, but I want nothing to do with Bethany. She's bad news. Just standing next to her reminds me what an idiot I was for falling for her.

Wouldn't it be great if you could erase the bite of things said by shitty people, just by acknowledging they're a terrible human? It should cancel it all out, any negative words or actions. But in my experience, it hasn't. I still remember all the awful things she's said and done, and I hate that I can't shake it off as her flaws talking, instead of wondering if maybe she had a point.

"You go across from me, Carson." She turns her head and gives me a totally fake, sweet smile. Then she looks past me to Dahlia. "Hi! I'm Bethany."

"Dahlia." She gives my ex a tight-lipped smile.

"You look, like, really, *really* familiar."

"We had English Lit together last year," Dahlia says.

"No. I don't think that's it." Bethany brings a finger to her chin like she's thinking. I still don't know for sure if she was behind the video or not, but she's trying to make Dahlia uncomfortable and I'm not having it, even if Dahlia has no idea that I used to date Bethany.

"Stop it, Bethany." I regret the words as soon as I say them because Bethany's smile turns smug.

"Oh my gosh," she says. "You're the girl from that video. Now the two of you together makes sense. No offense, but you're not really his type."

Dahlia's face can't hide the way Bethany's words hit.

"Actually, she is exactly my type, which is why I asked her to be my girlfriend earlier tonight."

Dahlia makes a choked, strangled sound and then hides it with a cough. I step closer and take her hand in mine. "Now that that's settled, can we get the game going again? Start at the opposite end this time."

I avoid the stares from my teammates and laser-beam evil eyes from Bethany, and eventually, the attention shifts from us as someone passes around a pitcher to refill our cups. I drop Dahlia's hand to get us both beer, but as soon as we're set, I put my arm around her neck and toy with her hair. I'm not sure why. Because I want to reassure her? Because I want to touch her? Because I want to piss off Bethany? Probably all the above.

I'm successful in at least two of those. Her skin feels so good—soft and warm, and being this close, I can smell her shampoo—something floral. It's enough to make me forget, or at least not care, that Bethany is shooting daggers in our direction.

We play two more games. Dahlia is perfection each time and I'm totally digging seeing her like this. It's not about Bethany at all when I pick her up and spin her around to celebrate three victories in a row. I'm just having a good time seeing her kick Brogan's ass.

She lets out a little squeal and then wraps her arms around my neck. Fuck it feels good to have her body pressed against mine.

Not hooking up. Not hooking up. Not hooking up...tonight.

I stop and slowly lower her to the ground. Her pupils are wide, and her breathing picks up as she slides down my body. I feel better than I have in months.

"Are you two playing the next round or going to make out?" Brogan asks.

It takes me a second to realize he's talking to us.

"What do you want to do?" I ask her.

"I can't chug any more beer," Dahlia says, and her delicate neck tightens as she swallows. Fuck, maybe we are going to make out.

"We're out," I tell them.

"Armstrong and I are out too," Bethany says.

Everyone ignores her.

"Quitting while you're ahead. Smart." Brogan smiles at us. "Nice to meet you, Dahlia. Have fun, you two."

I let Dahlia go ahead of me and flip Brogan off as I follow her. We stop by the keg, where I get another beer, then we run into some more of my teammates and guys I know from classes and partying together. I introduce Dahlia and everyone is great to her, but I can feel her closing off more with each second.

I thought we'd moved past her being shy around me, but I guess that was wishful thinking. I ask her a little about herself, her designs, even freaking Eddie Dillon, and she answers succinctly but doesn't provide any more details than necessary to answer the questions. I'm running out of ideas and this is officially going to end as the worst date ever. Or, fuck, Brogan's in my head. Worst non-date ever.

"Are you okay?" I ask, as I lead her to a quieter spot on the far side of the yard.

"I'm sorry. I know I'm ruining this night. I'm just so nervous. I heard two girls whispering about Felix's new girlfriend. Everyone thinks we're together. I'm so sorry. Rumors spread fast at a party."

"You're not ruining anything." I give in and touch her again, taking her hand and linking our fingers. "And you don't need to be nervous or sorry. Let them think we're together. Who cares?"

"If only it were that easy."

"It's been hours and no one has said anything about the video."

"Except your ex-girlfriend." She meets my gaze.

I guess that answers the question about whether she knew Bethany was my ex.

"Bethany's bullshit is about me. Don't pay her any attention. That's what she wants. She's sleeping with my teammate and trying to make me jealous."

"She wants you back," Dahlia says.

"No. Well, yes, but not because she really wants to be with me. She wants a reaction because it makes her feel like she still has control over me. That's all she wants. To feel like she has the upper hand." I gave into her drama too many times and now I'm paying the price.

"I'm sorry."

"Thank you, but you don't need to apologize for her bullshit."

"I can still be sorry. That must suck."

I smile at her. "I'm not ever going down that road again, so it doesn't matter what she says or does. Don't let her get to you."

"She's pretty."

I follow Dahlia's gaze across the yard to where Bethany is dancing with Armstrong. Sure, she's pretty, but she uses it like a weapon.

"So are you."

One side of her lips pulls higher than the other when she smiles. "You're a terrible flirt."

"I'm a great flirt." I move closer and rest a hand on her hip.

"You know what I meant."

The air between us is charged and maybe I've figured out how to make her more comfortable. Hint: it's with my fingers and mouth.

Keeping one hand at her hip, I bring the other up to her face and push back her hair, so I can see more of her.

"Felix," she whispers.

"Mhmm." I trail my fingers along her cheek.

"I'm not going to have sex with you."

"Not tonight, I know." I step closer, eliminating some of the space between us. "But we can do other things."

Her neck is so long and delicate and she smells so freaking good. I dip my head to press a soft kiss to her skin. She stills, but tips her head slightly, giving me better access.

"No, I mean, I don't know how to do anything. I've never… done it."

Her comment strikes me as odd, but I'm too busy kissing her neck. She tastes so sweet.

"Felix?"

"Yeah, baby?"

"Did you hear me, because it's really embarrassing and I don't want to repeat it if I don't have to, but it doesn't seem like you heard me."

I stand straight to look at her, but keep our bodies close. I repeat her last words. "You've never done it."

Oh fuck.

"Wait. You mean…"

Her face is so red, I know it's true, but I ask anyway. "You're a virgin?"

She squeezes her eyes shut. "Yes, but that's not all."

66

My brain isn't working well enough to figure out what 'that's not all' could possibly mean.

"I've never done anything. I've never even been kissed."

My expression must show my shock because, when she opens her eyes, she immediately hides her face behind her hands. "Oh god, I'm so embarrassed. I just didn't want you to kiss me and then I'd suck at it and the only thing I can think of that would be worse than you not kissing me, is if you kissed me and I was awful at it. I'm not a total moron; I know how to kiss. It's just that I've never done it. And you've kissed lots of people. Not a lot like I'm grossed out about it. Just a normal, college-guy amount."

I let her ramble because I'm still reeling. No knocking virgins—I get that there are all sorts of reasons a person decides to wait to have sex, but I was about to suggest we find a bathroom where I could finger her. And I probably would have scarred her for life. How in the hell has no one kissed her? I'm considering asking her, or maybe just taking her perfect mouth right here.

When she finally stops, she takes a deep breath. "I'm gonna go."

"Wait." I snap out of it as she takes a step away from me. "Don't go."

67

Chapter
TEN

Dahlia

DO YOU KNOW HOW HUMILIATING IT WOULD BE TO DIE from embarrassment?

I feel dangerously close to it as Felix's expression morphs between surprise and horror, then finally sympathy. Gross, sympathy is worse than horror. I don't want his sympathy. I want to go back to thirty seconds ago when he was kissing my neck and pressing his dick against my leg.

"You caught me by surprise," he says with a sheepish grin. "You're so hot."

"So only ugly people can be virgins?" I'm purposely goading him, but wait. Did he just say I was hot?

He makes a noise, something like a groan, deep in his throat, like what I imagine sex with him would sound like. Or maybe I'm still wishing we could go back to making out. Or almost making out. Sadly, I don't think him kissing my neck counts. But wow, it was fun.

"Of course not. But how is it possible that no one has kissed you?" His stare drops to my lips, and I plead (internally, of course) for him to put his mouth on mine.

"It's a long story."

"I've got time."

I glance around, hesitating to say more than I already have.

"Come on. Let's grab a drink first," he says and then takes my hand. This time, it feels way less sexual and more friendly. Ugh. There's a real chance I've been relegated to the friend-zone. I should have kept my stupid mouth shut. Violet was wrong. Rambling is not better than freezing up.

Once he has a beer, he leads me to a couple free chairs on the patio. Bethany and Armstrong walk by, but his ex doesn't even glance at us.

"Maybe she really likes him and just wants to rub it in your face a little. Not that I approve of that scenario either."

"Maybe," he says in a tone that tells me he doesn't believe that to be true. "Either way, it seems like she might have finally got the memo that I'm not interested." He looks at me with that heated gaze from earlier—the one before I told him I'd never kissed anyone. "She thinks I'm taking my new girlfriend home tonight."

I shrug one shoulder as butterflies swoop low in my stomach. I can't even entertain that thought because I will turn to a pile of goo right here. "I don't mind if she thinks that. It isn't like we're friends."

She didn't even remember me from class. I sat five feet away from her for three months.

He nods, then kicks one leg out so it rests against mine. "Tell me your story, Dahlia Brady. How have you never been kissed?"

"Now I kind of wish I had a drink." I run my palms along my thighs.

Felix leans forward and hands me his, then calls to someone nearby and asks for a beer. The guy hands him two cans from a cooler at his feet, without even blinking an eye. Felix opens one and sets the other between his legs.

"First of all, just know I am horrified that I told you all that, but since I did, the only way I can think to make it better is to tell you everything, so you know I'm not some sad girl you need to feel sorry for."

"I don't feel sorry for you," he says, without missing a beat. "I feel sorry for all the guys that fucked it up."

Damn he's good with the one-liners. How much he actually means? No idea.

"All of high school I had this huge crush on a guy in my grade. We were friends and I thought maybe we could be more, but it never happened."

"And nobody else tried to get your attention in all those years?" He shakes his head, disbelieving.

"They did…at first. I even went out with a few of them, but I wasn't into it. I had one of those crushes that you can't see out of, you know?"

"No, not really."

"Surprise, surprise, Felix Walters has never had an unrequited crush," I tease him.

His lips twitch with amusement.

"Well, anyway, the longer I went without dating anyone, the less people were interested. I sort of became this person that people didn't even consider."

"They just knew you'd say no."

"Maybe." I shrug again. "When I got to Valley, I thought it would be different. And at first, it was. I met a guy the second week of freshman year and we went out a few times."

"And he didn't try to kiss you?"

"He did try." I bite my lip. "We went to a party and then back to his house."

He's hanging on my every word.

"I was so nervous. I drank way too much and when he went to kiss me, I puked."

Felix laughs.

"Not on him or anything, I managed to run to the bathroom, but it definitely killed the mood."

"It happens."

"Does it? You've had a girl vomit when you went to kiss her?"

He's holding back a laugh and his blue eyes twinkle. "No, but I'm sure you're not the only one."

I hum my uncertainty. "And another time, I was hanging at this guy's dorm, and we were watching a movie and cuddling, and then he looked at me and I knew it was finally going to happen... until his long-distance girlfriend showed up at his dorm to surprise him."

"Oh shit." Felix covers his mouth with a fist.

"Yeah, I didn't know he had a girlfriend, but that was the end of that." I sigh and then laugh. "I even tried playing spin the bottle last year and the bottle never landed on me. I sat there for *an hour*, watching other people make out. It's a freaking comedy of errors at this point."

"There must be a hundred guys here." He waves the hand holding his open beer toward the party in front of us. "You're a beautiful girl. Any guy here would kill to take you home and kiss you until your lips hurt. Take your pick." His stare drops to my mouth again, but I notice he didn't lump himself into that category.

"Thanks."

"I'm serious. You're hot. I'm not the only one that's noticed, trust me."

He doesn't get it. Of course, he doesn't. He's Felix Walters.

"And yet, no one else has asked me out."

"Well, for the past couple weeks, you've been hiding. And before that, I rarely saw you out."

"Parties are a little intimidating. I'm better in small groups."

"So, then, we should do this again."

"Do what again?" I ask because all we've done is talk for the past couple hours.

"Go out. There's another party tomorrow night. I can introduce you to a bunch more people."

"That's nice of you, but—"

"But nothing, if you want this year to be different, then you have to try different things."

"I know. I do. And I will."

He runs his tongue along his bottom lip as he sits forward. "I have an idea."

All the nerves I felt earlier tonight are back.

"What if we kept hanging out?"

"I would probably fall asleep eventually." I cover a yawn that I've been holding back.

"I don't mean tonight. Tomorrow, the next night, the day after that. People already think you're my girlfriend. We just let them keep thinking that for a couple months."

"I don't understand."

"Think about it. We hang out. I can introduce you to people, and you'll get more comfortable. Plus, almost no one bothered you about the video when they thought we were out together. I'm good for your image."

I roll my eyes playfully. "Conceited much?"

"It's just facts."

It is, dammit. "What do you get out of this scenario?"

"I'm not taking home random girls, for starters. That shit is getting old."

"Your willpower is astounding," I say with a dry chuckle.

"I dig your sarcasm." He takes my hand and intertwines our fingers. My pulse picks up and the air suddenly feels muggy.

My mind reels. Does he realize what he's suggesting?

"Seriously, I could be good for you," he adds. "If people think we're together, the video will be completely forgotten in a week or two, and in the meantime, I'll help you do all the things you wanted to do but haven't yet."

"Help me?" My voice is shaky.

He nods. "Sure. Why not?"

So many reasons. "But we aren't really dating? I'm confused." And I think I'm hyperventilating.

"I think you're great," he says. Internally, I groan. That statement is the kiss of death. "But I'm not looking for anything serious right now."

"How come?"

"My sisters say that Bethany destroyed my *ability to trust women*," he says in a tone that suggests he thinks the phrase is bullshit.

I bite down on my lip to stop from smiling.

He notices and laughs. "It's okay. It's funny. But maybe not totally untrue. I just don't want to deal with the drama my senior year. Especially this semester. A lot is riding on this season."

"So, we pretend to date, but we're really just friends?" But we'd really be hanging out, and that's the part that I can't quite get over. I'd get to spend more time with him. Something I want badly, despite feeling awkward as hell around him.

And I think he might be right about the video losing steam if people think we're together. Somehow people see me as less pathetic for my feelings if Felix reciprocates them.

"Yeah."

No one would buy that. Me and Felix? Except, they did tonight. Even his closest friends.

"And what do you get? Really. Because we both know after I leave tonight, you could still find another girl to take home."

"I would never cheat on my fake girlfriend." He grins. His voice is more sincere when he says, "If it keeps Bethany from sleeping her way through my teammates to try to make me jealous, then that'd be great, too."

"Are you sure it won't make her try that much harder to

get you back?" Last time I saw her, she was making out with Armstrong on the dance floor.

"Trust me. She doesn't want me back. Not really. If she thinks I've moved on, sooner or later, she will too. She'll stop flaunting Armstrong in my face and hopefully find herself a soccer or baseball player to torture."

"Okay, but you could date anyone in this scenario. A girl you actually like."

"I actually like you."

"You know what I mean." I tilt my head to the side. Is he serious? I keep waiting for him to realize what a bad idea this is, but his thumb strokes the top of my knuckles, and he looks at me so eagerly.

"I don't know," I say, finally.

"Say yes, Dahlia."

My body tingles. "No fair using my name. You know what it does to me."

His smile widens. "Say yes, hot stuff."

My brows lift at the endearment.

"You are. That's what I'm going to call you so you don't forget it."

"I am so not."

He hums like I'm proving his point. "A couple months hanging out with me, and you'll see just how right I am. You'll have guys begging to take you out."

I can't even wrap my brain around that scenario, but I nod ever so slightly. "I have a feeling I'm going to regret this."

Chapter
ELEVEN

Felix

"TAKE A KNEE," COACH CALLS AT THE END OF practice.

I drop beside Teddy, catching my breath and wiping sweat from my forehead.

"We looked better today. Still a lot of work to do before our first game next month, but better." He continues detailing every mistake we made over the past two hours.

He isn't the kind of coach that softens the blow either. If you looked slow or tired, he's going to tell you. No, he's going to scream it at you. Some of the younger guys take it to heart, but I let it roll off me. When I screw up, no one is more pissed at me than me.

Today I was on, though. I found a rhythm that's been missing the past few weeks. I feel great, ready to lead my team to a championship season. I have to be. There's no other option. Everything I've ever wanted depends on it.

Maybe it's a stretch to think that my performance on the field is because of the deal Dahlia and I made, but something about the situation has settled me.

The more I've thought about it, the more I'm convinced it's a genius idea. She wants more than I can give her. Even if she won't admit it to herself. But I like hanging out with her and knowing she'll stop hiding because of that stupid video. And, fingers-crossed, Bethany will finally take a fucking hint and move along. I wasn't kidding about needing to focus and keep my head straight for football. This season is make-or-break time. I'll either get drafted at the end of college or this is it. This cannot be it.

There's only one little problem in our fake dating plan. The more time I spend with her, the more I want to kiss her and do a whole bunch of other things that would probably freak her out. I know it's selfish to take what I want when it's not real. She deserves better, which is why I pumped the brakes last night and didn't do something stupid, like suggest I be her first. I like her, but I've *liked* lots of girls. I'm sure it'll pass, and in the meantime, I can do something good for another person. Been awhile since I thought about anyone but myself.

After practice, I head back to the house to shower and get ready for the night. I'm meeting Dahlia at The White House. The basketball guys are having a big party tonight and their parties never disappoint.

Holly and Stella are hanging out in the living room with Teddy and Lucas when I finish getting ready.

"You look nice," Stella says, brows raised.

"Thanks." I drop down on the couch next to her. She's holding her phone out in front of her, and I lean in to look at the screen. "What's up, Ricci? Ready to get your ass handed to you this season?"

He scoffs. "As if."

We both smile as Stella rolls her eyes. My sister and Beau have been dating for almost a year now. He's a football player at Colorado, a rival college. It was a whole thing when they first started dating, but Stella's in love, so I guess I'm stuck with him. Still plan to kick his ass on the field, though.

I move out of the camera and look to Holly and Teddy. "Are you two going to The White House tonight?"

"Definitely," Holly says. "I want to meet your new girlfriend."

"She isn't my—" I start and then stop. It's going to take some time to adjust to my new relationship status. "I'm only introducing you if you promise not to make a big deal out of it. It's new, so it's not that serious. I'm still getting to know her."

All true, but not exactly the story I'm hoping to spin. Yes, I want other people to think that Dahlia and I are together and all about each other, but not my sisters. I know them. They'll get too attached and then be pissed at me for screwing it up. They don't know that I already have my exit strategy in place.

Six weeks. That's enough time for me to introduce Dahlia to everyone I know, take her to a bunch of parties, and get her comfortable with people. That takes us to parents' weekend. Dahlia didn't want to involve our families, which makes sense. Also, it's perfect timing with football. By October, it's an all-out dogfight, leading up to the conference championships. I won't have as much time for parties, and she won't need me anymore.

"What time are you heading over?" Teddy asks me.

"Soon, I guess." I kick Lucas with the toe of my shoe. "Want to come with me?"

"Yeah, sure. Gavin said some of the guys are doing century club."

"Oh no." Teddy groans.

Smiling, I shake my head at Lucas. "Every time you do century club, you do something stupid."

"Stupider than normal," Teddy corrects me. He isn't wrong.

"Like the time you tried to walk home from Phi Kappa Theta." The fraternity is at least five miles away. Luckily, a couple of guys on the team were taking a sober ride home and spotted him sitting on the road 'taking a rest.' He was passed out cold.

"Or the time you pissed yourself." Teddy lifts one brow and grimaces.

Lucas runs a hand along his jaw. "Okay, okay. That was two years ago. I've matured."

Stella laughs. "Earlier today you were watching cartoons and eating cereal out of one of those bowls with a straw."

"*Teen Titans* is awesome. And the bowl was a Christmas present."

"My bad." Stella holds up one hand, the other still gripping her phone. "You're the most mature guy I know."

"Let's not get carried away." Lucas stands and puts his left hand in the right sleeve of his T-shirt and proceeds to make farting noises.

I can't help but laugh as I get to my feet.

I hadn't really planned on partaking in century club, but that's about the only thing going on when we get to The White House. By the time I'm through several beers, the party is really going.

I send Dahlia a text to let her know I'm here and then, holding my phone in one hand in case she texts back, I decide to take a lap.

Jordan stops me as I'm making my way around the yard. I do a shot with him and some hockey guys out celebrating one of their teammates' birthday.

When Dahlia finally texts that she's walking over, I'm feeling good. I meet her on the patio. She's wearing another tight, little dress, this one pink, and a pair of white, platform sneakers that make me smile. Jane is at her side, and I tip my head to her in greeting before I move to stand next to Dahlia.

"I like your shoes."

"Thanks. They're the only part of me tonight that feels like me."

I nod slowly, trying to make sense of her words.

"The dress is Jane's, and Violet and Daisy did my hair and makeup. But the shoes are all me."

I smile at that. "What are you drinking tonight?"

"Oh, uh, just sticking with seltzer probably." She lifts the can in her right hand. Fuck, I must be drunker than I realized because I didn't even notice it.

"I probably should have done the same," I say as we move farther into the yard. "I came early and did century club."

"And you're still standing?" Dahlia's brows lift.

"Unlike you, I can handle my alcohol." I wink at her, and she blushes. "Truthfully, I only made it through about half a century."

"A quitter," she teases.

Jane's gaze pings between us. "Is it okay if I hang with you two for a while? I promise not to crash your whole night, but all my single friends aren't here yet."

"Definitely," Dahlia answers, then looks to me.

"The more hot girls, the merrier."

Dahlia snorts. "That's so sweet."

I really like when she goes all sarcastic on me.

The three of us stand around and drink with the other hundred or so people crammed into the backyard of The White House.

"So, Walters," Jane says, her tone immediately setting me on alert, "Dahlia filled us in about your plan."

Jane is eye level, in a pair of tall-as-fuck shoes, and her gaze is ice as she stares at me, thoroughly unimpressed. I don't know Jane well. She was always with Dahlia when I'd run into them at parties and stuff, but I was so focused on Dahlia that I don't remember a single word we've exchanged.

"Uhh…" I clear my throat. How am I supposed to respond to that? "All right."

"Do you have any hot friends who want to be my Cindy Mancini?" Her eyes crinkle at the corners.

"Cindy Mancini?" I mouth and look between her and Dahlia.

"I tried to pay a guy to date me once. It didn't go over well. I thought it would be very *Can't Buy Me Love*-esque, but he wasn't into it."

"It's an 80s movie," Dahlia fills in for me.

"I guess I missed that one."

"It's a classic. A young Dr. McDreamy pays the head cheerleader to pretend to date him and it makes him like super popular. But then it blows up spectacularly, as it always does. But they fall in love at the end."

I'm either too drunk for the speed at which Jane is talking or she's rambling faster than any human can process.

I look at Dahlia, silently asking, *Is she for real?*

"So, do you?" Jane asks.

"Do I…?"

"Have any hot friends you can hook me up with? Preferably taller than me, a junior or senior, no piercings—I don't trust guys with piercings, long story, don't ask, and he absolutely must know the difference between Taylor in her country era vs Taylor now."

"I can honestly say I don't know anyone that meets that very specific criteria, but I can introduce you to the guys on the team that are here."

"That would be perfect." She beams and looks at me expectantly.

My gaze slides to Dahlia, who's watching with an amused smile.

"She means right now."

"No time like the present," I say with a laugh, and glance around until I find some of the guys.

Lucas and Brogan open their stances to let us into the circle.

"Hey, guys," I say and point at Lucas. "You're still awake. Color me surprised."

He huffs a laugh and then looks to Dahlia and Jane behind me. He's as good of a candidate for Jane as any of my other teammates. I think he had kind of a thing for Stella before she got with

Beau, but otherwise, I've never known him to really be into a chick. He's more a man of opportunity. Of the *get drunk at a party and hook up* breed, so to speak.

Cindy Mancini? Close enough.

I clap him on the shoulder. "This is Dahlia and Jane. Jane was just saying something about that cartoon you like, what's the name?"

His eyes widen with delight as he looks to her. "You're a fan of *Teen Titans?*"

I expect her to lie, but she shakes her head. "No, I've never heard of it before."

"Oh." Lucas's face falls.

"But you can tell me all about it, if you want."

"Definitely." His smile is back, and he drapes an arm around Jane's shoulder and pulls her closer.

"Look at you," Dahlia says, "playing matchmaker."

"She didn't leave me much of a choice."

"She's like that. It's all part of her charm." She smiles. "Actually, she's pretty amazing."

"So are you."

She blushes. "I was thinking…about our arrangement. We probably need to set some guidelines."

"Guidelines?"

"Rules for our relationship. We decided on a timeframe, but what about rules for when we're at parties together?"

"I'm still not following."

She leans in a tad closer. "Are people going to keep believing we're together if we aren't touching or making out?"

Well, that gets my attention. I clear my throat. "Ah. Good point. Yeah, some PDA is probably necessary."

"I would do better with specifics."

"You want to set rules on what PDA is okay?"

"Please."

I blow out a breath and poke the inside of my cheek with my tongue. "All right. Well, uh, how's handholding?"

"Good," she says, smiling. "I'm good with holding hands."

I reach out with my left hand and take hers. "All right and… dancing?"

She nods.

"We should be good then."

"No kissing?"

My gaze drops to her mouth. "Sure."

"Sure to kissing or no kissing?" She licks her lips as her gaze darts to my mouth. "I mean, you've already kissed my neck, so I think that's okay. It can be our signature move. What do you think?"

I step closer, holding her stare, and then drop my head to place a soft kiss just above her collarbone. "Like that?"

"Yes." Her voice trembles.

"Anything else we need to decide?" I ask, lips still hovering over her skin.

"Yes."

Reluctantly, I stand tall and wait for her to continue.

"We need to hang out somewhere other than at parties. That's only one day a week, maybe two at most. That can't be the only time people see us together."

"What did you have in mind?" All my thoughts currently involve her in my bedroom so that's a no-go.

"Maybe lunch or coffee in University Hall a couple times a week."

"Lunch is usually when I work on homework or take a nap."

"Oh." She pulls her bottom lip between her teeth.

"How about breakfast at the Freddy dining hall? I eat there every morning with some of the guys on the team."

Her bottom lip slips free, and she smiles. "Okay."

"Okay? We're good?"

She looks nervous as hell, but nods. "Okay, fake boyfriend. I think I'm ready."

"One sec." I release her hand to get my phone out and then stand beside her as I snap a photo.

"What are you doing?" she asks as I upload it to my IG stories.

"Letting everyone know I'm out with my girl."

"Oh, god. I'm gonna be sick," she says. "Do I look okay in it? Maybe we should take another one in better lighting."

"You look perfect."

"Liar. But thank you."

That makes me chuckle. I pocket my phone and scan the party. I spot my sisters heading our way and the huge grins on their faces make me groan. "I'm sorry for anything that happens in the next thirty seconds," I say, just before Stella and Holly step up in front of us.

"What?" Dahlia asks at the same time Stella says, "Hi, big brother. Are you going to introduce us to your new girl?"

Like I have a choice.

"Hi. I'm Stella. This is Holly. We're Felix's sisters." The more outgoing of my sisters jumps right into the introductions. "You must be Dahlia. We're so excited to finally meet you."

Dahlia stares at them wide-eyed, a hesitant smile that's almost a grimace. "Hi. It's really nice to meet you both."

"We were just about to go inside and play Ring of Fire. You have to come with us."

"Yes!" Lucas calls. "I am so in."

"Stell, she doesn't like cards."

"It's okay," Dahlia says quickly. "I'd love to play."

I watch helplessly as Stella links her arm through Dahlia's and takes her away from me. My sisters and I are close. I love them, but I also don't really want them in the middle of this thing with me and Dahlia. Looks like they're not giving me a choice though.

Stella continues to commandeer Dahlia's attention while we play cards. As annoyed as I am, it gives me chance to sit back and watch her. Like when playing flip cup, she's competitive. Still quiet, but she sits forward, taking everything in. She's never the last person to do something. She's too observant for that. She is, however, terrible at rhyming. Twice she fails at that and has to drink.

It's all fun and games until some douchebag soccer player draws a queen and becomes the Question Master and starts asking people really cringe-worthy and inappropriate questions.

"Okay. I think I need to walk around," Teddy says, standing and waiting for Holly to do the same.

"I'm gonna head out." Stella checks her phone. "I have to be up early tomorrow for swim, and I want to call Beau."

"She means phone sex, right?" Lucas asks.

I groan. "Not something I want to think about."

"Bye, Felix." Stella hugs me, then smiles at Dahlia. "Nice to meet you."

"Yeah, you too."

"Do you have a ride?" I ask Stella. She and Holly live in the dorms, which aren't too far, but she shouldn't be walking by herself this late.

"Uber is pulling up now." She starts for the door. "Bye!"

Everyone disperses quickly after that.

"Sorry about that." I hang back as everyone heads out so I can have a minute with Dahlia.

"It's fine. I had fun. Your sisters seem nice."

"Nice," I try out the word. "Maybe to other people."

The backyard is still packed. We lose Jane and Lucas to the dance floor. I can't tell if they're into each other or not, but they seem to be having a good time.

Dahlia and I stand with Holly and Teddy on the patio next to some guys setting up a new game of beer pong, including the douche from inside. He's loud and obnoxious, and at a party filled with people being loud and obnoxious, that's saying something. I glare at him, but he's not paying attention to me. He's looking at Dahlia in a way I don't like. To be fair, I don't want him looking at her, period, but I know that's some caveman bullshit she doesn't need from the guy she's only pretending to date.

"You're that girl!" The guy elbows his friend. "That's her. I knew it. I've been wracking my brain to figure it out." He mocks Dahlia's voice as he says, "Felix Walters is stupid hot. I want to lick him all over. That was funny shit."

He starts in, repeating things from the video again, in that high-pitched voice that sounds nothing like Dahlia, and she's gone white next to me.

"That's enough." I edge in front of her.

"I'm just having some fun." He careens his neck to try to see past me to Dahlia. "I must have watched it thirty times or more."

"Dude, stop talking," I warn him.

"What are you, her bodyguard now?"

"No, I'm her boyfriend and you're making her uncomfortable."

"Her boyfriend? No shit?" He laughs as he takes a step and I feel Dahlia cower behind me, which snaps something inside me.

I push him backward to put some space between him and Dahlia, and then I get a shot in before he can get his balance.

"Felix," Holly shrieks.

His friends step in before I can land another punch, and Teddy hugs me, turning so he's protecting me with his body. I fight his hold, but he's a strong son of a bitch.

"All right," I say, still struggling to get free.

"You good?" Teddy asks.

No. "Yeah, I'm good."

He loosens his grasp and I shrug away from him. Dahlia stands next to Holly, the two of them watching on wide-eyed.

"Come on, let's get out of here." Teddy takes Holly by the hand, and Dahlia and I follow. We've only made it as far as the kitchen when Gavin runs in behind us. "Is everything all right? I didn't see it, but I heard you just punched a guy out."

My jaw tightens. "He's still walking around. Unfortunately."

Chapter
TWELVE

Dahlia

G AVIN OFFERS UP HIS ROOM IF WE WANT TO HANG OUT a bit while he kicks out the guy Felix got into a fight with, but I just want to go home.

"You'd think people would find something else to talk about, right?" Holly asks quietly as the guys say their goodbyes. "It's so last month's news."

A small laugh manages to bubble up in my chest.

"Seriously. Don't worry about it. That guy was an idiot."

"Thank you."

She steps forward and gives me a tentative hug. I like Felix's sisters. I like them a lot. Stella was fun and made me laugh, but Holly has a reassuring way about her that makes me appreciate her extra right now.

I lost Jane and haven't seen Daisy or Violet in a couple hours. It's still weird being at parties and not glued to their sides. Tonight was fun though. Up until that jerk ruined it.

"Do you want to catch a ride with us?" Teddy asks Felix.

"No. Go ahead. I'm gonna walk Dahlia home."

"It's okay. I think I can manage."

"I'm walking you home," he says, leaving no room to argue.

Outside, Holly and Teddy head in the opposite direction, so it's just me and Felix making the short walk next door.

He's quiet until we get near the front door. "I'm really sorry about tonight."

"It's fine. Nothing I haven't heard before."

"Yeah, but I promised it wouldn't happen when I was around."

The tic of his jaw tells me he's serious. He's blaming himself for that asshole.

"You can't control what other people say or do."

"Like hell I can't," he mutters.

A real smile pulls at the corners of my mouth. He's not used to people sucking. I bet everyone has treated him like a god from the time he could hold a football. "Did you hurt your hand?"

He looks down at it as if he just thought to check it out for himself. He opens and closes his fingers into a fist. "It's fine."

Without thinking, I reach for his hand and take it gently in mine to examine it. His knuckles are red and a little swollen. I run my thumb lightly over his injured knuckles. "Does that hurt?"

"No." His voice is deeper than it was a minute ago. He curls his fingers around mine to stop me from dropping his hand.

"Liar."

"It was worth it." Blue eyes hold mine captive. All night we hung out, but with so many people around, it didn't feel like this. Like I can't breathe. Having all of Felix's attention is a lot to handle.

Summoning all my courage, I whisper, "Do you want to come inside?"

He hesitates, and I panic.

"You should ice your hand. I have an emergency ice pack in the freezer for after those especially brutal practices and workouts."

His lips part. He's still holding my hand, and the reminder sends goosebumps racing up my arm.

He steps forward, gaze locked on my mouth. He leans in slowly, never taking his eyes off my lips.

"Dahlia! Oh my gosh. I just heard." An out of breath Violet comes out of nowhere, jogging toward us.

Felix takes a step back and our hands fall apart.

"I was dancing, and Gavin waited until the song ended to tell me." She takes a deep breath and looks between us, as if she's just realized she might have been interrupting something.

"I should go." Felix puts more distance between us. "Looks like the calvary has arrived."

I start to ask what he's talking about, but then I spot Daisy and Jane walking in our direction.

Violet opens the door and goes inside, calling over her shoulder. "I'll dig out my emergency bottle of black cherry vodka."

Felix shoves his hands in his pockets and disappears down the sidewalk before I can say goodbye.

Daisy glances between us as she gets to the door. "He looks pissed."

"Did he really take on three guys?" Jane asks.

I follow them inside and shut the door. "No. It was just one really jerky guy."

"I'm so sorry I lost you." Jane kicks off her heels. "You and Felix were talking, so I didn't want to keep being the annoying third wheel."

Violet comes back into the living room and the four of us sit on the floor, abandoning the furniture so we can sit closer together. She unscrews the top of the liquor bottle and pours each of us some in small, plastic cups.

"You guys didn't have to leave," I say.

"Of course, we did." Daisy nudges me with her knee. "We love you and we wanted to make sure you were okay."

"I am. Really. That guy was just a jerk." The more people Felix has introduced me to, the more I realize that most don't care. Am I still humiliated? Yes. But I'm done hiding.

"Well, in that case, give us the play-by-play of the fight. I'm liking Felix more and more. Anyone that would throw down for your honor." Violet inches closer. "Gavin banned that dude from ever coming to another party at The White House."

"Wow," I say. I didn't expect that.

"I cannot believe I missed it," Jane says with a shake of her head. "I leave you alone for five minutes."

I fill them in on the night and then the fight, as best as I remember it. It all happened so fast. One second I was wishing the ground would swallow me up and the next Felix was punching the guy. I hate to admit it because I'm generally anti-violence, no matter the situation, but it was amazing to have someone show up for me in that moment. And even more amazing for that someone to be Felix.

Sometime after one in the morning, I finally head upstairs to my room. The window in my room looks out toward the street. Cars still line the road in front of our house and a couple walks by, hand in hand, headed home from the party. The music has quieted, but the party is still going next door.

I stand at the window and watch for a few seconds, suddenly wondering if Felix went home or back to the party. He gave me his number, but I haven't used it yet. I change quickly and then climb into bed, phone in hand.

Me: Are you still up? Also, it's Dahlia.

I delete it before I send and try again.

Me: Thank you for tonight. I had fun. Hope your hand is okay.

89

I close my eyes and squeal as I press send. I immediately want to take it back. It's after one in the morning. Now I seem desperate and like I'm—

I jump when my phone pings with a new text.

Felix: I had fun too. My hand is fine. I wish I'd hit him harder.

Stupid butterflies in my stomach did not get the memo that punching people is bad.

Chapter
THIRTEEN

Dahlia

ALL EYES ARE ON US AS I WALK WITH FELIX THROUGH the dining hall to the football table Monday morning. Freddy dorm is where all the student-athletes live, so the dining hall is filled with jocks from every sport, and admirers who want their attention. I guess I fall into both categories, but I never got this kind of attention when I ate here freshman year.

"Lucas, can you scoot down?" Felix asks as he sets his tray on the table. He motions for me to take his buddy's seat as Lucas moves to make room.

"Thanks," I say and quickly sit with my tray.

"You brought the ringer," Brogan says. He and Archer are seated across from us. "Next time, you're on my team."

He smiles and then tosses a grape in his mouth.

"Hey," Archer says. His voice is quieter than Brogan's. Actually, everything about him is quieter than his friend. He draws less attention to himself, but he's actually really cute. Sharp cheekbones, full lips, and hazel eyes. His hair is long enough that it hides the hearing aids I caught a glimpse of the other night.

"Morning." I try to meet their friendly smiles.

Felix twists the cap off his Gatorade and takes a long drink before he says, "Find your own girl, Six."

Brogan ignores him. "You're on the golf team, right?"

"That's right," I say, surprised he knows.

"Walters mentioned it. He's all, my girlfriend is so hot, and my girlfriend is the best at flip cup, and my girlfriend is a kick-ass golfer." As he speaks, Brogan brings a hand to his chest and mimics Felix but in a high-pitched voice.

I can't help but chuckle. Brogan is this big guy, and his hair flops around and he looks absolutely ridiculous, but he doesn't seem to have a care in the world about who sees or hears him. When I grow up, I want to be Brogan Six.

"Shut the fuck up." Felix tries to laugh it off, but his face is a little red. He glances at me and winks. "All true, though."

"We were curious about you," Lucas pipes up beside me. "Our workout this morning included harassing your boy until he gave up all the details."

Now my face is red.

"Relax, hot stuff." Felix drops a hand to my thigh under the table, and I do the exact opposite of relax. "All good things."

The following week, classes start to get busier. More homework and assignments, plus Eddie and I finally connected and he gave me some concepts and ideas to work with for the look he wants me to create. I don't usually like having others weigh in so much on what I'm creating, but Eddie Dillon isn't a normal client. And if I want to make a career out of working with high-profile musicians, then I think I'm going to have to get used to it.

Felix and I have breakfast with his teammates every morning and text occasionally. The whole thing is beyond bizarre. I'm dating the captain of the Valley U football team. Sure, it's all for show, but suddenly, people know me and not because of the video. Or I guess, not just because of the video.

Thursday, when I get out of golf practice, I have two texts from him.

> *Felix: What are you up to tonight?*

> *Felix: Some of the guys are going to The Hideout around 8. I need my girlfriend.* 😏

> *Me: I can't. I'm stuck in the design lab all night. I have an assignment due tomorrow. Raincheck?*

I stare at the screen until he responds.

> *Felix: Sure.*

I'm disappointed by his one-word response, but since I really do have a lot to do, I put my phone away and get to it.

The design lab is quiet tonight. Violet was here earlier, but she went to meet up with Gavin. I don't mind the quiet. It's just me and another junior design major, Robby. He has in ear pods and hasn't so much as looked at me since the single chin jut I got when he walked in.

I have to create a mood board for class, one that will be the inspiration for a design I'll create in class this semester. I decided to do menswear, since I'm currently obsessed with dressing Eddie. If all goes well, maybe he'll actually wear some of my creations.

My concept is three pieces. Pants, a shirt, and jacket. All with a timeless, casual vibe. My mood board has pieces like Levi jeans, black pants, jean jackets, hoodies, Hanes T-shirts. Nothing you would expect to find in a celebrity's closet, but high-end designers recreate these items time and time again, putting their spin on them and charging more for the higher quality material and craftsmanship. And I combed through all the paparazzi photos I could find of Eddie (a really *terrible* job, let me tell you). His look is all over the map. I think he's still finding his image. But he always seems to go back to the classics.

I also included fabric swatches for the materials I plan to use. A polyester and spandex blend in gray, white cotton, and black faux leather. At first, I thought I wanted to do a faux leather, but now that I have it on the board, it doesn't feel right. It's too obvious. *A rockstar in a leather jacket, really impressive, Dahlia.*

I spend another hour combing through jackets online for inspiration. I settle on a simple green light cotton work jacket with a zipper. It's simple but trendy, and I think with my other pieces, it just might work.

I always struggle with mood boards. They're great in theory, but I do my best designing on the fly. Yes, it results in several throw-away pieces, but there's something about the process that unlocks my most creative ideas.

Satisfied for now, I set my board aside and pull out my laptop. I have three very rough sketches for a pair of pants I want to make for Eddie.

I get to work making the first design. I fall into a rhythm, cutting, pinning, sewing. I forgot to get his measurements, so I guess. The mockup is just to show him the idea. He looked at the illustrations already and approved the concept, and told me to pick whichever I liked best.

I'm finishing up the waistband and am about to add a button when the design lab door opens. It's been hours since I saw or talked to another person and the knock back to the real world startles me.

And the last person I expected to see is standing at the door.

"Felix," I say his name as if my brain is still trying to process that it's really him and I didn't fall asleep at my workstation, and am currently dreaming he's here.

Felix, or maybe Dream Felix, smiles. A half-smile. He does

that a lot. Few things get a full smile out of him. I always smile fully. Happy-looking people get less attention.

"You're really here," he says, as he takes a few more steps into the lab.

"Where else would I be?"

"I thought working at the design lab was code for you dodging me."

"Why would I…?" I start, but he's closer now and his scent hits me. Definitely not a dream.

Chapter
FOURTEEN

Felix

TWO HOURS OF SITTING AT THE HIDEOUT, EATING AND drinking, shooting the shit with my buddies, and I couldn't stop thinking about Dahlia.

When Brogan asked where she was (the fourth person in an hour) it hit me how in such a short time people have gotten used to her being with me when I go out. It's like when I was with Bethany. If I was somewhere without her, people would wonder why. Except in Dahlia's case, I think they're asking because they like her. Nobody really liked Bethany. Maybe to gawk at, but it wasn't the same. My teammates actually like being around Dahlia. I didn't realize how nice it would be to have a girl that fits in with all the other people in my life so well.

And I guess as I sat there with my buddies, I realized how much I wanted her there too.

I screwed up Saturday, hitting that guy and almost kissing her, so I don't expect that she's going to want to go to another party with me without a lot of groveling on my part.

"After Saturday night, I guess I wouldn't blame you for not wanting to go. I'm really sorry." I scan her work. A poster with images and fabrics glued to it, and what I think are a pair of pants lying on the table in front of her. I've never been in this building before. I didn't even know where it was. I had to ask Violet when I stopped by their house. I assumed that's where Dahlia really was.

"I'm not hiding out or avoiding the world. I really had a lot to do."

I nod and lean against one of the black tables that surround the classroom. "I see that."

My stare lands back on the black fabric in front of her. She's resting one hand on the material and standing partially in front of it, like maybe she doesn't want me to see. "What are you working on?"

"Oh, uh." She turns and steps an inch back to give me a better view. "A pair of pants. They're for Eddie. Or, well, it's just a mockup."

"You got the job. That's amazing." Warmth spreads through my chest.

"Thank you." She tucks a strand of hair behind one ear and ducks her head slightly.

"Congrats. I knew you would."

"Well, he's giving me an opportunity. There's no guarantee that he'll wear anything I make."

"He will." I smile at her when she finally looks up timidly. "I know it."

"So, why again did you track me down?"

"I feel bad about Saturday. Let me make it up to you."

"You don't need to feel bad. It wasn't your fault."

"I failed. I don't like failing."

She laughs lightly. "You don't control the whole world."

"Real bummer, I know."

"How do you want to make it up to me?" she asks.

"I heard Sigma is having after hours. I need my girlfriend with me."

She glances down at her cut-off jean shorts and sneakers. Today's shoes are another pair of Jordans—these look older though, a little more worn than the pair she had on that night at The Hideout. "I can't. I'm a mess."

"You look great."

She shoots me a look of disagreement, but I think I have her convinced, until she frowns. "And I really should finish this. I told Eddie I'd send him photos by the weekend."

"It's only ten-thirty, the party won't start for a bit. How much longer until you're done?"

"I don't know. An hour, maybe. I need to do some finishing touches and then beg Robby to try them on for me."

"Robby?"

She looks over her shoulder to a guy sitting at a table on the other side of the room. I hadn't even seen him.

"Well, I could swing back by and pick you up when you're done?"

Dahlia looks at Robby again and then me, chewing on the corner of her lip. "I have another idea."

"Oh no." I hold my hands up. "I don't think that's a good idea."

"Please? You're about Eddie's height and build, and it'll get us out of here quicker."

I hold back a groan, but then she gives me this wide-eyed, hopeful look, and I know I'm going to do it.

"Fine, but we are closing down that party tonight."

"How late is that?" she asks, then shakes her head. "Never mind. It doesn't matter. I'm willing to suffer for my art."

I huff a laugh. "Going to a party with me is suffering?"

"I don't do well without sleep."

"What time is your first class tomorrow?"

"Eight."

"I'll have you home by three."

She groans.

"Two-thirty."

She still doesn't look pleased.

"Two. Final offer."

"Deal." She beams. She points to a partition in the back of the room. "You can change there."

"Never had to do someone a favor to get them to party with me before," I say as I head back there.

"Just lose the jeans. You can keep your shirt on."

Shaking my head, I go behind the short screen and drop my jeans. I can see over it and I watch Dahlia work at her station while I do. She's got this frantic energy about her when she's really into something.

"I think you just wanted an excuse to see me mostly naked," I say, walking back to stand in front of her in just my boxer briefs and T-shirt. I'm comfortable with my body. Years of sharing a locker room with dozens of guys, most with no qualms about walking around totally nude, has made sure of that. But there's an excited thrum coursing through me as her gaze rakes over me.

"I was going to bring you the pants." Her face is red, and she won't meet my eyes as she hands them to me.

I chuckle. "That makes more sense."

Flustered, she's quick to say, "It's no big deal. I've worked with male models before. Be careful. There are still pins at the bottom."

I carefully pull on the pants. She watches my every movement. She's hesitant at first to touch me. Her hands come forward and then she pulls them back. She walks around me to check the fit, I guess. Seconds tick by and she doesn't say anything.

Finally, she brings her fingers to the front of the pants where a button would go. She holds the material together and then runs her other hand down my thigh. Every muscle contracts on reflex and my dick twitches. A hot girl is touching the front of my pants.

She's basically undressing me. Yeah, yeah, I know it's the opposite but tell that to the dirty fantasies flashing through my brain.

"Eddie is a little bigger than you," she says.

"Way to ruin the moment," I mutter under my breath. That killed any movement south.

"I mean taller. What are you, six-two?"

"And a half." That half inch seems super important right now.

"How do they feel?" She's standing so close, fingers still brushing my skin as she holds the material together at my waist.

"Good." I clear my throat. "They feel good."

"Okay, hold still." She leans around me to get something from the desk behind me and her boobs press into my chest as she does.

Aaaand, we're back in business. I wonder how these pants are going to look and feel with an erection. If it were anyone but Dahlia, I'd be convinced she was fucking with me or doing it on purpose. But I know that isn't the case. She's so unassuming, so naive in a lot of ways. The other night she had no idea when people were checking her out or being a little too friendly. I could tell. Usually when a girl notices a guy giving her attention, she alters her behavior. A little more hair touching, more smiling and dainty laughs. But Dahlia didn't do any of that. She has no idea, and that turns me on so freaking much.

I'm in a haze of lust-filled thoughts when she squats down in front of me, her face eye level with my crotch. Jesus fucking Christ.

I wonder if she'll be honored or horrified when my dick is tenting these pants. Before it fully inflates, she works a safety pin through the front of the pants and stands.

"Okay." She smiles at me so innocently. "Walk around in them. I want to see how they look while you move."

"Walk around? Just walk?"

"Sashay, prance, whatever floats your boat, Walters." She crosses her arms over her chest and amusement twinkles in her eyes. "And lift up your T-shirt a little bit. Eddie likes his shirts tighter than the one you're wearing."

"Now I know you're fucking with me." But I do it.

"Good. Walk the length of the room. Eddie uses the entire stage when he performs. He moves around and dances. I need to see what the pants look like in those scenarios."

I do as she asks and start walking slowly away from the table. "You into this guy?"

"Eddie Dillon?" She laughs.

"Just saying, you know an awful lot about him."

"It's my job." She follows behind me, eyes on my ass. "Can you stop there and move in place a little?"

"Uhh…" Still holding the hem of my T-shirt up with one hand, I absently run my other hand through my hair.

Suddenly EDM music starts playing in the room. Robby wears a mischievous grin as he watches along with Dahlia. "Show us what you got, Walters."

"This is not the kind of stuff Eddie Dillon sings. Even I know that."

Robby moves to the beat likes he's up in the club. He struts toward Dahlia and takes her hand. I expect her to hesitate or wave him off, so imagine my surprise when she starts to dance alongside him.

Neither of them are even looking at me for a few seconds as they get into a rhythm dancing together. Dahlia looks up at me first then breaks away from Robby, facing me and silently encouraging me.

"I don't dance," I say.

"Just humor me."

Cursing myself for agreeing to this and not just going to the party by myself, I shuffle side to side.

Dahlia's smile is immediate. "Good. Try some things like jumping, raising your hands over your head, lunging."

"Lunging?"

"I'm going through a mental list of all the things Eddie does on stage."

I lift my hands over my head. Then jump. "He lunges?"

"You know, like this," she says as she holds onto a pretend microphone and lunges forward on one leg, like she's crooning for an audience.

"Oh no, I think it's more like this." I do my own take, adding in a fist pump.

She hasn't stopped dancing and now we're standing close.

"You're not bad."

"It's my secret talent. Eight years of dance class."

"I can picture you in a sexy little leotard."

She rolls her eyes and then does some sort of spin that sends her hair flying around her shoulders.

I close the space between us, and she startles, while nearly colliding with my chest. She hesitates for only a beat before dancing with me the way she did Robby. He's a way better dancer than I am, but it's just the closeness I'm craving.

Her face tilts up and our eyes lock. She holds my stare. Our bodies are millimeters apart. I place a hand at her hip and because I'm greedy, glide my thumb along the band of her shorts and let it slip just under so that I'm touching bare skin. "I have a secret talent too."

"I don't think it's a secret." Her voice is breathy.

It takes everything in me to pull away from her. I give her a playful wink as I force my feet back. "Not that."

"What is it?"

"I'll show you sometime," I say, then raise my hands at my sides. "Did you get what you needed?"

Chapter
FIFTEEN

Dahlia

"THANK YOU SO MUCH FOR DOING THAT," I SAY TO Felix as we step out of the design lab.

"It'll be worth it when I see you cutting it up on the dance floor at Sigma." He glances over and smiles at me. "Why'd you stop dancing?"

"It got too hectic. I was doing golf as well, plus taking AP classes." I shrug. "Are you going to show me your secret talent now?"

He flashes me a wide grin. "In time."

"Fine." I huff dramatically. He holds the outside door open for me and I step out into the night. "Do you mind if we stop by my house first? I want to drop off all my stuff."

"For sure. What are your roommates up to tonight?"

"Daisy and Violet are hanging with their boyfriends and Jane had a bunch of homework."

We're both quiet as we walk across campus and toward the street that runs in front of my house.

When we get to a dark spot, where the streetlights are too far apart to light the sidewalk, Felix finally breaks the silence. "You walk this alone at night?"

"No, not usually," I admit.

"But you planned to tonight?" He raises both brows.

I never plan for it, but sometimes it happens. Driving to campus is a pain. Parking near the design lab is a nightmare, and usually one of the girls is with me, so we have the whole safety in pairs thing going on.

"I would have walked fast and avoided any scary-looking people."

"Oh yeah? That's your safety plan?" His voice still has a concerned edge, but one side of his mouth lifts.

"And don't forget about my sick dance moves. I'd hit 'em with a pirouette or maybe a couple brush kicks."

"I don't know what those are, but I'm doubting their effectiveness."

Me too. Plus, I seriously question whether either of those skills have stuck with me, but I like the response it gets from Felix. It was fun hanging out with him in the design lab. Aside from home and maybe the golf course, it's the place I feel most comfortable. It made me more relaxed around him and now I'm looking forward to going to the party.

"I'll be quick," I say as I hurry up to the front door. "I just need to toss everything in my room and change."

"You don't need to rush," he says as I open the door.

Daisy is sitting in the living room on the couch, Jordan too. Seltzer and beer cans litter the coffee table and they're both holding cards.

"Hey," they say in unison.

When Felix steps in behind me, Jordan stands to greet him.

I walk through the living room to the kitchen. Jane and Violet are doing homework at the table. They both look up as I enter.

Jane smiles, and Vi says, "You worked late. Did you finish your design for Eddie?"

"No, but I got a good start."

Felix steps closer to the kitchen, sort of lingering between the two rooms. "Who's up for after hours at Sigma?"

"Can't tonight," Jordan says. "Daisy has a test in the morning and needs help studying." He gives his girlfriend a wink.

"I'm going to crash early," Violet says. "Classes kicked my butt this week. I'm heading to Gavin's now."

She starts to collect her things and I look to Jane. "Want to come with us?"

"No." A crease forms at the bridge of her nose as she scrunches it. "I'm not up for being the third wheel."

"You know it isn't like that," I fire back.

"Pass." She shakes her head.

"Okay, then." I look to Felix. "I'm gonna change."

"Want a beer?" Jordan asks him from his reclaimed spot on the couch.

While Felix goes to take the offered drink, I head upstairs. In my closet, I quickly strip out of my shorts and T-shirt, and then flip through my dresses and skirts. After hours' parties are usually pretty casual, but I don't like the idea of walking in with Felix and not looking amazing. I might have an invisibility superpower, but his god-status shatters it. People will be staring at him, and by extension, at me. Plus, I also want to look good for him. I know this whole thing is fake, but I like him. I can't help it. He's Felix Walters.

I narrow it down to two options. I'm holding each one in front of me, while standing in front of the floor-length mirror in my room, as Jane knocks and then cracks open the door.

"Need help?" she asks with a small smile.

"Yes, please." I pull her inside.

I try on each while she stares into my closet.

"The black one," she says. "You look effortlessly gorgeous in it."

"Okay." With that settled, I quickly run my fingers through my hair and then dab on some lip gloss and add a layer of mascara.

When I'm finished, Jane sits on my bed, picking at the comforter.

"Is everything okay?" I ask.

"Yeah," she says in a tone that disagrees with her statement.

Felix is waiting for me, but he has a beer, so I cross the room and sit down on the bed in front of her. "What's wrong? You seem down. You know you can come with us, right? Felix is more the third wheel than you."

"I know I'm your soulmate, but that boy is totally into you and that makes me the third wheel. And I really can't. I still have to write a paper for my Nineteenth Century Music Theory class."

"How much more do you have to do?"

"All of it." She smiles sweetly and then grimaces. "This week has sucked. I swear all of my professors got together and decided to pile on homework and tests this week."

She starts to get up, then squeezes my hand. "You look amazing. He likes you. I'd bet my life on it. Now go have fun. If you stay the night with him, promise to text."

My face warms at the thought. "I'm not staying at his house."

"Please do. I want to hear all the details tomorrow. It'll be my reward for finishing this paper." She groans a little. "I don't even have a topic yet. Ugh."

I hate seeing her like this. Jane has always had my back. I don't think there's anything she wouldn't do for me.

"Do you remember that night last year when the four of us stayed in and helped you study for your philosophy test?"

She laughs. "How could I forget? The three of you got so drunk."

"That was unintentional." I laugh too at the memory. "But you aced that test."

"Yeah." She shrugs. "You were so entertaining, I studied way longer than I would have on my own."

I grin really big. "It was a fun night."

"Oh no," she says, finally realizing where I'm headed with this jog down memory lane.

"Oh, yes."

Much to my surprise, Felix doesn't bat an eye when I tell him I need to stay in tonight with Jane. She can write the paper on her own, I know this, but I also know it's what she'd do for me. Besides, Vi is gone for the night, and Daisy and Jordan are preoccupied, which means it's up to me.

We're standing just outside the house, where I can talk to him without Jane overhearing.

"I'm sorry. She seems sort of down and she needs to finish a paper, so I'm going to stick around. Sorry about making you try on the pants. I guess I didn't hold up my end of the bargain. I promise you can keep me out late this weekend."

He chuckles and the movement makes his chest lift. "It's all right. Lucas texted and said Sigma was a bust anyway."

"You're welcome to stay and hang out."

It's worth noting, there's no world in which I would have believed he would take me up on that, but Felix nods slowly and rolls his bottom lip behind his teeth. "Yeah, okay."

I stare up at him for too long, the words not quite sinking in.

"Was that not the answer you wanted?" He smirks.

"Sorry. I didn't think you'd want to. Chill nights in don't seem like your style."

"That's not true at all," he says, brows tugging together. Hmm. I guess I just assumed that because when I see him, it's always at parties. There's a lot about Felix I don't really know.

I push open the front door and step in with a smile. "We decided to stay in."

"Word on the street is that Sigma is dead," Felix adds as everyone looks at us.

Jordan is the first to speak. "Cool, man, grab another beer and help me quiz Daisy."

Chapter
SIXTEEN

Dahlia

F OR THE NEXT TWO HOURS, WHILE JORDAN AND FELIX
pepper Daisy with questions for her physics test and I help
Jane come up with ideas for her music theory paper, I use
any free minutes to start a running list in the Notes app on my
phone of things to ask Felix.

"I think that's it," Jane says, voice full of glee as she raises her
arms over her head. "I'll read it over one last time in the morning,
but I don't think it's too bad. We're a good team."

"Duh."

She smiles and sneaks a glance at Felix. "I told you he liked
you."

Her words fill me with too much hope to accept. "He and
Jordan are friends, and you heard him—Sigma wasn't worth
going."

"Uh-huh." She stands and heads into the living room. "I'm
finally done. How goes the studying?"

"If I don't know it by now, I don't think I ever will," Daisy says.

"You know it," Jordan reassures her. It's sweet to see how much he hypes her up. Everybody needs a hype man, or woman.

Felix straightens and our eyes meet.

"I'm so tired," Daisy whines. "Knowing my luck, I'll oversleep and miss the test."

"No chance." He stands and pulls her to her feet. "I have three alarms set. You're gonna wake up and you're gonna kill that test, sweet Daisy."

She lifts up on her toes to kiss him. Jordan scoops her up and tips his head toward the rest of us. "Night, girls. Thanks for hanging out tonight, Walters."

"Later," Felix calls.

The three of us watch Jordan carry Daisy upstairs and then Felix smiles between me and Jane. "I guess it got pretty late," he says. "I should go too." He pulls out his phone. "Good to see you, Jane. Thanks for tonight, Dahlia."

And with that, he starts for the door.

"Wait," Jane calls, "getting an Uber this time of night is a pain. You either get the creepy old guy who wants to chat non-stop or some weird, young person whose car smells like they help transport dead bodies. Stay here. You can sleep on the pillow fort."

Felix's brows rise and a smirk plays on his lips. "The pillow fort?"

"Oh, it's epic. You have to see it. Dahlia and I built it." Jane starts up the stairs, leaving Felix no choice but to follow.

"I know what you're doing," I whisper-hiss as I pass by her in the doorway.

She grins and sing-songs, "You're welcome!"

Felix walks into my room and toward the many blankets and pillows spread out on the floor between my bed and the window.

"Woah," Felix says. "This is…I don't even have words."

Jane grins. "Awesome, right?"

"Is this for the many guys you lure back to your room, hot

stuff?" Felix asks as he sits down in the middle of it. He lies back and crooks a hand behind his head. He looks silly and yet still so hot.

"Just my number one, boo," I say, then cringe. Did I just use the word *boo?* "Jane is the only person who's slept there."

"I get chatty when I've been drinking." Jane smiles. "Dahlia got tired of me falling asleep in her bed while I was talking her ear off."

"I did not!" Even if she does thrash around in her sleep, I never would have said anything. Jane's parents were really strict when she was younger, and she never did sleepovers with friends. I love giving that to her.

Jane ignores me and continues talking to Felix. "So we made me a little fort. I lie there and we gab about boys, you know, all the usual girl-talk stuff."

He adjusts a pillow. "It's like indoor camping."

"Minus nature," Jane scrunches her nose, "anyway, I'm so tired." She fakes a yawn. "Night, night."

She goes, shutting the door on her way out.

"She's something," Felix says, smiling after her.

"She really is." I stand at the edge of the fort, not sure what to do. "You don't have to stay if you don't want."

"Are you kidding? This might be more comfortable than my bed." He sits up, but instead of getting to his feet, he takes my hand and tugs me down to the pillows with him.

I land, not gracefully at all, beside him. "Really?"

"No." He laughs. "But the company is better."

I settle into the blankets. There are something like fifteen of them, plus a half-dozen pillows. Jane even bought a little stuffed teddy bear for her second bed.

"I like your room." Lying on his back, he looks around the space.

"Thanks." It isn't big, so there isn't much furniture. My bed, a desk, and a nightstand. The only thing on the wall is this season's

Valley U golf tournament schedule and mini Polaroid pictures of me, Jane, Daisy, and Violet over the past year.

"What's your room like?" I ask, staring up at the ceiling. Felix's body lies alongside mine, a pleasant warmth radiates off him.

"Well, it doesn't have a pillow fort."

"Missing out."

"No kidding."

I elbow him. "Really, give me a visual. I realized tonight I don't know a lot about you, outside of football and parties."

"That's all there is to know," he says, but I notice his jaw tics.

"Tell me about your room."

"Okay." He turns his face to look at me. His tongue darts out to wet his lips. Felix has a great mouth. It's almost too wide for his face. I think that's why I always notice his smile.

"It's a little smaller than yours. The bed is pushed against one wall. The TV and PlayStation are set up on the other side and eighty percent of the time, my clothes are sitting in the laundry basket on the floor because I don't want to fold or put them away." A real, full smile takes over his face now.

"Anything on the walls?"

"A poster," he says with a little reluctance.

"Of?"

He squeezes one eye shut and grimaces. "Me."

"What?" I giggle.

"Lucas started it. He put one up as a joke; the guys all thought it was hilarious. I took it down, but then two more appeared. Took those down, and—"

"Three more appeared?"

"Yeah." He laughs. "So I left one up and they've stopped pranking me."

"Isn't that weird when you bring girls back to your room?"

"I doubt any of them have noticed," he says in a tone that suggests he's annoyed by it, but no one is making him hook up with random chicks.

"What else do you want to know?" he asks.

"I made a list."

"Oh man, I better get cozy then." He kicks off his shoes and turns on his side. The movement puts him so close, I can't think.

"It's in my phone." I sit up. I can breathe a little easier without his mouth taunting me. "Which is downstairs."

"Maybe just ask me the ones you remember," he suggests with a playful smirk. He grimaces a little as he adjusts his back.

"Okay, for starters, how do you go out so much? You never seem worried about classes or homework. And I know from Jordan and Gavin that even the men's sports don't get preferential treatment from professors like I assumed."

He grins. "Maybe *they* don't."

"So, you're just more special?"

"Oh, I definitely am." His smile is so big and magnetic, I find myself leaning forward. "I got injured right before my freshman year. Had a thing with my elbow and couldn't play. It sucked, majorly, but since I was useless, I took something like eighteen credit hours both semesters that year. And I took summer classes. This year is a breeze. Just the way I need it to be."

"You're an art history major, right?" It surprised me when I saw it listed below his roster photo on the Valley U football website.

"That's right."

"Why art history?"

He shrugs, then adjusts again. "The plan has always been the NFL, but if by some chance that doesn't happen, I thought that was the safest bet. My parents own a gallery in Scottsdale."

"You'd be happy doing that?"

"Fuck no. Anything but the NFL will feel like a disappointment."

When he squirms this time, I say, "You don't have to lie down here and pretend it's comfortable."

"No, it is." He lets a little of that discomfort I saw in flashes settle over his features. "My back is tight. I meant to roll it out after practice, but I was in a hurry to get to The Hideout and hang out with my girlfriend before I knew she was going to blow me off."

I laugh. "Turn over."

He hesitates, but when I motion for him to flip, he does.

Lying on his stomach, I inch forward until my knees rest against his hip. I press my hands to his back. "Here?"

"Little higher."

I adjust.

"To the right an inch."

My fingers glide over and my heart races at the simple contact. "Yeah, there."

As I press in, he groans.

My pulse races and skitters as I massage his back. Warmth seeps through his T-shirt as I work on loosening up the tight spot in his back.

When I can find my voice, I say, "That's a lot of pressure to put on yourself for football."

"I can handle it." He turns his head and winks. "What else was on your list? I could talk about me all night."

"I'm having a hard time remembering," I say, which is true. My skin buzzes with electricity. He's here in my room, lying on the floor, so casually and comfortably, and flirting with me. At least I think that's what's happening. It's a little hard to tell with Felix because he's so charming. I'm not even sure he knows he's doing it.

We fall silent. My hands work and I feel his back loosening up, but my emotions are getting more jumbled. Anxiousness mixed with confusion, a heavy dose of lust and angst. I do what I always do when it all becomes too much to keep in. I blurt out the thing I shouldn't say. "Jane thinks you like me."

My hands still, and he rolls over onto his side again. He stretches and says, "Thanks. That feels better. Great, actually."

"You're welcome."

An uncomfortable beat passes between us. But before I can

blurt out anything else, he lifts a hand and lets his fingers tangle in my hair. "I do like you."

"You know what I mean. *Like* me."

"I do." He fingers a strand of my hair by my ear and his knuckles graze my neck.

"But…"

"I'm not the guy for you, but that doesn't mean I don't wish that I were."

That fuels a thousand more questions. Ones I'm not sure I'm brave enough to ask, but if I don't, I might hate myself later.

"If you like me, then why aren't you the guy for me?"

"You need someone to give you all the experiences and fun you've been waiting for. Someone that will make you feel special and treat you like the absolute baller chick that you are." The way his blue eyes focus on nothing but me turns my insides to liquid. "That's not something I have time for or would even be any good at."

I think he's wrong. He already makes me feel that way. Just being with him is the most exciting thing that's ever happened to me.

Felix sits up so his face is inches from mine. My heart stops and I hold my breath. Is he going to kiss me? Finally? I move just a fraction closer. Gently, he brushes the pad of his thumb over my lower lip, but he doesn't bring his mouth to mine. Instead, he says, "Don't settle for less, okay? You deserve that."

Chapter
SEVENTEEN

Felix

I WAKE UP LYING FLAT ON MY BACK WITH MY PHONE vibrating in my jeans pocket. Dahlia is curled up beside me. We must have fallen asleep talking. The last thing I remember is her going downstairs to get her phone and then proceeding to ask me the twenty or so questions she'd compiled. Things like what I did for fun on nights I didn't party (PlayStation or hang with the guys) and why Bethany and I had broken up (she wanted more than I could give with football and school).

I felt bad not being completely honest on the last one, but it's the root of it anyway. She wanted the face of the football team, the guy heading to the NFL, but not the guy busting his ass to make it happen or the guy underneath all that. She never made a list of questions to ask me about myself. She hardly asked me anything, at all. Ever. Nah, Bethany never tried to get to know me. That should have been my first red flag, but honestly, I'm so used to people only caring about football that I didn't see it right away.

Carefully, trying not to jostle her awake, I slide my hand into my pocket to get my phone and then silence it. Dahlia's eyes are still closed, dark lashes fan out over her fair skin. Her perfect pink lips are parted slightly. My already hard dick twitches at the sight of her, all gorgeous and sweet.

She never did change last night, and the black dress is bunched up higher on her hips, giving me an eyeful of upper thigh. I have the same overwhelming desire to kiss her as I did the other night. It's a problem of my own making, I realize. I asked her to be my fake girlfriend, even though I really want her. But I'm not gonna lead her on. She's not just some girl I can hook up with and walk away. Dahlia could never be that girl. Even so, last night was… nice. Just hanging with her, talking and laughing.

I roll away from her slowly and get to my feet, then pull on my shoes and send a quick text to Teddy to ask him to bring my bag to the gym for weight training this morning. She still isn't awake, and I feel bad about leaving without saying something, but I know she doesn't have to be up for a couple hours still, so I give her one last look and then slip out of her room.

"You missed a hell of a party last night," Lucas says. "I've never seen so many people at an after hours party."

"What'd you do last night and where'd you end up crashing?" Teddy is full of questions this morning. He's like this now that he's dating my sister. She asks him, he asks me, and I am too tired to dodge.

"I hung out with Dahlia last night and I stayed at her place."

Teddy and Lucas stare at me, matching curious expressions on their faces.

"What?" I close my locker and push past them for the weight

room. It's just down the hall from the locker room. The beat of the music is louder with every step.

"Wait, wait, wait." Lucas jogs to keep up with me. "I need way, way more information."

"That's all you're getting."

"What happened to 'it's new and not that serious'?" Teddy asks from my other side. Damn these guys are chatty this morning.

"It's not," I say, as we get close to the weight room. "It was late, so I crashed there."

Coach has a special kind of torture waiting for us this morning. Occasionally he likes to mix things up and it always sucks a giant, hairy cock. Today, instead of lifting heavy in our usual routine, he throws a high intensity interval workout in for funsies. No one has fun. Except maybe him. Jump rope and burpees in between every set of bench press and squats. Fuuuuck. The only positive is the guys are too winded to keep questioning me about Dahlia.

The rest of my day doesn't really improve. I fall asleep in my European Modernism class and then run into Bethany in University Hall on my way to get a coffee to stay awake for my next class. I was able to avoid her before she tried to talk to me, but seeing her still just strikes a nerve.

One more class, practice, a mandatory team study hour, a shower, and a glorious nap later, I'm ready to go out. A thrum of something I can't quite pinpoint hums just below the surface. Annoyance or frustration. I can't put my finger on it, but I need a night to really cut loose.

The baseball team is having a party tonight. The party is at Lambda Chi since their off-campus house was condemned last year. A lot of the baseball guys are a part of that fraternity.

"Twenty bucks for a cup or ten if you agree to participate in the other festivities." A young guy, a freshman by the looks of him, recites like he's done it a hundred times already tonight.

"Festivities?" I ask as I pull out my wallet.

"Kissing booth," he says.

I feel both brows rise. "Seriously?"

Lucas snorts. "I'm totally in."

The kid looks back to me.

"No way."

He continues on, unphased, "Tickets for the booth are one dollar or six for five. There's another table inside if you change your mind."

"I'm good," I say.

We pay and head inside. Both of us with a pink cup for the keg and Lucas with a wristband and a time slot to work the kissing booth.

"Six kisses for five dollars?" I smirk at Lucas. "You're the cheapest date ever."

"But think of how much action I'm going to get tonight." He straightens. "I need to find someone with a breath mint or some gum."

"You're crazy, man," I tell him as we fill up our cups.

The kissing booth is hard to miss. It's dead center of the party. There are two people sitting on stools—a guy on one side and a girl on the other. A line of people snakes around the yard with people already waiting. And everyone else is gathered around to watch. It's like these people don't know they can just kiss for free. Or go home and watch porn.

"Hey, not everyone has a Dahlia. You're lucky. Uncomplicated but still all the benefits. Plus, she's cool as hell."

That thrumming under my skin intensifies.

"Oh, speaking of, there she is." He nods his head, and I follow his line of sight to see her walking in with Jane. Her eyes are glued on the kissing booth. I quickly glance to the people currently kissing and chuckle. Most people have done a closed mouth sort of lingering peck. Lips smashed together for three to five seconds. But one couple is really going at it. They're full on making out, and when I look back at Dahlia, her eyes are wide, and her cheeks are flushed.

"You think she took a time slot?" Lucas asks with a taunting smile.

"Fuck off," I toss over my shoulder as I head toward her.

"Hey, you guys made it," I say when I get to them. I'm relieved to see that Dahlia isn't wearing a wristband and I don't see any tickets in her hand. Jane, on the other hand, has one ticket pinched between her thumb and pointer finger.

"Just one?" I ask Jane as I take Dahlia's free hand and interlace our fingers.

"One is all I need tonight. I have my eye on this guy that lives here and rumor has it all the Lambda Chi guys had to take a slot." Jane makes a noise that's something between a squeal and giggle. "I'm going to see if I can find him."

With a wave, she's gone and I'm alone with Dahlia.

"Drink?" I tip my head toward the keg.

"Definitely," she says, tearing her gaze away from the kissing booth. Her cheeks are flushed.

As more people arrive, the main attraction loses some of its focus. A game of beer pong starts up, then the dance area starts to fill with people. Dahlia and I walk over to where some of the guys are hanging out. From our position, we can't make out much of the kissing booth, but occasionally, there are hoots and hollers, indicating someone is really going at it up there.

We're standing in a circle with my buddies, she's leaning into me and I'm holding her hand. I can't resist running my thumb along her delicate fingers. It's such an innocent touch, but nothing I do with her feels harmless.

She's wearing another dress tonight—this one a light purple that hugs her curves and dips low in the front. I'd bet money that it's another item out of Jane's closet. It doesn't seem like something

Dahlia would have picked out. Don't get me wrong, she's still wearing the shit out of it.

She seems more at ease the more time we spend together. A week or two ago and she never would have leaned against me so casually. I have a perfect view down the front of her dress and I'm struggling to be a gentleman.

I'm not paying attention to the conversation, but when everyone starts laughing, I snap out of it. Dahlia looks up at me. Somewhere along the way, she stopped being as shy about making eye contact, too. I like having her attention.

Her sweet smile is a drug. Holding my gaze, she sweeps her hair off her shoulder. The movement pushes out her tits and one strap of her dress falls.

I have a theory. She's trying to kill me.

I lean down and press a soft kiss just above her collarbone. Her skin dots with goosebumps. I tell myself I'm doing it to sell the fake girlfriend thing, but as badly as I want to keep going, I know that isn't completely true.

When Lucas gets back from his slot at the kissing booth, he's all smiles. "Did you guys see the line of girls for me?"

"I expected everyone to scatter, if I'm being honest," Brogan says. "But I guess there's no limit to what people will do for charity."

"Pshha." Lucas side-eyes him. "I'm sexy as hell and kiss like a dream. Ask any one of them."

The guys and I all laugh.

"I'm serious," Lucas protests.

"Sure, man," Brogan says. "Whatever you say."

Lucas looks to me for help. "Tell them."

"How would I know?" I ask, still chuckling.

The laughter from our buddies gets louder.

"We live together. You've seen me with girls. Or rather, heard. We share a wall. You must have heard." He nods his head like this is proof that he's an amazing kisser.

"Dude, I have not been listening to you have sex through the walls."

His jaw drops. "I hear you all the time. Or I used to."

"Well, this got super weird." Archer chuckles.

"I can't believe you won't vouch for me." Lucas crosses his arms over his chest and looks between me and Dahlia. "Well, let's see how it's done then. Show me how the legendary Felix Walters does it."

"What?"

"Kiss her. Let's see how it's done."

Immediately, Dahlia's face takes on a pretty pink blush.

"Fuck you. We're not making out so you can watch."

"When has that ever stopped you?" Lucas scoffs.

He's not dropping this.

"You're a great kisser, man. That's what the girls *all* scream from the other side of the wall. Happy now?" I grit out.

"No, no. Let's see the master work," Lucas says.

Someone starts chanting, "kiss, kiss, kiss" and soon, they're all joining in.

"I hate all of you." I turn, angling my body so I'm facing Dahlia, then step forward.

"Sorry about this," I whisper as I lean down and touch my lips to her cheek, just above the corner of her mouth. It's a ghost of a kiss, so soft I'm not entirely sure she could have even felt it. But damn, I felt it.

Their response is immediate. "Boo!" and "I kiss my grandma like that."

"Aww, come on," Brogan says. "Kiss your girl for real."

"It's okay," she says quietly, giving me the go-ahead. She tilts her head up to me in invitation. It'd be so easy to swipe my lips over hers. I'm faintly aware of the guys, still staring at us and chanting, "Kiss, kiss, kiss."

I've thought about kissing her no less than a hundred times

in the past thirty seconds alone, but I'm not going to steal her first kiss to prove a point to my buddies.

I step away from her and flip them off. "Sorry, boys. I'm not a show pony."

An uncomfortable moment passes as the guys quiet, then look between me and Dahlia. When I dare to glance in her direction, I immediately wish I hadn't. The pink in her cheeks has intensified. I embarrassed her, but she doesn't want her first kiss to happen like this.

"I need to use the bathroom," she says quietly, wearing a fake smile.

I drain the rest of the beer in my cup in one swallow. I try to keep my demeanor cool and casual, but as soon as she's gone, Brogan asks, "What the hell was that about?"

"Nothing. I'm just not kissing on command."

"Then why not kiss her because you want to?" Genuine confusion is plastered all over his face. "Did something happen? Or are you just not into her anymore?"

"Nothing happened and of course I'm into her. Dahlia's amazing."

"Yeah, well, you might want to tell her that because she looked like you publicly refused to kiss her. Oh wait…"

Fuck. I glance toward the door. As soon as she gets back, I need to talk to her. Hell, I never thought I'd be finding excuses not to kiss a chick. Especially one I'd sell my lucky jock strap to really kiss.

The longer she's gone, the more anxious I am to talk to her. Seconds and minutes feel like an eternity. I'm about to go find her, when Lucas says, "No fucking way."

My head snaps to him. He points toward the kissing booth and then elbows me. "Maybe you're not such a good kisser after all, Walters. Your girl decided to get a little extra."

And there she is, halfway up the line, clutching a ticket in her fingers, head held high and determined.

Chapter
EIGHTEEN

Dahlia

WHAT THE HELL AM I DOING?

My heart races with excitement and nerves. I feel reckless standing in this line, but it's a welcome emotion from the embarrassment of Felix refusing to kiss me.

His friends looked surprised at first, then confused. I doubt they believe we're together now after he wouldn't even kiss me. My skin itches with the humiliation of it. The man hooks up with every other chick on campus like it's no big deal but won't even press his lips to mine to save face? How depressing.

I trudge forward. Only four people are in front of me in line. I can't believe I'm going to kiss some random guy who's kissed fifty or more people before me and doesn't even know my name. It's not the way I saw my first kiss going down, but it doesn't matter anymore. I just need it to be done.

Someone grips me by the arm, and I spin to see Felix glaring down at me. "What are you doing?"

"What does it look like I'm doing?" I tear my arm away, but my voice doesn't have any hard edges. I'm not mad at him. This is my fault. I never should have agreed to this fake dating scheme. I can't pretend to date Felix and not develop real feelings for him. I already have if I'm honest.

"Don't do this. Not here. Not like this," he pleads.

"Why? Because you want me to hold out for some big, special moment or because you don't want your fake girlfriend to kiss someone else at a party?" I remember the speech he gave me last night about not settling for less than I deserve.

"Both."

"Tell me, was your first kiss some big, special moment?" My voice rises.

His face scrunches up, giving me my answer.

"I don't understand. I like you. You like me. Everyone thinks we're together. What's the big, damn deal?" My stomach rolls with a possibility I hadn't considered. "Or did you just say that you liked me because you felt sorry for me?"

"What? Of course not. I'm just…" He struggles to finish the sentence. His stare darts to the front of the line then back to me.

"Not the guy for me. Got it." I take a step as another person gives their ticket to the person at the front of the line collecting them and then walks toward the guy sitting on the stool handing out kisses. Only one more person ahead of me now. The nerves kick in, but I'm not backing down. I just want it to be over with, so guys like Felix don't look at me like I'm some fragile person they need to handle with care.

"Dahlia. Fuck." He takes my elbow again and guides me out of the line. "Fine. I'll do it."

"Don't do me any favors."

"I'm not. I want to, but not here."

"What are you waiting for? Candlelight and mood music? It's not that big of a deal to me." I'm taunting him a little, but I can't help it. After he rejected me in front of his friends, anything but him kissing me here feels like a consolation prize. And who's to say he won't just change his mind again later? No, this is my chance to finally kiss someone. I'm doing it, even if it means giving up my fake boyfriend.

"Next," the guy taking tickets says.

I hesitate, giving Felix one more chance. His silence tells me everything I need to know.

"Next please."

I turn from him, disappointment suddenly stronger than the nerves about kissing a total stranger in front of the entire party. I hold out my ticket and take a step, but I'm suddenly being pulled backward. My chest collides with his, but Felix doesn't give me time to recover before his mouth covers mine. His lips are soft, but they press into mine hard and commanding. His fingers curl around my hip in a bruising hold, like he's afraid I'm going to pull away. I don't. I melt into him. The hand at my hip glides around to my back and squeezes me against him at the same time his tongue slips into my mouth.

Any nerves I had about kissing him are doused in the flames his touch ignites. I'm not kissing Felix. I'm being kissed. He is in total control and I'm just along for the ride. A really, amazing ride.

My head spins, my heart races, and a thousand butterflies have taken residence in my stomach. Candlelight and mood music would have been completely wasted because I'm not aware of anything but him. His chest pressing into mine. His hands strong and commanding. The light scruff on his face that scratches in the most erotic way every time he tilts his head. The faint taste of beer and mint on him, and the soft groan he makes as he pulls back.

I'm out of breath and there's a buzzing in my ears. I'm still leaning against him and super thankful because my legs are weak. My eyelids flutter open and I look into his gray blue eyes.

He doesn't look away, but one hand comes up to where both of mine rest against his chest and he plucks the ticket from my fingers. "I think that's mine."

"What if I bought six for five dollars?"

One side of his mouth lifts. "You're trouble, hot stuff."

With that, he links our fingers and tugs me with him, away from the kissing booth.

I might have been lost in my own world during that kiss, but when we get back to Felix's circle of friends, it's obvious they were not. And the circle has grown. All eyes are on us. My face is on fire and my lips tingle.

"Well, damn, Walters," Brogan says, fanning his face. "I felt that all the way over here."

Lucas lifts his hands and then mocks bowing down to him. "I'm not worthy."

Felix shakes his head and chuckles. "I hate you all."

The rest of the night, I'm glued to his side. Maybe it's all the hormones raging through me from that kiss, but I feel more like his real, fake girlfriend now. I stand a little taller beside him. And Felix is freer with his touches. In fact, he can't seem to stop touching me. He's either holding my hand or has his arm around my waist, but he doesn't try to kiss me again. Which is too bad because I really, really want to kiss him again.

Sometime around one, the kissing booth is officially done, and not long after, people start trickling out. We're sitting at a table watching other people play cards. I'm sitting on Felix's lap, and he has one arm draped around my hip.

I'm covering a yawn, when he asks, "Are you ready to go?"

"So sorry. I'm having fun, promise."

"Nah, don't be. Too many nights of staying up late. Let me walk you home."

It's about three blocks away, weaving through campus, and we could easily get a sober ride, but the night is still warm, and I'm not in any hurry to leave Felix's company, so I agree.

Once we're out of the party, our steps slow.

"Plans for tomorrow or can you sleep in?" he asks. Our fingers brush accidentally, and he shoves both hands in the front pockets of his jeans.

"I have practice, but not until ten. You?"

"Same, practice at noon. Then hopefully taking the most epic nap ever." He smiles, removes his hands from his pockets and takes my hand. My pulse races at the simple touch. Except too late I realize he's leading me across the street like a protective big brother. I hold on a little tighter, so he isn't tempted to drop my hand as soon as we get to the other side. There's no reason to hold hands where no one can see us, but I want to all the same.

My house is in sight before I'm ready to say goodbye. The living room light is on, and I know Jane left the party before us and is either in her room or mine waiting to hear how the night went.

He squeezes my hand and stops in front of my house. We're here, but I'm not ready for the night to end.

"Do you want to stay over?" I ask, saying the words all at once before I lose my nerve.

"I should probably go home and let you get some sleep."

Who needs sleep? I'll sleep when I'm dead.

He steps forward and wraps his arms around me. I melt into him, letting my head rest on his chest and squeezing his sides.

"Thanks for walking me home." I tilt my head up, still pressed into his chest. His blue eyes flash over my mouth, and for a second, I think he might kiss me again.

His lips brush softly against my forehead and then he steps away. "You're welcome. Night, hot stuff."

Chapter
NINETEEN

Felix

S ATURDAY AFTER PRACTICE, SOME OF THE GUYS END UP AT
our house. Brogan and Archer show up, then some freshmen,
including Armstrong. I think he and Bethany are done.
Teddy said she was at the party last night with some baseball
guy. I never even saw her, which is a first. I usually have a radar
that points me directly to her. It reads something like: Warning—
Danger ahead! But last night the only person I remember is Dahlia.

That kiss was…well, fuck, it was hot. It might have been her
first kiss, but in a weird way, it felt like mine too. Or at least the
first real kiss in a long, long time. When's the last time I kissed a
girl without taking off her clothes? Sadly, I can't remember.

I could have *just* kissed her for hours. I seriously considered
it, but continuing to kiss her complicates things in a way I'm not
ready to act on. Being someone's first kiss is one thing, but anything beyond that feels too heavy for our agreement.

By eight o'clock, my house is filled with teammates and some of their girlfriends. My sisters are over too. Most people are drinking, but it's calm and casual.

I haven't talked to Dahlia all day, which isn't odd. We've gone a day or two between texting since we started hanging out, but as I look around my house at everyone laughing and having a good time, I keep wondering what she's doing.

I finally give in and hit her up.

Me: What are you doing?

Hot Stuff: Jane and I just left Taco Bell. 🖤 🖤 🌮 😋 🖤 🖤

I laugh at her exaggerated use of emojis.

Me: Tacos sound great. Now I'm hungry.

Hot Stuff: Oh, they were delicious. What are you up to tonight?

Me: Not much. Want to see for yourself what a night-in looks like? Fair warning, half my team is here. But it's chill.

Hot Stuff: I'd love to. Is it okay if I bring Jane?

Me: Of course.

Hot Stuff: Right. I forgot. The more hot girls, the merrier.

Me: Exactly!

Twenty minutes later, she and Jane walk through the front door. Lucas is overly excited to see Jane. He scoots over, directing people to move, so she can sit next to him on the couch. Dahlia walks over to me, swinging a bag in her hand and wearing a flirty smile that looks like the fun kind of trouble.

"I brought you my extra tacos." She holds up the bag in front of me and the smell hits my nose.

An involuntary groan slips out. I reach for it, and she lifts it just out of reach, taunting me.

"Don't tease me, hot stuff. I would do very bad things for those tacos right now."

She loves pushing my buttons. Little does she know, she pushes most of them without even trying. Everything about her just hits a little different. But right now, as she purposely tries to get a reaction out of me, I'm more than happy to oblige.

I lunge, but instead of going for the bag, I loop an arm around her waist and bring her down onto my lap. She giggles and squeals, still holding the bag as far away from me as possible.

"You're in trouble now." I tickle her sides and she immediately brings her elbows closer to try to stop me.

"You didn't say the magic word." She's squirming on my lap, which does not go unnoticed by my dick.

"Is the magic word tacos?" I ask.

"No."

My fingers dance up her rib cage again. "Is it Felix Walters is a god among men?"

She laughs. "That's not one word."

"I know, but it was worth a shot. Plus, I just wanted to throw it out there, so you'd know it was okay if you were feeling that too."

"Your ego is impressive."

"All of me is impressive," I say before I can think better of it.

She just giggles.

"Please, hot stuff, may I have your leftover tacos?"

She brings the bag closer. "Was that so hard?"

Right now, everything about me is hard. Thankfully, this time, I stop the words before they leave my lips.

She starts to get up, but I curl an arm around her waist and shift, so she's sitting on my leg while I set the bag on the other. There are three tacos inside, which makes me wonder how many she ordered in total.

"How was practice?" I ask, right before I take a bite out of the first one.

The guys have noticed my food and I have to kick several of them away when they try to steal one of my precious tacos.

"It was good. I shot thirty-six on nine holes."

"That's awesome." I lift one hand in a fist, and she bumps her wrist against mine.

"Thanks. How was yours? Don't you have a game coming up soon?"

"First one is next weekend," I reply. "Are you coming to cheer me on?"

"Maybe. I have a tournament Friday and Saturday at Gold Canyon. What time is your game?"

"I couldn't tell you, but it's probably online."

"It's *probably* online?" She arches a brow and digs out her phone. A few taps later, she says, "Eight o'clock. I should be back by then."

"Sweet." I lift up my wrist again, and she taps it with a laugh.

It's easy to be with Dahlia. Even easier to flirt and play. Sometimes, like last night when I walked her home, I have to rein myself in and be careful about how far I take things so I don't lead her on. And sometimes, like right now, I just want to say fuck it. I like chilling with her. Why does it have to be more complicated than that?

I crumple up the last taco wrapper and toss it in the bag, then sit back with a satisfied moan. "Thank you. Best second dinner I've ever had."

I get another laugh out of her, but I can barely hear it over the guys screaming at the PlayStation.

"Wanna see my room so you can knock another thing off that list of yours?" I already told her what it looked like, but it's hard to talk to her out here.

"Oh." She sounds surprised by my offer. "Yeah."

Stella looks over as we stand and start for my room. "Hey, no stealing her away. I need to talk to Dahlia."

"You do?" Dahlia asks, a faint smile pulling at her lips.

"Yeah. Holly and I wanted to see if you and your friends wanted to sit with us at the game next weekend?" She holds up both hands. One pretends to block Holly from view and the other points in her direction. "This one is making us go super early, so we get the best seats."

"Yeah, that would be great," Dahlia says, glancing at me like she isn't sure if it was the right thing to say.

"All settled?" I ask my sister.

She aims a pleased smile back at me. "If I say no, are you going to let her hang out with us instead of dragging her to your room?"

"Drag?" I cock a brow. "As if."

I take a couple steps away, and when Dahlia doesn't follow, I lean forward, taking her arm and dragging her with me toward my room to the sound of laughter from my sisters and teammates. Fuckers.

I shut us inside and then shake my head at her. "Thanks a lot, fake girlfriend. They think I've got you in here against your will."

Her soft giggles fade as her eyes leave mine to scan the room. "No one would ever look at the two of us and think that."

I don't like that assessment of us, but before I can find the right words to voice it, she's walking up to the infamous poster of my face. It's large and hangs on the wall above my desk. And since there isn't much else to look at it in here, there's really no missing it.

Her delicate fingers rest on the white wall next to the poster. She glances back over her shoulder at me. "It really is a great photo of you."

"Thanks." I plop down on my bed. Dahlia continues to walk around the room, taking in every detail like she's analyzing it for hidden clues. She holds up an unopened bag of black licorice. "And I was just starting to like you. Black licorice, really?"

"Oooh. I forgot about those. Toss that here."

She does and then comes to sit on the edge of the bed, still wearing a disgusted look over my candy preference.

I tear open the bag and pluck one out. I rip off a piece with my teeth and then shake it at her. "Don't look at me like that. I didn't judge you for the awful EDM music you like."

"That was Robby's music, not mine."

"Uh-huh. I saw your sick dance moves. That was not the first time you've listened to house music and got your groove on."

She laughs quietly and smiles at me. "Black licorice is gross."

"Untrue. Plus, it's lucky."

"Lucky?"

"Yep. I've been eating it before every game for as long as I can remember."

"Your pre-game meal includes candy?" She looks at me with this sassy, disbelieving look on her face that makes me smile bigger. I really like having her here in my space.

"Not a lot of candy. Black licorice should be savored, not devoured." I eat another chunk. "One or two vines the night before."

"How did that become your pre-game ritual?" she asks, staring at me like she's riveted by the backstory. I'm not sure anyone's asked me before.

"In high school, we'd stop at this gas station across from the school before away games and load up on junk food and snacks for the bus ride."

"Super idea." She laughs again.

"Young and dumb, but I guess we had stomachs of steel. Anyway, one day I grabbed a bag of black licorice and ended up having a great game. I threw over six hundred yards and ran in two touchdowns myself. It was just one of those rare, epic nights." I shake the licorice at her again. "All thanks to black licorice."

"Sure. It had nothing to do with your hard work and talent."

"What's your pre-tournament ritual?"

"I don't really have one," she says. "I guess I follow the same warm-up routine."

"That definitely doesn't count." I sit up straighter and set the bag of licorice aside. "There has to be something you do, no matter how small or silly, to bring you luck before you play."

"So, you admit it's silly to think black licorice is responsible for your game performance?"

"I absolutely did not admit that. Come on, you don't have any lucky charms?"

"I really don't think so," she says, glancing up through her thick, black lashes. "Is that strange? Am I the weird one here? I have rituals, but nothing like a special food I have to eat or a rabbit's foot I carry in my pocket."

"You're not weird. Just obviously less superstitious than me."

She makes a soft noise like a hum, then her gaze circles the room again. "I like it, and you described it really well. Right down to the laundry basket full of clothes."

"I don't spend a lot of time in here." Although now that the season is starting, I will be here more than I have been. I don't party at all during the week when we have a game the following weekend. I'll kick back on Saturday nights after we play, but the other six days, I'm completely focused on football.

"I spend so much time in my room," she says. "I always have. My parents used to joke and say I locked myself in my dungeon for days at a time."

"I get bored by myself."

Her lips part, like she's about to hit me with some smart-ass comment about boring myself, so I lunge for her. My arms circle her waist and my fingers tickle her sides as I bring her down on top of me.

"So not fair." She wriggles and squirms.

I relent, but keep her close. She glances up at me and the smile on her face dims slowly as our gazes lock. Her chest rises and falls as she catches her breath. I try, and fail, not to look at her lips. Soft and pink and begging to be kissed.

She shifts slightly off me but doesn't look away. "Are you going to kiss me again?"

"I hadn't quite decided," I admit. I know I shouldn't. It complicates things and that's the last thing either of us needs.

"But you want to." Her brows pull together, like she's questioning her own assessment of the situation.

"I've wanted to kiss you since the first time I met you."

She sits up now and adjusts her ponytail by pulling on the loose strands with both hands. "That can absolutely not be true."

"It absolutely is. And you couldn't get away from me fast enough." I smile as I think back on it. I couldn't decide if she was repulsed or intimidated by me. Sometimes I'm still not sure her feelings don't toe the line between the two.

"I was dumbstruck. I've never been able to talk to guys, but it's worse with you."

"You don't seem that nervous around me now."

"That's because I've already done all the most embarrassing things I can imagine in front of you."

I laugh lightly and tug on the end of her hair. I like it up and out of her face, where she can't hide behind it.

"I'm still nervous around you, though," she says. "Just not quite as bad. Like I don't feel like I want to throw up."

She no longer wants to vomit when she's around me, as in, there was a time she did feel that way? It's weird progress, but I guess I'll take it.

Chapter
TWENTY

Dahlia

ON WEDNESDAY NIGHT, I HAVE AN EARLY DINNER WITH the girls and then head up to my room. We leave tomorrow morning for Gold Canyon, even though the tournament doesn't start until Friday. We'll get to the host course Thursday afternoon, hit the driving range, maybe play a few holes, then go to sleep early so we can be up in case we're in the first group to tee off.

I finalize and submit some homework, triple-check I have everything I need for the next two to three days, and I'm in bed by nine, bag packed and by the door so I can grab it and go in the morning.

My internal clock isn't ready to go to sleep yet, though, so I pull out my laptop and find something to watch. I pick the first thing I see, some unsolved mysteries-type show. All the lights are off in my room and the house is quiet downstairs. Daisy and

Jordan were going out, Violet headed over to Gavin's, and Jane went to the library to study.

I'm not sure how much time passes. Enough that I'm deeply engrossed in the suspicious and alarming way a young girl went missing without a trace when a scraping noise outside gets my attention. I hit pause and train an ear toward the window. Living next door to The White House, I've gotten pretty used to random noises at all hours of the day and night. Whatever it is, stops, so I go back to my show.

But a few minutes later, the noise is back, and this time, it's louder. Closer.

I set my laptop aside and get up. I'm sure it's nothing, but I still pad slowly over to the window. A foot away from it, I look out to the street. I don't see anyone, and everything looks like it always does. I guess this is what I get for watching a creepy true crime show before bed.

My shoulders relax and I take a step closer to admire the clear, quiet night. Suddenly, a dark head pops up out of no-where. Glowing eyes stare through the glass pane and the knock that comes a millisecond later sends me jumping backward and screaming.

The floating head on the other side screams back, then laughs. "Shit, you scared me. Little help here, hot stuff."

I hurry to open the window, and Felix pulls himself inside.

"I scared you?! What are you doing?"

"Nobody was answering downstairs."

"So you climbed up to my window? Why? And how?"

"It was easy, actually. I climbed onto the fence around your yard, and then from there, I was able to pull myself onto the porch roof." He smiles proudly. "I brought you something. I brought you two somethings, in fact."

"Is one of them a new heart because mine feels like it's going to explode at any second. Holy crap. What if you'd fallen?"

"Worried about me? Aww. That's sweet. I was perfectly safe the whole time. Promise." He makes an X over his heart.

Pulse still racing, I shut my laptop to cut off the ominous music from the show and then flip on the overhead light in my room.

"I'm sorry," Felix says as he sits on my bed. "I didn't mean to go full-on psycho stalker, but I wanted to see you before you left."

"Maybe call next time?" I offer.

"Noted." Grinning, he pats the bed. "Now, come here so I can give you your gifts before your heart explodes and I scaled your house for nothing."

His playful side is endearing and impossible to resist. As the shock wears off, my surprise turns to delight that he's here. We haven't hung out all week, except breakfast with his teammates. He's had extra practices and meetings leading up to their first game of the season Saturday, and I've had a similarly busy schedule, trying to get schoolwork done and prepping for the tournament.

When I sit, he turns so we're facing one another. It isn't until now I realize how little I'm wearing. Thin sleep shorts and a tank top with no bra. I pull a blanket from Jane's fort and wrap it around me before I sit beside him. Excitement finally zips through me. "You got me a gift?"

"Two." His expression is all boyish pride. He's so pleased with himself and I'm dying to know what he could possibly want to give me that's worth climbing into my window at night. "Which do you want first, right pocket or left pocket?"

His hands disappear behind him.

"Right," I say, then watch eagerly as he pulls something out of his back pocket and places it in front of me.

My stomach flips as he sets the red licorice on the bed between us.

"You got me licorice?"

"Red licorice," he clarifies. "You made your opinion on black licorice very clear the other night, so I got you cherry-flavored."

My gaze flicks between him and the candy. I'm a little thrown and a whole lot delighted.

"I'm sure you don't need luck to kick everyone's ass this weekend, but a little luck never hurt anyone."

"Thank you." I trail my fingers along the package, trying to name all the feelings coursing through me at the thoughtfulness of his gift. I'm not sure anyone has ever given me a gift like this. No, I know no one has. I would remember it. I pick up the licorice and hold it protectively in my lap. "What's in the other pocket?"

His smile grows impossibly bigger, and I'm nearly giddy with anticipation.

"This one is technically a gift for you and me. Another good luck charm, if you will." He pulls out a wad of blue fabric and holds it up. As the material falls open, I take in the Valley U Football across the front of the jersey. A replica of the ones the team wears.

"I love it," I say. Then he flips it around and my stomach bottoms out. It has his last name and number. Walters #10.

"Players' girlfriends all wear them at the games." He tosses it at me. "You don't have to wear it if you don't want to."

"No, I want to." I don't care one bit that it's part of a ruse to make people believe we're dating when we're not. I'm going to wear Felix's jersey on game day.

"Good," he says. "Because I can't wait to see you in it."

We play thirty-six holes on Friday, then eighteen on Saturday. The fall season is generally more casual. It's a chance to work on things, while still staying in a competitive mindset. I've been working on my short game since last spring, and it shows in the improvement of my overall score. I finish tied for third, and Valley takes second overall.

"Plans tonight?" Harper asks from where she sits next to me

in the van on the way back to Valley. The mood is light. Everyone seems happy with their performances and we're all eager to get home and enjoy our Saturday night.

No one more than me, though.

"Yeah, I'm going to the football game. You?"

"Oh, right. You're dating Felix Walters now."

My face warms as I smile.

"Good for you. He's gorgeous. All that dark hair and those arms." She sighs. "*Forget about it.*"

"He's pretty great," I say, feeling a little breathless just talking about him.

"Yeah?" she asks, cocking a brow.

"You seem surprised."

"I mean, don't get me wrong, I haven't heard anything otherwise, but usually when people talk about him, it's just about how hot he is or how great he is at football. I don't think I've ever heard someone say anything about his personality. But if he's good to you then I'm happy to hear it."

"You don't think it's odd that we're together?"

Harper and I aren't super close. We've gone out to parties together a few times, but we each have our own friend groups we hang out with most of the time. But we've spent enough time together on long bus rides and practices that she knows me well enough to know my usual dating pool would not include the captain of the Valley U football team.

"Well, I saw the video, so I know he's your type."

I suppress a groan. No one at practice said anything, but I should have known that was just them being polite. "Of course, you did."

"Whose type isn't Felix? I'm not even dating men right now and he's my type."

A small laugh escapes. Harper's sexuality is ever-changing. She says she's still figuring it out. Not that it's any of my business, she just offers updates randomly in our conversations.

She elbows me. "You're beautiful and sweet, and you have a gorgeous backswing."

I snort at the last compliment. "I doubt he cares about my golf swing."

"I guess he had to have one flaw." Her smile brightens. "But seriously, if you weren't his type, then I'd say he's a very dumb man. And I doubt a successful guy like Felix is dumb."

"Thanks, Harp."

It's almost eight when the bus pulls to a stop in the back parking lot of Ray Fieldhouse. I hurry to grab my stuff and leave. Jane is waiting at the house for me so we can walk over to the football field. Of course, Coach takes forever giving us one last 'good job' pep-talk before going over the schedule for next week.

The football field is two blocks south of the fieldhouse. I can hear the noise of the crowd and the crackle of the announcer over the loudspeakers, though I can't make out any distinct words.

I run, as fast as one can with a set of golf clubs and a bag strapped to their back, through the lot and then across the street. Jane throws open the front door of our house before I get there.

"I'm sorry." I pant as I drop my backpack to the floor and then, more gently, set my clubs down. "I swear Coach was driving ten under the speed limit the entire drive back like he knew we all had plans and wanted to mess with us. I'm sweaty and gross and I need to find something to wear for the party after the game."

"I've got you covered. Outfit is laid out on your bed."

"Thank you." I hug her around the neck. She's always so ready to help me, even before I ask.

"You're welcome." She laughs lightly as we pull apart. "Now, hustle young lady. We have a football game to get you to so you can cheer on the star player."

My stomach does several flips.

Twenty minutes later, I am showered, dressed, and descending the stairs to head to the game.

Jane sits up on the couch and drops the magazine she was

flipping through on the coffee table. "Oh. My. Gosh." She punches each word.

I run a hand over my stomach and fist the soft jersey in my hands. It smells faintly of Felix, and the scent is making me nervous, as if he's standing right in front of me. "Is it okay?"

She doesn't speak as she stands and walks over to me, and her silence makes me panic, thinking this is all a terrible idea and I look ridiculous.

Then Jane's lips pull into a huge smile. "This is going to be amazing."

Chapter
TWENTY-ONE

Dahlia

B Y THE TIME WE FIND STELLA AND HOLLY INSIDE THE
stadium, the game has already started. The noise is loud
and the energy electric.

"You made it!" Stella scoots down to make room for us. "I almost had to fight a guy to save these seats."

"Thank you," I say.

She waves me off. I reintroduce her to Jane. Holly leans over from Stella's other side. She's wearing the same Valley U jersey I am, though I'm sure hers has Teddy's name and number on the back. "Hi, guys." Her red hair falls over one shoulder. "I'm glad you're here. Felix is already having a great game."

None of us try to talk beyond that. It's too loud. The Valley U cheerleaders shout from the sidelines in front of the student section. The band in their blue and yellow striped shirts take up one entire section, instruments out and ready. The crowd is on their feet, clapping and screaming along with the cheerleaders.

It's overwhelming and amazing. My pulse races in rhythm with the bass drum as I find Felix on the field. Dressed the same as everyone else, white pants and a blue jersey, he looks nothing like the others, though. At least not to me. I could pick him out by his posture and build alone.

He has a presence, especially now as he barks out commands from behind the line of scrimmage. He claps his hands and then the ball is there. He shuffles backward, poised to throw as he surveys the field. When he sends it sailing through the air, I continue to stare at him. The way he watches the play unfold in front of him. His poise and concentration doesn't end until the crowd cheers. Felix's body relaxes and he claps before unclasping the chin strap on his helmet.

It's only then that I look down the field to see another guy picking himself up off the ground in the end zone with the ball in hand.

Holly is screaming louder than anyone else around us. She has her hands cupped around her mouth as she calls, "Good job, Teddy!"

I glance back to the field in time to see him point at her as he runs off the field in front of us. She yells even louder. Stella laughs and winces. "Geez, Holl. I'm gonna need to invest in ear plugs."

During the switch from offense to defense, I lose track of Felix. Blue jerseys cover broad shoulders all down the sideline. I scan names and numbers I don't recognize until Felix's dark hair catches my attention. He's not looking at the field, but at me. My heart skitters and skips as his mouth pulls into a smile, and his gaze drops to my jersey. *His* jersey.

Anxiousness I hadn't even realized I was feeling since I walked in finally eases, replaced by excitement. I'm standing in the crowd with the star quarterback looking at me. I smile back, lift one hand, and mouth 'hi.' He replies with a wink before turning back to face the field.

Someone claps me on the shoulder. I turn, ready to glare

at whomever is touching me, but when I do, I see a couple guys smiling at me.

"Your guy is on fire," one of them says.

My guy.

I turn back to the field, a little dazed. Never in a million years could I have imagined this. Real or fake, I'm going to be riding this high for a long time.

I learn from Felix's sisters that UTEP isn't very good and was supposed to be a nice, easy start to the season, but Valley is just making them look silly. Felix connects pass after pass with ease, and the defense shuts their offense down easily. The restlessness of the crowd dies off a little as the game nears the end of the second quarter with us up by more than forty points, but the student section is still on their feet and ready to cheer on Felix every time he steps onto the field.

Everyone loves him. I knew that before today, but being surrounded by it is an entirely different thing. Guys cheer for him as loudly as the girls do. He's the star of the team in their eyes, no doubt about it.

At halftime, Stella and Jane save our seats while Holly and I go up to the concession stand.

"How long have you and Teddy been together?" I ask as we stand in line.

The immediate smile on her face is contagious. "Eight months, but I've been crazy about him forever."

"You're cute together. It's easy to see he's just as crazy about you."

"So are you and my brother. After Bethany royally fucked him over, I thought it would be a long time before he trusted someone again."

"What do you mean she royally fucked him over?" I think back to everything Felix told me about his relationship with Bethany, which admittedly wasn't much.

"Where to begin." Holly blows out a long breath. "All she

seemed to care about was going out where people could see them together. And she'd post every little thing on Instagram. I had to stop following her because one time she took a video of him going down on her."

My eyes widen in surprise. "What?!"

"You couldn't see anything. The camera was aimed on her face, but she rasped out something like, *My man works just as hard off the field as he does on,* and added enough tongue and kitty emojis to get the point across."

"Gross."

"Yeah, major ick. To be honest, I never thought he liked her that much. But maybe that's because I didn't really like her. He was upset when things went down though, so he must have felt something for her."

"So, what happened? Why did they break up?" I'm dying to know more details.

"He really hasn't told you any of this?"

"He said something about her wanting more than he could give with school and football. I didn't press for more," I admit.

"Eh, I get it. I don't want to know anything about any of the girls Teddy even so much as looked at before we got together."

I huff a small laugh as we move up closer to the front of the line. I'm anxiously waiting for more information, any little tidbit to better understand Felix. Maybe it will help me understand why he's so hesitant to date (really date) anyone. And why he won't kiss me again.

"We were all at a party. Things had been tense all night. They were fighting about something. Felix was really upset. I don't know what started it, but then she started saying these awful things to him in front of everyone. How he was pretty to look at but had the personality of a rock. And how she had been trying to hold out for his NFL contract, but she just couldn't pretend anymore. She basically made it seem like she was using him for a paycheck."

My stomach twists and white-hot jealousy jolts through me

with a heavy dose of anger. She had this great guy and only saw him for the money he'd make someday. No wonder he isn't interested in another relationship.

We grab our food and start back for our seats.

"You know what," I say, pausing outside the restrooms, "I need to pee. Go ahead. I'll meet you back down there."

"You don't want me to wait?"

"Nah, I'm fine."

"At least let me take your stuff." She reaches for my hot dog and soda.

"Thank you."

She smiles, juggling two drinks, a hot dog and popcorn as I disappear into the restroom.

I groan at the line of women waiting and seriously consider holding it until after the game, but I really have to go and the line is moving fairly fast, so I decide to stay.

I've been standing in line for a few minutes when the girl in front of me turns and smiles. I smile back politely.

She looks a little shy as she asks, "You're Dahlia, right? Felix Walters' girlfriend?"

"Umm…yeah," I say like I'm not sure I am, then I smile. "Yes. Yes, I am."

"He's having a great game. I'm Francine. My boyfriend is Cody, he's a freshman." She turns to show me her back, which is when I realize she's wearing a jersey just like mine. They really are the standard attire of girlfriends, it seems.

"It's really nice to meet you."

"You too," she says as a toilet flushes and then a stall door opens. "I guess I'll see you around."

I'm smiling to myself as I stand at the front of the line. I can't believe someone just recognized me by name in the bathroom. It's surreal and even more surreal that they know me because I'm Felix's girlfriend.

It's finally my turn. I go and then head to the sink to wash my hands. And there she is. *Bethany*. She comes out of one of the stalls, the same way other women might strut down a runway. She tosses her shiny blonde hair over one shoulder as she steps up to the sink next to me. While she washes her hands, she stares at her reflection, turning to see every angle. She's so busy checking herself out that it takes her a beat to see me.

Her gaze flicks to me, away, and then back. She laughs as she stands tall. Drying her hands with a paper towel, she slowly scans my outfit.

"Look at you," she says, voice full of fake sweetness. I'm having a hard time meeting her eyes and not thinking about all the awful things she said to Felix. "Nice jersey. I wore it better, but I think we both know that."

It's hard to argue with her. She's gorgeous. A truly awful human wrapped up in a very pretty package.

I shrug and try to ignore her. Bethany is not used to being ignored.

She steps closer, wedging herself between me and the sink. Her voice lowers and is filled with venom. "Felix may have plucked you out of your boring, dull life to feed his ego for a while, but sooner or later, he's going to get tired of being with someone so… forgettable. And when that happens, you'll go back to being no one."

I don't want her words to hit me so deeply, but they do. I'm frozen in place. I can't make all the angry words bubbling up inside me come out. Instead, it's hot tears I feel pricking the back of my eyelids.

The worst part is, she's right. Bethany is just lashing out and saying whatever she can to hurt me, thinking I'll cower and give him up. She has no idea how close she is to the truth. Because in a month, our agreement will be over, and I'll go back to my life, him to his. I was never going to get to keep him, but she's just made me more determined than ever to enjoy every minute until then.

She tosses the paper towel in the trash and brushes past me.

After she's gone, I wait an extra minute, getting myself together, before I head out.

I almost run directly into Holly.

"Hey." I force a smile at Felix's sister. "You waited."

"I didn't want you to fight the crowd back to our seats alone." She hands me my drink and food. "Did Bethany say something to you? I saw her come out before you, looking smug and evil."

I can't bear to repeat the conversation, so I lift one shoulder in a shrug and start for our seats. "I think that's her everyday look."

Chapter
TWENTY-TWO

Felix

"Yo, Walters. Awesome game," some guy yells and then tosses a beer in my direction as I walk through the front door of my house.

"Thank you." I catch it, tap the tab a few times before I pop it open, and then drain half the cold can in one long gulp.

Adrenaline from the game still pumps through me. We're ready to take this season by storm and UTEP was just the first stop. They're probably the easiest team we're going to play, so we can't get too far ahead of ourselves, but for tonight I'm just going to enjoy it.

I make my way through the living room to more pats on the back and congratulations. Teddy and Holly are standing in the kitchen. My sister smiles as I approach.

"Nice game," she says.

"Thanks." I take another drink from my beer. "Have you seen Dahlia?"

She hesitates and the smile slips from her face.

"What?" I ask, sliding my hand into my jeans pocket to get my phone. I didn't explicitly ask her to come over tonight, but I assumed she knew I'd want her here. Looking up from the field and seeing her cheering me on in my jersey was almost as good as winning the game. Shy, beautiful Dahlia wearing my name and number across her back, and everyone knowing she's mine—hell fucking yeah. I could get used to that.

I'm already tapping out a text to her when Holly says, "Oh, there she is."

I look up in time to see Dahlia and Jane walking toward us from the front door. Another hit of adrenaline surges through me, but then it comes to a screeching halt when I see she's changed out of my jersey. Major bummer. I was looking forward to getting an up-close view of her in it.

"Hey," I say, stepping forward to hug her. "I was just texting you to make sure you were coming."

"Of course." Her arms wrap around my neck to hug me back. "Congratulations! You were amazing!"

Emotion is still running high, nerves raw, and I don't have my usual armor on to distract myself from how good it feels to have her touches and attention, her praise. Lust shoots straight through me and my chest tightens. I set my beer down and then lift her off the ground, spin her and listen to the sweet laughter that leaves her perfect mouth.

When I stop moving, I meet her gaze. "Hi." It comes out gruffer this time.

"Hey," she says back, a little breathless.

I set her back on the ground but keep hugging her. "How was your tournament?"

"I got third," she says, a hint of pride in her voice.

"Amazing. Must have been the licorice."

More of that sweet laughter filters out. "Must have been."

"We need to celebrate." I pull back reluctantly, say a quick hello to Jane, and then grab them both a seltzer from the fridge.

"Black Cherry. Nice." Jane's lips tip into a pleased and, all too knowing, smile.

I shoot her a wink, then take Dahlia by the hand. The three of us go outside. The loud music and wall of people we find out there fits my mood perfectly tonight.

I stop not far into the chaos and lean closer to ask, "How do you want to celebrate?"

"Whatever you want. It's your night. I already celebrated. We stopped for dinner on the way home from the tournament."

"That is not celebrating."

She rolls her eyes playfully. "It's all I need. Tonight is about you. All these people are here for you. You're really incredible out there. I could barely look away."

Fuck, I can't describe how good it feels to hear those words from her.

"Well, I wanted to celebrate by gawking at you wearing my jersey all night."

A hint of something like embarrassment flashes across her face.

"You look gorgeous," I reassure her. "Just, you know, even more gorgeous when people know you're mine."

I have no filter tonight. Something I should probably try to rectify before I get entirely too carried away.

She lifts our raised hands. "I think they still get the idea."

The three of us stand around talking and drinking, but I get yanked into other conversations far more often than I want. Buddies want to say good game and teammates want to celebrate.

I lose Dahlia and Jane when I get pulled inside to do a shot with my teammates.

Holly catches me afterward. "Where's your girl? She didn't leave, did she?"

"No, she's outside."

"Is she okay?" The expression on my sister's face takes me back to earlier when I asked if Dahlia was at the party. Like then, Holly looks nervous or anxious or something.

"Why wouldn't she be okay?"

"It might be nothing," she says quickly. Too quickly.

"What the hell happened?"

"At halftime, Dahlia and I went up to get snacks and use the restroom."

I motion with my hand for her to get to the point.

"I was waiting for Dahlia outside and Bethany came out just before her, looking far too pleased with herself. I asked Dahlia about it, but she shrugged it off. I saw the expression on her face though. She was upset. I have a bad feeling Bethany said or did something to her."

I grind down on my back molars.

"What are you going to do?" Holly asks.

"I don't know. Find Dahlia for starters."

"I'm sorry," Holly says. "For what it's worth though, I really like Dahlia. Your taste in women has improved."

"She's great," I say through gritted teeth. "Which is why I need to go find her."

"Don't screw this one up," she calls after me with a laugh that I know is meant to lighten the mood but fails.

Fucking Bethany has crossed a line this time. She can shovel her bullshit at me, but not Dahlia.

I find my girl in the same spot I left her with Jane. The latter is saying something and Dahlia smiles in response. I scan her outfit seeing it differently now. Jean shorts and a plain white tank top. It's what she wore to the game, minus one important article of clothing.

I reach them, wrap my arm around Dahlia's forearm, and pull her toward me. "Can I talk to you a second?"

Jane tips her head. "I'm gonna go dance."

Dahlia nods to her and then looks at me, confusion marring her face. "What's wrong?"

"Why aren't you wearing my jersey?"

"I took it off after the game." Her brows tug together, and she smiles. "I'm sorry. I didn't realize it was such a big deal."

"Did Bethany say something to you?"

Her smile drops instantly and rage wraps around my spine.

"What did she say?"

"It doesn't matter." Her words tumble out and her face tilts down, breaking eye contact.

I slide my fingers along her neck and lift her chin with my thumb, so she'll meet my gaze. "What happened?"

"She was trying to hurt my feelings or make me mad, so it would come between us and ruin our night. I'm not going to let it. You shouldn't, either."

"What did she say?" My tone is hard, but I run my thumb along her cheek softly.

"That I would never look as good in your jersey as she did." She tries to hide it, but I see the spark of hurt those words caused. She covers it by faking a smile and adding, "It's fine. I'm fine."

"It's not fine." I scan the yard looking for my ex. Surely, she isn't dumb enough to show her face at my house after saying something like that to Dahlia. Except, of course she is. I find her on the dance floor with a couple of her friends.

"I'll be right back."

Dahlia latches onto my arm. "No. That's what she wants."

"She doesn't get to say shit like that to you. Nobody does. Do you understand?"

"People talk shit. I'm hardly the only person that Bethany has been a bitch to, I'm sure."

"I don't care what she says to other people. She's not saying shit like that to you."

"You know what I want?"

"What?" I ask, voice still tight.

"I want to enjoy tonight. No drama, just the full Felix Walters experience. I want to celebrate like the guy I'm with just won his first football game of the season."

"We can do that as soon as I tell her to get the hell out of my house and never come back. That's what *I* want to do."

She closes the gap between us. Her tits pressing into my chest momentarily distract me.

"No, I want the real experience. You treat me like you're afraid I'm going to break. Would you run over there and chew out your ex for some random girl?" She shakes her head. "I'm stronger than you think. I can handle a mean girl and I can handle you kissing me again without thinking it means something more than it does. So, for tonight, can we just hang out, celebrate, and you treat me like you would any other girl you were dating?"

"You aren't any other girl."

She groans. "That's exactly what I mean. I really am. Less experienced, yes, but it doesn't make the things I want any different."

I hear what she's saying, but I can't pretend that I don't know that I'm the first guy she's kissed or that she hasn't had sex. And I definitely can't pretend like she's just some random girl I'm hanging out with for a night. Or that my ex didn't try to hurt her to get back at me.

"You said that we would do all the things I wanted to do but hadn't yet. That you would help me do them. I want to be a girl hanging out with the guy she likes at a party."

It's my turn to groan. I don't think she knows just how much I've held back.

Her navy blue eyes widen and her voice lowers. "Please?"

"All right," I agree. I'm positive this is a terrible idea, but it would be nice not to triple check every thought or action when I'm around her for one night.

The huge smile she flashes at me and the immediate lust that shoots through me in response make me second-guess my decision. I'll aim for somewhere in the middle of what she wants

155

and what I want to do. Slinging her over my shoulder and taking her to my room for a quick fuck is the latter, so I lace my fingers around her lower back and look down the front of her tank top.

"What are you..." she starts and then laughs. "Are you looking down my shirt?"

I bring my gaze back up to meet hers. "I've been trying not to stare at your tits all night, hot stuff."

She laughs again.

I blow out a breath. "The full experience, huh?"

She nods excitedly.

I am definitely in trouble.

Chapter
TWENTY-THREE

Dahlia

FELIX AND I JUMP AROUND THE PARTY. EVERYONE WANTS to talk to him and congratulate him on the game. And I'm happy to stand at his side and watch him take it in. In all honesty, he's far more humble than I expected him to be. He takes their kind words and changes the subject, asking about them, if they're someone he knows or, if not, he defers to one of his teammate's performances. I've heard how Teddy ran in a thirty-two-yard touchdown with three guys sprinting after him no less than five times.

Tonight, Felix's dark hair is covered by a black hat, turned backward, and he's wearing another plain T-shirt—also black. His wardrobe isn't very creative. It's all plain, one-colored tees and jeans. And yet, I wouldn't change a thing. His clothing highlights just how handsome he is by not pulling your attention away.

When I asked for the full Felix Walters experience, I'm not sure I knew what I was getting myself into. He's barely touched me any differently than the other nights we've hung out, but something has shifted between us. His words are freer, so are the scorching glances he sends my way in three, two, one…

My stomach flips when our eyes meet. Every few seconds he turns his attention back to me. He looks at me like he's ecstatic that I'm here. I wonder if that's how he makes everyone feel. Maybe this is just part of the experience. It wouldn't surprise me. He has charm for days and that smile…damn that smile makes me forget my own name.

His hand slides around my waist and he hooks his thumb through a loop on my denim shorts.

"It was good to see you, man," he says to the guy in front of him. "We're gonna head in. My girl needs a fresh drink."

"Lucky guess or using me as an excuse to get away?" I ask as he pulls me toward the house.

"I didn't like the way he was looking at you."

"He wasn't looking at me at all."

"Oh, he definitely was. You were just too busy staring at me to notice."

My cheeks heat. He stops, thumb still attached to my shorts, and tugs me closer.

"Don't be embarrassed. I pulled you away so I could stare back at you." His gaze locks on my lips and holds. "I've never been so annoyed that people want to talk to me."

"Woe is you." I laugh and rest my arms on his shoulders.

He turns his head and playfully bites my bicep, then kisses it. "Do you want another seltzer? I put an extra case in my room for you."

Goosebumps run down my spine from his lips on my skin and the thoughtfulness of his action.

"Yeah." My voice is quiet and breathy.

His stare locks onto my lips again, but then he steps away. "Come on, hot stuff."

In his room, Felix shuts the door and then goes over to a

mini fridge next to his desk and pulls out a beer for him and a seltzer for me.

"Thanks." I take the cold can and hold it in both hands. The air conditioning is blasting and I shiver, goosebumps dotting my arms.

"Cold?" He sets his beer on the desk and then rubs both of his hands down my arms.

"A little."

Moving a step closer, he continues to warm my cool skin by running his palms up and down from shoulder to forearm. The music and noise from the party drift faintly in, but it's just the two of us all alone, and he's looking at me like he can't decide if he's going to let himself kiss me.

I will not beg, even though I really, really want nothing more than to feel his lips on mine again.

"Stop looking at me like that, hot stuff," he warns in a low voice that sends another round of goosebumps popping up along my bare skin.

"Like what?" I can't drag my stare away from his mouth.

"Fuck," he mutters under his breath as he finally drops his head and brushes his lips over mine. He lingers there. A low groan vibrates in his chest. "You have no idea how bad I want to do all the things you're thinking right now."

"Then do them. I know what this is between us." I know that this is all temporary. Pretending to be together and his feelings for me. Will I be sad when both are over? Absolutely, but it's not enough to stop me.

He chuckles softly. "That's good because I sure as hell don't anymore."

With another soft kiss that does absolutely nothing to quell the desire blooming inside me, Felix backs away. He goes to his closet and comes back with a black hoodie. "My lucky sweatshirt."

"You have a lucky sweatshirt?" I take it from him and hug the fabric to my chest.

"Absolutely." He takes it back and lifts it over my head and then down over my body.

I work my arms through and he tugs the hem so it covers my torso. It's too big. The sleeves hang over my hands and it's so long that it looks like I'm not wearing any pants, but it's so comfortable, I'm already dreading taking it off.

"Does luck transfer to the person who wears it?"

"I'm not sure. I've never tested it. You're the only person to wear it." He scans me from head to toe. "We should get back out there. You can test out your luck with some flip cup."

I lift both brows as I smile back at him. "I was thinking more along the lines of it helping me *get lucky*."

He blanches like he can't believe I said that. "Fucking hell, hot stuff."

Felix doesn't drop my hand as he pulls me out of his bedroom and back to the party. Jane lifts her arms over her head when she spots us. "All my favorite people are finally in one place!"

Daisy and Jordan are sharing a seat, and Violet is sitting in another chair while Gavin stands next to Jane. The two of them are on a team against two of Gavin's roommates, Noah and Jenkins. And some of Jordan's hockey teammates are gathered around watching.

All my friends glance to my hand, where I'm still holding Felix's.

"Hey," he says, jutting his chin to the guys. "You made it."

"Wouldn't miss it." Jordan offers him a hand. "Congrats on the game."

"Same to you," Felix says. "Heard you beat ASU."

"We destroyed ASU," Jordan's teammate and roommate Liam says as he drapes one arm around his boyfriend's shoulders.

"And Jordan got a hat trick." Daisy beams with so much pride it makes the rest of us smile back at her.

"You are my hat trick, baby." He kisses her so hard, I can practically feel it.

I want someone to kiss me like that. Like I'm their everything. Maybe that's too much to expect from a guy I'm fake dating, but when I catch him looking at me, the intensity in his gray eyes makes it seem not so crazy.

After Gavin and Jane finish their game of beer pong, we decide to play flip cup. I think Felix gets off on watching me kick everyone's ass. It's me, him, Jane, and Lucas, against Daisy, Jordan, Violet, and Gavin.

Daisy calls off after two games, which is what I should do, since my body tingles from the alcohol, but I'm having too much fun.

Jordan goes with her, and Brogan and Archer take their spots. I like Felix's teammates. Especially when they start fighting over me. Brogan and Lucas are currently playing rock, paper, scissors to decide whose team I get to be on.

Felix wraps his arms around me from behind and nuzzles into me, nose running along the column of my neck. "Everybody wants you, hot stuff. Not sure how I feel about that."

"It must be the lucky sweatshirt. I think it's working."

His hands slide under the bulky material. Cold fingers tease the bare skin along the band of my shorts. "It's definitely working."

I turn in his arms. Maybe it's the alcohol, but I feel braver in my actions around him tonight. I rest one hand on his bicep and squeeze the hard muscle. "I like your arms."

"Yeah?" He seems amused by my admission.

"And your eyes. And mouth. And the way that one piece of hair always falls onto your forehead."

His smile grows. "That's a lot of things. Sounds like you might like me."

"I do, but not because of any of those things."

His forehead knits in confusion.

"You're a good guy. A great guy, actually. You're talented and you work hard, but you know how to have fun too. I like a lot of things about you now that I think about it. Want the full list?"

161

His mouth falls into a straight line and his throat works with a swallow. "I don't feel like such a good guy right now. All my thoughts are very, very bad."

His hands around my back slide up and under my tank top. My face flushes at the contact.

"Tell me."

His answer is to flick my bra clasp open. I let out a little gasp. My nipples harden as the material loosens around them. Calloused, outstretched palms glide up higher on my back. His thumbs inch around until they brush side boob.

No one can see anything, except that Felix has his hands up my sweatshirt, but the fact he's touching me where anyone can see is hot.

"Are you two gonna keep playing or make out?" Lucas asks.

Without tearing his gaze from mine, Felix says, "Make out."

My pulse races and my heart is hammering in my chest.

"To be clear," he says as he brings his mouth closer. "This isn't part of the Felix Walter's experience."

"No?"

"Uh-uh. This is the Dahlia Brady effect. Totally different thing. You drive me completely fucking crazy."

I'd doubt his words if he wasn't looking at me like he can't tear his gaze away. I lace my arms around his neck and bring my body flush against his. His rough palms continue to caress my back and sides as he slants his mouth over mine.

A moan slips from my lips and he swallows it, letting out one of his own as he deepens the kiss. It's slow and sweet. He takes his time, unhurried, almost reverent.

My fingers twist in the hair at the nape of his neck and I lean up on my toes to kiss him harder. The frantic need building inside me wants to savor, while at the same time it shouts for more.

I'm vaguely aware of Jane catcalling behind us, but I just smile and keep on kissing Felix.

He grunts as he finally pulls away. He drops his forehead against mine as we catch our breaths.

"Wow," I say, my heart refusing to slow even as the world starts to come back into focus. "The Dahlia Brady effect is strong."

His hands lower back to the top of my shorts and he presses a kiss to my temple. "You have no fucking idea."

Chapter
TWENTY-FOUR

Felix

"DON'T GO. IT'S STILL EARLY," DAHLIA SAYS AS JANE hugs her goodbye.

"It's not that early, my friend. And I'm beat." Jane meets my gaze over Dahlia's head. "You've got her?"

"Yeah," I say, nodding. "I got her."

Jane steps toward the front door where Gavin and Violet are waiting for her, kisses her hand and holds it out. "Love you. Call me if you need anything."

When the door closes behind her, Dahlia turns to face me. "Are you sure it's okay that I stay?"

Okay? Is she serious?

"Definitely. I'm not done kissing you yet."

"Oh." Her face lights up. Tipsy looks good on her. Cheeks flushed, big, goofy smile, and eyes only for me.

"Want another drink? More flip cup? I bet one or two more wins and you could make Brogan cry."

The party is still going strong outside, but we both stopped drinking some time ago. Her, because she didn't want to 'get so drunk she wouldn't remember kissing me' and me, because I couldn't hold a beer and grab her ass with both hands at the same time.

"No." She shakes her head with a small laugh. "I don't think I have it in me."

On cue, she yawns.

"Come on. It's been a long day." I take her into my room, then grab a water and some Advil. "Take these before you fall asleep."

"I don't want to sleep yet. I was promised more kissing."

"Okay, then take these before I kiss you again."

She does and then climbs onto my bed.

Fuck. I rub at the back of my neck. Her blonde hair fans out over my pillow and her long, bare legs curl up on top of my comforter. I know she has shorts on, but it seriously messes with my head thinking about sliding my hand up her smooth thigh and underneath my baggy sweatshirt to find her completely bare.

"Tonight was amazing." She spreads her arms out wide so that she takes up most of the bed. Her head falls to the side to look at me. "Did you have fun?"

I kick off my shoes and then press one knee onto the bed, holding myself up over her. "I had a great time."

The happy smile that curves her lips hits me square in the gut. I really did have a great time, and I want to keep having a great time, but worry is trickling in that I'm taking things too far. I know she wants me, but we're jumping lines I never intended to cross. At the same time, I feel like it was all inevitable. I was never going to be able to spend time with her and not want more and more.

She brings a hand to the middle of my chest. "What are you thinking?"

"So many things."

"That you want to kiss me?"

I nod.

"And get me naked?"

165

So badly. My cock strains against the front of my jeans. I give her another nod.

She sits up, forcing me back onto my heels. I'm too busy staring at her perfect mouth and soulful dark blue eyes to realize what she's doing until she lifts the black sweatshirt up and over her head. My gaze goes to her chest. She glances down and laughs, then slides the straps of her still unhooked bra down each arm and pulls it out from underneath her tank. Her nipples poke against the thin white fabric of her tank.

When it looks like she's going to take off the last layer, I stop her by taking her hands in mine and pinning them above her head. The movement pushes her onto her back, and I cover her body with mine.

"If you take off that shirt, then it's game over." My dick is crushed between us and throbbing.

"And that's bad?" Her chest rises and falls quickly.

"I told you, I'm not done kissing you yet."

I love kissing her. It's fun and playful, and somehow competitive. Who can drive the other crazier. And that somehow pushes away any shyness from her. When my mouth covers hers, we're just two people that can't get enough of each other. She claws at my shirt, trying to bring me impossibly closer, and meets my kisses with the same frantic need coursing through me.

It's hard to remember to take things slow when I want to claim every inch of her, but I do. I kiss her long and slow until her fingernails dig into my biceps and she lifts her hips to get the friction she so desperately wants.

I roll off her but keep kissing her. My dick is leaking in my boxers. If she keeps rubbing against me, I'm gonna come in my fucking pants.

"Felix," she rasps, tearing her puffy lips away from mine.

"Mmmm?" I drop my head to kiss her collarbone.

Instead of replying, her delicate fingers slip under my T-shirt and hover just above the button of my jeans. If I shifted even an inch, she'd be palming my cock. My abs tighten and it's hard to breathe. Some guy with way more restraint than me, murmurs, "Turn around."

"What?" Her gaze darts to mine and a little of that uncertainty creeps in.

"On your other side." I help move her so she's facing the wall and I spoon her from behind. She holds herself rigid, still unsure, but as soon as I slide my fingers up the front of her tank top she sinks into my touch.

"I've been dying to touch these all night," I say as I cover one breast with my palm and squeeze.

She arches her back, pressing herself into my hand.

"That feel good?"

She nods frantically.

"Let me hear you, hot stuff." I need her words to ground me in this moment. Plus, some part of my ego loves knowing she wants me. Her want feels different than other girls I've hooked up with. Better, more genuine somehow.

"It feels so good," she says.

I tweak a nipple, rolling it between my thumb and finger, and press my lips to her shoulder. She moans and tries to push back into my dick again. I'm a bump and a rub away from coming, so I slide my hand down her stomach and cup her pussy through her shorts.

Her body stills and then shudders. "Oh, god."

"If it's too much, let me know."

She lets out a shaky breath.

"Dahlia?"

"Don't stop," she says.

I curl my fingers inside the leg of her jean shorts until they brush against her damp panties, then trace a circle on her clit through the material. "You're so wet."

"The Felix Walters effect," she says quickly.

I kiss her neck, then move my hands to the top of her shorts.

I swear my hand shakes as I pop the button and pull the zipper down. I don't take her clothes off but push my hand down the front of her panties until my fingers glide through her slick heat.

"Felix." My name comes out in a plea.

"I've got you. Nice and slow. Say the word and we st—"

"Don't you dare stop."

I chuckle. "All right."

Sweat beads up on my forehead as I push in and out of her. She soaks my fingers, grinding into my hand, and moaning so sweetly. I want to hear that noise on a loop for the rest of my life.

Her movements are jerkier as I increase the pace slightly, and her breaths are ragged. "Felix."

No, I take it back, that's what I want to hear on a loop for the rest of my life. My name said on the brink of orgasm.

"I think I'm gonna," she pants.

"Come for me, Dahlia." I rub the heel of my palm against her clit harder as her body begins to tremble.

Her moans fill my room and echo off the walls. I'm torn between wanting to swallow those pretty noises, so no one else can hear, and reveling in the sound.

She curls forward into a ball as her body goes soft. I move my hand up around her waist and pull her back against me.

"Fuck, you're gorgeous when you come."

A pretty flush creeps up her neck.

"No need to be embarrassed, just straight facts."

She turns around, her face inches from mine. "That was incredible. You're incredible. This entire night has been…incredible."

I lean forward and place a chaste kiss on her lips.

"Do you want me to…" she trails off and glances down at the obvious bulge in my jeans.

"You just look at it another couple seconds and I'm gonna blow in my boxers."

"For real?" She stares hard like she's trying to gauge my seriousness.

"Truly." I wrap my hand around her neck and bring my mouth back to hers, then get up from the bed.

She sits up, leaning against one elbow.

"I'm just getting some water. You need anything?"

"No." She sits up and buttons her shorts.

I grab a water and take a long drink, then set it on the nightstand. Her lacy, white bra is on the floor at my feet. I pick it up and hold it in the air, then swing it around.

The mood is still thick with sex, but I'm trying desperately to lighten it with a few silly antics. My dick is deflating so slowly though. Probably because her nipples are still saluting me and I'm holding her sexy-as-fuck lingerie.

She comes up onto her knees and then sits back. She's thinking hard about something and I'm not sure I want to know the answer, but I find myself asking anyway. "What's going on in that pretty head of yours?"

"Isn't that uncomfortable?" She points to my crotch.

Incredibly. I toss her bra on the bed. "I'm fine."

"Can I…" Again, she doesn't finish the sentence.

She doesn't need to for my dick to resurrect his plan for release. I roll my lips behind my teeth and stare down at her.

"I can't tell if you're holding back for my benefit or yours." Her voice is quieter, but she holds my gaze as she says it. "Is this still about me deserving more?"

"No." I run my hand through my hair. "I mean, partly, yeah. You don't need to do anything for me. Making you come is the hottest thing I've done in a really long time." Ever, maybe.

"What if I want to?"

"Want to what?" I need to hear her say the words so we're crystal clear on what's happening. We've already gone farther than I planned. The Felix Walters experience would have ended an hour ago with me coming in her mouth and then sending her home. This isn't that. But I'm not sure she knows that.

"I want to make you feel as good as you made me feel." Her

words send lust tingling down my spine. "I want to touch you. If you want me to."

"Of course, I want you to." I run my thumb along her bottom lip.

She reaches forward with unsteady hands to unbutton my jeans. I stop breathing as she pushes them down and then hooks her fingers into the waistband of my boxers.

My hand falls away from her mouth so I can take off my T-shirt.

She smiles up at me when I'm standing naked in front of her. "You really are stupid hot."

"Right back at you."

I love the way my words make her flush. It makes me want to tell her a million more times until she gets used to the compliment.

"So gorgeous," I rasp. "No one has ever looked better wearing my jersey."

Surprise shows on her face, but the expression is followed quickly by disbelief.

"Or in my bed."

My plan to keep going is thwarted when she wraps her fingers around my shaft. Her touch is soft and tentative, but I'm already so keyed up that it pulls a long groan out of me.

In no time at all, I'm gritting my teeth and fighting off the orgasm that's racing to the finish line far too fast. And shit, I forgot to grab a towel or something.

"Hand me my shirt."

She keeps pumping me as she reaches for my shirt. The movement sends her long, thick hair falling onto my dick and that is my undoing.

I barely get her out of the line of fire and cover myself with the black wad of material before I'm unloading into it.

She continues watching with rapt interest as I clean up and toss the shirt in the hamper. Her face is lit up with excitement and her lips are still puffy from our marathon make-out session earlier. Her hair is slightly disheveled, and her clothes are wrinkled.

No one has ever looked better. Full stop.

Chapter
TWENTY-FIVE

Dahlia

"**M**ORNING." FELIX WRAPS AN ARM AROUND MY waist and tugs me back against his chest.

"Morning," I murmur back, wiggling closer. I can't get over the feel of him spooning me. He got me off like this, we fell asleep talking like this, and now waking up like this? There's a good chance I've died and gone to heaven.

His hand skirts up the front of his sweatshirt. Why yes, I did put it back on before going to sleep. I figured it worked its lucky magic last night, might as well soak up all of it I can. He cups my breast and squeezes gently, while pressing into me from behind. My body heats instantly.

"I dreamt of these last night," he says as he moves his hand over to give the other boob the same treatment.

"You dreamt of my boobs?" I ask through a giggle.

"Oh yeah. They're perfect."

"You haven't even seen them."

He hums and rolls on top of me. Once he's there, Felix scoots down so his face is at my belly button. He lifts the sweatshirt and tank and presses a kiss there. My stomach tightens and a delicious tingle shoots through me. He works his way up so slowly, trailing kisses up my stomach, that by the time he gets to my nipples, the anticipation is killing me.

His mouth is warm as he covers one, palming the other. He flattens his tongue and licks a circle, then closes his teeth over the sensitive bud.

I arch into him. "Holy crap."

He says something from underneath the sweatshirt and tank, but I can't understand him.

"I can't hear you over the ringing in my ears. Oh god, don't stop."

He gives my nipple one long lick and then pokes his head out.

"I said they're perfect. I now have official confirmation." He winks as he pushes my shirts up and then dives back in, licking and sucking, biting.

I'm writhing beneath him. Is it possible to orgasm from this alone? Because it feels *real* possible. Especially when he shifts and his hard length hits at the perfect spot between my legs.

He groans with me. I forgot I can touch him. My hands have been clutching the sheet, but I move them to his back. His corded muscles bunch and flex as he grinds slowly into me while still lavishing my breasts with attention.

Pounding on the door startles me.

"Rise and shine, asshole. Leaving for breakfast in twenty," Lucas says, then knocks once more.

"Go away!" Felix calls, but it comes out all garbled because he doesn't bother removing his mouth from my chest.

"Felix!" one of his sisters, I think it's Holly, shouts. "Get up or I'll make Teddy break down your door."

"Unngh." Felix sucks hard on my right nipple before popping off and meeting my gaze. "I'm sorry. I completely forgot. I have to go to a breakfast thing this morning."

"It's the most important meal of the day," I quip. My pebbled nipples are wet, and the cold air makes me shiver.

"Fuck food. I want to stay here and devour you." He ducks his head to kiss my breasts again.

"They won't really break the door down, will they?" I ask, just a hint of nerves creeping in. I mean, it's pretty obvious what we're doing in here, but I'm not sure how I feel about his roommates seeing us.

"It's real possible, hot stuff." He looks up and grins. "Don't worry. I won't let them see your perfect tits." He pulls the sweatshirt back over his head. I love the way his light scruff feels against my skin and the warmth of his mouth, the playful bites and searing hot sucks.

I don't want to leave his bed. Don't want this incredible night to end. I asked for one night and he gave it to me, but what happens next? Do we go back to pretending to date and keeping our hands (and mouths) to ourselves?

When we get the five-minute warning yell and coordinating knock on the door, Felix reluctantly pulls away.

"I really hate them right now." His hands glide down my waist and he sits back, still straddling me. "You're a fucking goddess. I could worship those tits all day."

I don't know what to do with all the compliments he's piled on me. It's surreal to consider he might actually mean them. But, uh, tit worship? Yes, please.

He's all disheveled dark hair and stormy eyes. He slept in a pair of black sweats that leave his chest and arms on display. There's also the serious bulge in his pants.

I've seen other dicks. Not in person, but online, in movies, Justin Bieber paparazzi pics, whatever. Nothing could have prepared me for Felix. He's long and thick and gorgeous. The Felix Walters experience does not disappoint.

"Stop looking at me like that, babe." He pulls my tank and

sweatshirt down to cover me but keeps running his hand along the curve of my waist.

"Like what?" I taunt him a little. I can't get over the rush it is having a simple look or touch get him all riled up. I made him hard. *Me.*

"Like you want to climb me like a tree and lick me all over."

My face heats. That's exactly what I want to do.

He groans and climbs off me, readjusting himself while staring at me lying on his bed. "Next time, we're staying at your place."

The promise of next time makes my stomach flip.

"You don't think Jane would break down the door?" I arch a brow as I sit up. I run a hand through my tangled hair as I look around for my bra.

"Good point, but you know, the more hot girls, the merrier."

My jaw drops, and he falls forward, perfect six-pack flexing, as he laughs.

"So not funny." I stand on the bed and launch a pillow at him.

"It was a little funny." He grins at me, easily dodging all three of his pillows I toss at his head.

When I'm out of ammunition, he lunges for me. He grabs me around the legs and tosses me over his shoulder. He smacks my butt as he stalks over to the door of his room. Once we're there, he lets me slide down until my face hovers in front of his.

I place a hand over my mouth. "I haven't brushed my teeth."

"Morning breath won't save you now."

"What about breakfast?"

He presses me against the door. "They can't break it down if we're standing in front of it."

Ten minutes later, lips tender from all the kissing we've done for the past twelve hours, Felix and I emerge from his bedroom. I'm all out of sorts with reality. I can't believe I spent the night with Felix. We crossed off so many firsts for me, and it still somehow doesn't feel like enough.

I duck into the bathroom after him and finally swipe some toothpaste over my teeth, gargle some mouthwash, and clean the black smudges from underneath my eyes. When I step into the living room, Felix, his roommates and sisters are all sitting around waiting on me.

Felix jumps up. "Are we ready?"

I hide behind him, running my fingers through my hair. I'm sure I look every bit the part of a girl who spent all night and morning making out.

"I'm starving." Stella gets to her feet, followed by the rest of the group.

"Hideout?" Lucas asks, spinning his keys around one finger.

Everyone agrees and we head out the front door.

"Dahlia and I are going to take my car. We'll meet you there," Felix says, taking my hand and guiding me toward his orange Corvette parked at the curb.

"Don't get lost," Stella warns with a knowing look.

Felix opens the passenger door for me.

I pause before climbing in. "I'm coming?"

"You thought I was gonna kick you to the curb this morning?" He arches a disbelieving brow.

"Umm..." Kind of, yeah. Or at least drop me off at my house and go about whatever he had planned for the day.

"Well, fuck. Even I'm not that big of an asshole." He chuckles. "Besides, I want to stare at your puffy lips a little longer. I love knowing they're all swollen and red from me."

Proving his point, he steps closer, backing me into the side of the car and kissing me stupid until the others honk and yell out their windows for us to hurry up.

"Come to breakfast with me and then after, I'll drive you

home. I'd invite you back here, but I have to go to the fieldhouse later for film review."

"Yeah, of course. I have stuff to do today, too." Like catch up with Jane. She's sent a dozen texts already this morning.

He swipes his lips over mine once more and then steps back.

At The Hideout, I slide into a booth next to Felix. Lucas is on the other side of him, with Holly, Teddy, and Stella across from us.

Someone orders a pitcher of mimosas, but Felix and I stick to water.

Felix raises his glass. "Happy birthday, Teddy."

"It's your birthday?" I ask the big guy across from me.

A shy smile tugs at one side of his mouth, and he nods.

"Oh my gosh." I elbow Felix. "I had no idea. Happy birthday."

"You didn't tell her why we were having breakfast?" Stella asks.

"I thought I mentioned it." He grins as he takes a drink.

"Uh-huh." Lucas snorts. "Because it sounded like you two were doing a whole lot of *talking* in there this morning."

My face flushes. Felix drops an open palm to my thigh.

We order lots of food and the conversation is light and fun. The guys talk about last night's game, Holly forces us all to sing Happy Birthday to a red-faced Teddy, and I quietly take it all in. I'm enjoying seeing this side of Felix. He's relaxed and happy, and his touches come easier now, like he's no longer putting up a wall between us. I'm still in his sweatshirt. The only way I'm giving it back is if he physically removes it from me.

"Dahlia, are you coming to breakfast with us on parents' weekend?" Stella asks.

My gaze flicks to Felix. "Umm…I'm not sure."

Holly glances between her brother and me, and with no malice in her tone says, "Do you two ever come up for air long enough to talk?"

I blush harder.

"You have to come," Stella adds. "Our parents will be so excited to meet you."

Felix doesn't seem at all concerned that his sisters are inviting me to meet his parents. His hand remains steady on my thigh.

"If Felix won't invite you, then I will." Stella grins. "Be my date."

"I didn't invite her because I forgot about it," he says casually.

"Actually, I can't anyway," I say. "I just remembered I have a golf tournament and I think my dad is coming up to watch."

Felix looks to me. "A tournament at Valley?"

"Yeah."

One side of his mouth lifts. "That's cool. Can I come watch?"

"No," I say quickly.

He scoffs. "Why not?"

I laugh and the honest reply slides out before I can stop it, "Because you're very distracting."

Chapter
TWENTY-SIX

Dahlia

"I'M SO JEALOUS I COULD DIE," JANE WHINES FROM WHERE she lies on the pillow fort next to my bed. "I came home alone and fell asleep watching *Fresh Prince of Bel-Air* reruns."

"I love that show."

"Don't patronize me. I was eating a microwaved burrito while wearing sweats, and you were getting busy with Felix."

I snort a laugh. "It was a pretty great night."

I'm curled up on my side, still wearing Felix's lucky sweatshirt, but freshly showered. Jane came running to my room for details minutes after I walked through the door.

"When are you going to see him again?" she asks, hugging a pillow to her chest.

"I don't know. We didn't make any plans."

"Invite him over tonight." Her eyes light up. "Oooh, we can watch *Can't Buy Me Love!*"

"I don't know." I wrap the strings of the hoodie around a finger. "I don't want to be the girl that turns into a clingy bitch the second we start hooking up."

"You're not just hooking up."

"I don't know what we're doing anymore," I admit. "But everything Felix has told me is that he doesn't do relationships. He doesn't have time and Bethany really fucked with his head."

"Evil bitch. She's lucky you didn't tell me about the bathroom stunt until today. I'd like to rip her hair out strand by strand."

"Honestly, same."

We fall quiet. I'm tired but can't stop replaying things from last night over and over in my head. Jane sits up quickly. "We should order loads of takeout and have a girls' day. I'll text Daisy and Violet."

"They're busy," I say.

"No, they're not. They're with Jordan and Gavin. They're always with them. I'm glad they're in love and everything, but we need a girls' day." Her thumbs fly over the screen of her phone, and I don't bother trying to talk her out of pulling our friends away from their boyfriends. When Jane has an idea, there's no stopping her.

And in less than an hour, the four of us are sitting around the living room watching an old Sandra Bullock flick with takeout from three different restaurants. Daisy and Vi pepper me with questions about Felix. It's exciting to be the one with something to contribute to our conversations. I've always been the one listening and asking the questions about the guys they're dating. It's the perfect end to an incredible weekend. Great friends, a cute romantic comedy, and greasy food.

I don't hear from Felix Sunday night, and Monday I have to skip breakfast to see my advisor. My fingers itch to text him, but I refrain. I'll let him make the next move. See? I can do this. I can casually date with no expectations.

Except, I have this low-level anxiety that grows as each hour passes without hearing from him. What if he decided that he's done with me and our arrangement? What if I never get another chance to hang out with him one-on-one, or kiss him. I run my fingers along my lips, remembering what his mouth felt like on mine.

After classes, I head straight to the golf course. I played well last weekend at the tournament, but it's just giving me more motivation to push harder. We have our home tournament coming up and I would love to win with my dad watching.

He's the reason I started golfing. I was Daddy's little girl, through and through. And he loved golf. At first, I only played so that I could spend time with him. We'd get up early on a Sunday morning and meet up with some of his friends, play eighteen and then have lunch.

Dance was my first love. But somewhere along the way, things changed. I found I liked being outside. I liked the solitude and quiet atmosphere on the course. And I loved the challenge. It didn't come as naturally to me as dancing, and I had to work really hard to improve. I still remember the first time I shot a lower score than my dad. I remember the smile on his face and the exhilaration I felt from years of consistent practice finally paying off.

That feeling was magic. I didn't have aspirations of playing in college, though. In fact, the only reason I did freshman year was because I got a scholarship, but I think it's helped keep me sane. When everything else has felt hopeless, I've found pieces of myself out here.

And now that I'm seeing the payoff again, shooting lower scores than I ever have at tournaments, my competitiveness wants to push it even further to see how much more I can improve.

"Will you record my swing? I want to check something." I hold out my phone to Harper. Practice is over, but we're both still hitting balls.

"Your swing is looking great," she says, but takes my phone and stands behind me to capture video as I get into position with my three wood.

I take a deep breath, swing, and watch the ball sail down the driving range.

"It looks damn near perfect to me." Harper holds out my phone, and I take it.

"It feels like my hands are drifting as I come down from the backswing." I slow the video down, examining every frame for flaws.

"Stop overanalyzing. You're playing great. Lean into whatever magic you've found and don't tweak so much you lose it."

"So basically, rely on luck?"

She laughs. "Luck is just hard work with a sprinkle of good karma."

"I thought it was preparation meeting opportunity?"

"Eh, I like my version better." Her lips pull into a satisfied smile at her own answer.

"Well, I've never been that lucky, so I think I'll stick with the hard work part and hope karma or opportunity finds me."

I tee up another ball, but before I can get into position, Harper says, "Oh, I don't know about that. I think you might be the luckiest chick I know."

She glances at me over her shoulder with a sly smile then out to the parking lot that runs along the side of the range. I follow her gaze until I find the object of her interest.

Felix leans against the hood of his orange Corvette, arms crossed over his chest, staring back at me. His lips curve when he realizes he's been spotted, and he lifts one hand in a wave.

I wave back dumbly, heart racing.

"What is he doing here?" I ask more to myself than Harper.

"I don't know, but whatever it is, I hope it ends with you riding him in the front seat of his car. He is straight-up obsessed with you, and I am so here for it."

"He is not obsessed with me."

"He's looking at you like a man *obsessed*."

I shove the club in my bag and head toward him. When I get within ten feet, he pushes off the car and stands tall.

"Hey." He shoves both hands in his pockets. It looks like he came straight from his own practice. Black athletic pants and a gray Valley U Football T-shirt. His dark hair is a little messy and windblown. He's still the hottest guy I've ever seen.

"Hi," I reply tentatively, looking around for some explanation for his appearance at the campus golf course. "What are you doing here?"

"You said I couldn't come to your tournament, but you said nothing about watching you practice." His grin is wolfish, and my stomach does a little flip.

"Yeah, well, it extends to practices."

"In that case, your coach called practice fifteen minutes ago, so technically, I'm just a guy hanging at the driving range watching some badass girl hit the fuck out of a golf ball. You gave me goosebumps a couple times."

"How long have you been here?" I know my face must be bright red because it's on fire.

He chuckles. "Long enough to be impressed."

"Why?"

"You're amazing."

I shake my head. It's fuzzy with his presence and compliments. "I mean, why are you here?"

"I didn't hear from you today. Wanted to make sure you were alive."

"You're here for a wellness check?" I feel one brow lift.

Felix laughs again, this one silent but shaking his chest. He removes his hands from his pockets and steps closer. "What are you doing tonight?"

"I was going to work at the design lab. Why?"

"Hoping you could hang out. The rest of my week is slammed with practices and meetings."

"I have a design I need to finish for tomorrow." I've never

wanted to blow off homework so badly. "Maybe I can finish in an hour or two and then we can do something?"

Something like kiss until my lips hurt again. I've missed that feeling.

"I have to crash pretty early. Coach was pissed at practice tonight and called an extra workout for tomorrow at the ass crack of dawn."

"Bummer."

"Yeah." He nods slowly. "Can I drive you home at least?"

"I live down the street," I say, fighting a smile. I can actually see the house from where we're standing.

Felix waves a hand toward my abandoned golf bag. "You've got all those heavy clubs."

He walks with me back to get my stuff. Taking my bag from me, he groans. "Fuck. They are heavy."

"Maybe you're just weak, Walters," I tease.

With that, he hooks the bag over one shoulder and then scoops me up, carrying both me and the clubs across the range.

"Oh my gosh, put me down. People are staring," I whisper-hiss.

"No can do, hot stuff." He tips his head toward Harper and a few of my other teammates who lingered after practice. They watch with surprise and amusement. He raises his voice to speak to them. "Everything is fine. Don't worry. She just got a little weak in the knees at the sight of me. Isn't that sweet?"

"Oh my gosh, Felix." I hit him playfully in the chest.

His smile is broad as he stalks away. He doesn't put me down until we've reached his car. I adjust my skirt that rode up as he carried me and straighten my tank top.

Felix puts my clubs in the back of his car and then leans against it and pulls me to him.

"I can't believe you did that. They are going to give me so much shit tomorrow."

"I guess I better make it worth it then." He slides a hand around the back of my neck and uses it to guide my lips to his.

He makes this sexy, little noise every time we kiss. It's a sort of gruff hum that comes from deep in his throat, but somehow, I can tell he's smiling when he does it.

His grasp around my neck is gentle, but his mouth crushes mine. I lean against his chest and drape my arms over his shoulders. His tongue tangles with mine as he circles my waist with his free hand. Long fingers splay out over my lower back and graze my ass. Two inches lower and he'd be under my skirt.

I have enough wherewithal to know that standing in the middle of a parking lot with half my teammates watching isn't a super idea. I'm winded when he pulls back. He winks. "Ready, babe?"

Ready to make out in his car? Ready to scrap my evening plans and go home with him? Yes, to all of the above. But apparently, I'm too dazed to answer.

He shoots me a half smile and steps away from the passenger door so I can get in. "Come on," he says. "I'll drop you at home."

I chance a glance in Harper's direction as I move to climb inside. She gives me two thumbs up and flashes me the biggest smile.

Felix gets behind the wheel, starts the car, and then leans over to brush his lips against mine again before he puts it in reverse.

And I think, maybe I am the luckiest girl alive.

Chapter
TWENTY-SEVEN

Felix

THURSDAY AFTER PRACTICE, I STAY TO GET IN SOME MORE conditioning. It's the only way I'm going to sleep tonight. We don't play until Saturday, but we leave early tomorrow morning to travel to Flagstaff. One bad night of sleep and I'd probably have enough adrenaline to get me through. Two nights of shitty sleep, though, and I won't be sharp enough to get it done. So tonight, I need total exhaustion on my side.

Teddy stays with me, going through the motions more to keep me company and make sure I don't overdo it than because he needs it.

When I stop for water, he collapses on the field. "How are you still standing?"

"Obviously I'm in better shape than you."

His mouth falls into a straight line, but my ribbing gets him back on his feet. The sun set some time ago, and without the lights on the field, it's getting hard to see.

"Are you stressing NAU this much?" He ducks his head and wipes his forehead on the sleeve of his T-shirt.

"It's not just NAU," I say. "It's every team from here on out. I want to finish strong. No regrets, no looking back and wondering what could have been, ya know?"

"Yeah." He nods. "I get that. And we will. No one works harder than you. Not in all the years we've been playing together. We're ready. *You* are ready."

I try to let his words ease the nerves pinging around my ribs. Since I was eight years old, all I've wanted is to be a football player. My mom would make my sisters and me answer that question on the first day of each new school year. She had one of those chalkboard signs where she wrote our names, which teacher we had that year, how old we were, how tall, and a bunch of other details I can't remember. Even when we got to junior high, she'd bribe us with chocolate chip cookies or something until we'd agree to stand in front of the sign and have our picture taken.

Every single one of those photographs I'm standing in front of the same black chalkboard sign, proudly stating that I was going to be a football player when I grew up. Through buzzed hair, a mohawk, a scraggly attempt at growing facial hair, popped collars, there's even one where I'm rocking an eyebrow piercing. My appearance shifted over the years, but my identity never has. I'm a football player. It's all I've ever dreamed of being.

I shake out my legs. I don't know how much more I have in me tonight, so I finally relent. "Yeah, you're probably right. Ready to get out of here?"

"Of course, I'm right," he says and claps me on the shoulder. "Do you want to grab dinner? I'm starving."

"Yeah." I blow out a long breath. I'm dog tired, which is exactly where I wanted to be.

We gather our things and head for the parking lot. I'm dragging, which is the only reason Teddy spots her before me.

His elbow to my side nearly knocks me over. Fuck, I might

have overdone it. But when I glance up and see Dahlia waiting next to my car, I perk right up.

"Hey," I say, smiling wider than I thought possible twenty seconds ago.

"Hi." Her timidness around me still surprises me. It fades the more time we spend together, but she always approaches me like she's not sure if I'm going to be pleased to see her or not. Spoiler alert, I'm always fucking pleased to see her.

She smiles at Teddy and pushes a lock of her blonde hair behind one ear. "Hey."

"Hi," he replies back to her, then says to me, "I'll catch you back at the house."

Teddy hops into his truck and I toss my bag in my car and then lean against it to keep my wobbly legs from collapsing.

"I'm sorry for the surprise attack, but I wanted to give you this." She holds out my black sweatshirt.

"Thanks." I take it without removing my eyes from her. She's in a golf skirt and tank top, similar to what I saw her in on Monday. It's cute and sporty and her boobs look incredible. I try not to stare directly at them but fail miserably. "Coming from practice?"

"Yeah, well, sort of. I stayed a little late to work on a few things. Then I had to go straight to campus for a group project meeting." She glances around. "Are you just getting done for the night?"

"I stayed a little late to work on a few things, too."

"Excited for the game?"

"Honestly?" I run a hand through my hair. "Scared shitless."

"What?!" Her mouth curves with a surprised smile. "Why?"

"NAU is tough this year. One of the better teams we'll go against this season."

"Aren't you, like, the best college quarterback in the country or something?" The genuine confusion on her face as she tries to understand why I'm nervous about this weekend's game is adorable. And something I've gotten used to. On the outside, I'm all confidence because that's what my team needs. But the reality of what this season means for my future has me a little freaked out. You can go from being number one to some guy who could have been great in an instant.

"What are you doing for the next couple hours?" I ask her.

"Nothing. Why?"

"Hang out with me for a while? I've barely seen you. Archer and Brogan have also noted your absence at breakfast. Real bummer vibes from them."

She laughs. "I'm sorry. Monday I had to meet with my advisor, Tuesday I overslept, and…anyway, yes, I'd love to hang out."

I take her to my place first so I can shower and change, scarf down a sandwich and protein drink, and then we sit around with my roommates. Lucas and Teddy are playing video games. I opt out so I can keep my focus on Dahlia.

"How was your week?" I ask.

"Good. Just school and golf. Yours?"

"Good. Just school and football." I sling an arm around her back and let my fingers brush against her shoulder. "What are you girls going to get up to this weekend?"

"I'm not sure. It sounds like it's going to be pretty quiet around campus."

She's right. The football and basketball teams are both traveling, and I ran into Jordan at the dining hall today and he said the hockey guys are doing some team building event upstate Saturday and Sunday.

"I need to do curfew check in about thirty minutes. Want to come keep me company?"

"Curfew check?" she asks, brows pinching together.

"I go by the dorms and make sure the guys are in their rooms and ready for tomorrow. The bus leaves early."

Lucas coughs into his hand, "Overbearing asshole."

I flip him off, stand, and pull Dahlia to her feet.

"You personally check that every guy on the team is in by curfew?" she asks.

"Not every guy, but most of them."

"I already talked to Archer and Brogan," Teddy says. "They're in and ready to go."

"Thanks, man," I tell him.

Dahlia and I get in my car to head back to campus. She looks over from the passenger seat and smiles at me. I move one hand to rest on her thigh. The more we hang out, the less fake it all feels, but I'm not about to add that to the list of things to dissect right now.

I park in the lot behind Freddy dorm. I could call the guys and check in instead of stopping by, but I really don't mind. It gives me something to focus on. Sitting idly and waiting for the time to finally get on the bus is torture.

"Oh, wow. I should have brought a jacket." She huddles into herself as she steps out of the car.

Chuckling, I reach in and grab my sweatshirt, then toss it to her.

"It'll be dirty for tomorrow."

"Oh, I hope so." I wink and a pretty blush paints her cheekbones.

As we walk, I take her hand and lace our fingers together. When we get to the front entrance of the dorm, I pull her off to the side and back her against the building. She giggles in surprise, seconds before my mouth descends and captures hers.

I don't know what this girl's done to me. It's only been a few days since I've kissed her, but it feels like an eternity.

I use the strings of my hoodie to pull her even closer. I'm reconsidering my evening plans. Kissing her until I pass out might be the way to go.

We pull apart when a group of loud guys walks out of the dorm. They give us, or rather her, a long look, taking in her wet, puffy lips and bare legs. I clear my throat and send them a death glare.

They scurry along and I glance back at Dahlia. "Ready?"

She's smiling, a knowing glint in her eyes. "Did you just pee on me?"

I bark a laugh into the dark night. "Pee on you? Is that a kink of yours? Because it's not something I'm into myself, but I might be willing to try it once."

She punches my arm. "You know what I mean. Those guys barely looked at me and you glared at them and stepped in front of me like you were marking your territory."

"Oh, that's what you meant. Then, yeah, I was absolutely peeing on you."

Still laughing, I take her hand and we walk into the dorm. A lot of the guys live in Freddy since the entire dorm is student athlete housing.

"Did you live in Freddy your freshman year?" Dahlia asks.

"Yeah. You?"

"Yep. Room 107."

"Really? I was 123. Damn, I knew I should have stayed in the dorms another year. We would have been neighbors. I could have borrowed a cup of sugar or something."

She laughs. "When have you ever borrowed a cup of sugar?"

"Well, never, but I might have tried a line like that to talk to you."

The shake of her head is disbelieving. "I would have probably gone out and bought sugar just in case you asked. And then froze if you actually came to my door."

"You don't freeze around me anymore." I lift our joined hands and kiss the top of her knuckles.

She watches my mouth brush against her skin. "Trust me, internally, I'm still freaking out."

We stop by all the first-floor rooms. The guys are in, chilling, ready for tomorrow. Then Dahlia and I head up to the second, and so on. Only one guy is missing, and his roommates vouch for him that he's at the library finishing an assignment he needs to turn in before we leave.

It's all gone so easy and fast. Kissing Dahlia between rooms, checking on my guys, kissing her some more. Pretty perfect way to spend a night.

"Is that it?" she asks as we push out of the front doors of Freddy. She almost sounds as disappointed as I feel.

"Yeah. I text the guys off-campus. It's really the young guys I worry about."

"You're a good captain," she says.

"Thanks." Her compliment hits me unexpectedly. She isn't the first to say it, but I believe her in a way I've brushed off the same words from others.

We're almost back to my car when she says, "I got some news today. Eddie liked the pants. And he wants to fly me out and meet with the wardrobe people for the tour."

I stop in my tracks and stare at her. "You waited all night to tell me this?"

Her shoulders lift in a small shrug. "I was waiting for the right moment."

"Dahlia, that's incredible." I wrap her up in my arms. "We could have celebrated."

"No, really. It's okay. I knew you'd be busy tonight."

"I could have at least taken you to dinner or something."

"This was perfect. I got to see another side of you." When I don't say anything, she adds, "It must be hard trying to keep so many people in line while taking care of yourself and what you need to do to prepare for a game."

"It's actually easier having something else to do, other people to worry about instead of myself."

She smiles. "I guess I get that. Golf is different. We cheer each other on, but we don't look out for each other the same way that you do for your team."

"Well, I guess it's a good thing you have me then."

"Why's that?"

"Because I'm always looking out for you. Whatever you need, hot stuff."

"Whatever I need?" She leans forward, lips hovering over mine.

My chest tightens as her lashes flutter closed and she kisses me. Her voice is breathy when she speaks again. "I think I could get used to that."

Me too. Fuck. Me too.

Chapter
TWENTY-EIGHT

Dahlia

On Saturday afternoon, the girls and I are having a perfect chill day. I had practice this morning, then when I got home, the four of us went to brunch, followed by a yoga class at the student rec center, and after we have all been working on homework spread out in the living room while watching movies and just hanging out.

"This is so nice," Jane says. She's sitting, legs crossed, in the middle of the floor in front of the TV. "I need all your boyfriends to leave town on the same weekend more often."

"Or you just need to start dating a basketball player." Vi grins. "Eh?"

"Or a hockey player," Daisy chips in.

They all look at me.

"What?"

Laughing, Vi asks, "How are things with your football player?"

"Good." I focus entirely too hard on the sketch in front of me. "We're just…you know, keeping things casual. It's fun."

I thought I loved being able to talk about boys the same way they all do, but being in the hot seat right now is excruciating. Technically, I think we're still fake dating, but we're making out for real. I started to ask him last night, but he seemed really stressed about the game, and it didn't seem like the right time to bring it up.

Speaking of the game, I pick up my phone and check the score. A proud smile breaks out wide on my face. "They won the game."

"That is not the face of a casual anything." Daisy uses her pencil to point at me. "But I love him for you."

"And you for him," Jane says. "He needs a girl that sees him for more than being the star quarterback. And you need someone to remind you daily how absolutely incredible you are."

I snort a laugh.

"I'm serious," she insists, voice climbing. "I've heard some of the things that man says to you. He thinks you're amazing and he gets off on letting you know it."

My face heats. "That's just Felix. He knows how to make people feel good. I think that's why he's such a good quarterback. He sees people, knows their strengths, and wants to help them be their best."

"Good quarterback skills and good boyfriend skills." Violet stands and holds up the dress she's been working on for the past couple hours. It's a beautiful dark pink with a square neckline and thick straps. Vi loves designing and making dresses. Beautiful gowns with long skirts or decadent layers. And the details are always stunning. The pink one she's holding up is no exception.

"He's not really my boyfriend, but agreed. He's the best. And that's gorgeous," I say, changing the subject.

Jane sighs dreamily. "I wish I could pull off that color."

"You can pull off any color you want," I say pointedly. She can. I've seen her in hunter orange and beige and every color in between.

"No. My skin tone does better with lighter shades of pink. That'd look great on you, though, Dahlia."

It's not like anything I'd pick for myself, but since I started living out of Jane's closet a month ago, I've been wearing a lot of dresses that I never would have imagined myself in.

"Try it on," Vi says. "I'm dying to see what it looks like on someone."

"Ooooh, should we put on *Pride and Prejudice* and make it a whole thing?" Daisy asks, excitement clear in her tone.

Saturday nights hanging at home, watching old movies, drinking wine, eating junk food, and trying on dresses used to be a regular occurrence. I've missed it. And from the looks on my friends' faces, I think they have too.

Thirty minutes later, we've pulled out all of Violet's dresses (we keep them in the coat closet because no one needs a coat in Arizona ten months out of the year), opened two bottles of wine, and cued up Darcy and Elizabeth on the TV.

The movie is really just background noise at this point. We've seen it so many times, I can practically quote it word for word.

I do try on the magenta dress and then a black one, a green one, before going back to the magenta.

"I knew that one was perfect for you." Jane winks at the same time my phone buzzes on the coffee table.

I reach for it a little faster than usual.

"The winning QB?" Jane asks, a smile in her tone.

"Yeah. They're on their way back."

"What time will he get in?"

"Not until late," I say, rereading his text and tapping out one of my own.

Felix: *Thanks for the good luck text. Hope you know you're now a part of my official pre-game good luck charms. Gonna need one of those texts before every game. How's Valley? Tell* *me everything I'm missing. I'm too amped up to sleep and I'm on this bus for the next four hours.*

Me: Campus was pretty dead earlier today, so I don't think you're missing much.

Felix: What are you doing tonight?

Me: Watching Pride and Prejudice with the girls while drinking wine and trying on fancy dresses.

Felix: I'm missing seeing you in tight, sexy dresses?

Me: Yep ☺

Felix: Pictures or it didn't happen.

Me: Oh, it happened.

Felix: Take pity on a tired, horny man, hot stuff.

Me: A minute ago you were amped up. Which is it, Walters?

Felix: Whichever gets you to send me a pic.

"You're totally blushing." Vi tosses a piece of popcorn at me, drawing my attention to my roommates, who are all staring at me.

"He wants me to send him a picture of the dress."

"A photoshoot for your man?" Jane asks. "That sounds like a fab idea. Let's do your hair and makeup too. We'll make him cream his pants on the bus ride."

"That's a truly terrible image." Vi scrunches up her face.

"But a great idea," Daisy says. "Jordan has been begging me for new spank bank photos."

"You send him nudes?" Vi's mouth falls open in shock, and I choke on my wine.

"No, well, okay, fine, I have, but I meant photos of me in all your amazing dresses. It really does something for him seeing me all done up. This one specifically." She flounces the red skirt.

"It's because he's imagining ripping it off you," Vi says. "But don't let him rip that one."

"I can't even begin to tell you how jealous I am of all of you," Jane says. "Maybe I should take some sexy photos of myself and spam my contact list."

"No," we all tell her at once.

"Why not? I need someone to come rip off my dress and kiss the crap out of me. I'm the only one in this house not getting kissed. It's a real disappointment."

I hug her. "There is a great guy out there for you, I know it. And you don't need to spam all your contacts to find him."

In the end, I give in to their whims and we spend an hour taking photos of the four of us in our living room. Hair and makeup done like we're going out, each of us in our favorite custom Violet dress, and all of us a little bit tipsy.

I don't send any of them to Felix though. I'm not sure why. I guess I'm nervous that his reaction wouldn't be as excited as my friends' boyfriends. And why would it be? He's not really my boyfriend, and in a couple weeks we have to go back to being just friends. I'm not sure I can do that knowing he has sexy photos of me on his phone. Jordan called Daisy seconds after she sent him a pic, and Gavin's response was so dirty, I can't bring myself to repeat it. I love that for them. They are goals.

But even though I didn't send him a picture, Felix and I have been texting on and off all night. His bus is still more than an hour away when I climb into bed.

Me: How's the ride?

Felix: Long. Boring. Teddy is passed out beside me. No one wants to entertain me tonight.

Me: I'm entertaining you.

Felix: Yeah, but you're holding out on me.

Me: You've seen me in a dress before.

Felix: Your point?

Me: Should have taken a photo then.

Felix: Good idea. Next time you're over, how about you pose for a few in the dress and then slowly take it off. You, topless, sprawled out on my bed, pretty dress on the floor. *groan*

Me: Sorry, you're gonna have to memorize that image if you want it to last.

Felix: Already done, babe. Already done.

I fall asleep at some point during our texting and wake up to knocking on my window.

"It's me, hot stuff," Felix calls through the glass.

I push my messy hair out of my face and walk over to let him in.

"Is this a thing now?" My voice is rough with sleep.

"I didn't want to wake up the whole house," he says as he climbs inside and pulls the window shut behind him.

"Just me?"

"Just you." His hair is messy and the Valley U football T-shirt he's wearing is wrinkled. He still looks insanely handsome.

He plops down on my bed, then blows out a breath and rolls his neck. "I am beat."

"I bet." I lie down next to him. "Not that I'm complaining, but uh, why are you here?"

He lets his head fall so our faces are only inches apart. "I was hoping I was going to catch you in that sexy dress you were taunting me with."

I glance down at my sleep shorts and tank. "Sorry to disappoint."

"Not at all." One of his big palms comes to rest on my upper thigh. "I might be too tired to peel you out of some big, complicated outfit anyway."

"Too tired to get a girl naked?" I arch a brow.

"Okay, fine. Never that tired." He guides his hand around to grab my ass. "But I am enjoying this outfit quite a lot."

He pulls me on top of him and then wraps his free hand around the back of my neck to bring my lips to his.

Warmth spreads through me. I'm falling for him. I know I am and that it's going to hurt something awful when it's over, but at least I'm sacrificing my heart for some amazing experiences.

A deep groan rumbles in his chest as my hips roll. His dick is already hard and tenting his athletic pants, and the thin fabric of my sleep shorts provides very little barrier. Both of his big hands grip my thighs, and he grinds me over him until I'm panting, muscles quivering.

I break apart from our kiss. His eyes are hooded with lust and the way he looks at me makes my breath catch.

"I, uh, I bought condoms."

His hands still.

Before I can lose my nerve, I add, "I've thought about it. I'm ready and I want it to be you."

"Dahlia." He sits up and brushes my hair out of my face. His grayish blue eyes are stormy and his face twists like he's in pain.

"If it's because you don't want to, then I won't say another word."

His brows lift. "You know that isn't it."

"Then we're on the same page." I sit up and meet his stare head-on. "Look, I know what we are, or what we're not, but I trust you. I like making out with you. You're good at everything and I don't want my first time to be some awkward hookup with a guy that's crappy in bed. You might not be the guy for me, but you're an amazing guy, and that means something."

"I don't know," he says, but I can see the wheels turning in his head. He wants this too.

"Will you just think about it?" I ask. "We have two more weeks and then…"

I can't bring myself to finish that sentence. At least out loud.

Then we go back to our regular lives. Him as Felix Walters, star quarterback, and me as…just me again. But me with experiences that I'll remember forever.

"Yeah," he agrees. "Yeah, I'll think about it."

He flips us so he's on top of me and kisses me again. It's sweeter this time, less hurried, and I know it's not happening. At least not tonight.

Over the next week, Felix and I hang out a lot. He's slept at my house every night. Just slept. Well, okay, not just slept, but we haven't had sex. On Friday afternoon, we're having lunch with his teammates in the dining hall, but after everyone else heads to class, we hang back.

His leg rests against mine under the table and he hooks his foot around my ankle. "Any plans for tonight?"

"A friend of mine from high school is dating a guy here at Valley. She's coming for the weekend and we're meeting up for dinner tonight."

"That's cool," he says, then narrows his gaze as he smiles at me. "What were you like in high school?"

"I don't know. Like I am now, I guess."

"So, awesome and hot?"

Laughter spills out of my mouth. "You're too much."

With a wink, he leans forward and presses his lips against mine. The butterflies in my stomach that seem to always be present when I'm around Felix, flutter and swoop as I get lost in his kiss. He pulls back far sooner than I want and looks at me like he wants more details.

"I was the same. I've always been more reserved and quieter than my friends."

"How come?"

I think about that for a second. "I'm not sure. I imagine some of it is just part of my personality, but the first time I can remember people referring to me as shy was in the fourth grade. My dad switched jobs halfway through the school year and my family moved across the state."

"You were the new girl," he says and waggles his brows.

"Yeah. And can I just say that all the movies and books make it seem way more fun than it actually is? Making friends is not something that's ever been that easy for me. It takes me a while to get comfortable around new people. Half the girls thought I was stuck-up, and the others thought I was weird."

"I'm sorry," he says. "I would have been your friend, hot stuff."

"No, you wouldn't have." I roll my eyes and shake my head. I think I have a pretty good picture of what young Felix was like and we would not have run in the same circles. "I had this really unfortunate haircut that looked like a blonde mushroom on top of my head, and I had an early growth-spurt, so I was taller than all the guys in class for a year or two."

An amused smile tips up his lips as he wraps a finger around a long strand of my hair. "I don't think any of that would have mattered. Enough time around you and I would have felt it."

"Felt what?"

"This." He motions between us. "We're the same. Different, but the same."

I'd like to think he's right, and that under any circumstances, Felix and I would have been friends, but I'm not so sure.

"Did you always want to be a designer?" he asks, pulling me from my thoughts.

"No. For a long time I thought I was going to be a dancer. But even back then, I was making my own leotards and booty shorts."

His smile widens. "We definitely would have been friends. No way I wasn't befriending the new, hot, dance girl."

"You're something else."

He glances at the time and then turns in his seat and places either leg around mine, closing me in. "I should get going, but I really don't wanna."

I lean into his chest. I don't want him to either. He wraps both arms around me. "Two days without you. How am I going to survive?"

I smile, but don't respond. It feels so real between us, so perfect. If I had a boyfriend, this is exactly what I would want it to be like. I love that we can sit and talk like friends, but that neither of us can keep our hands off the other. It's the best of both worlds in a way I didn't realize was possible. And maybe it isn't. Maybe the reason things are like this is because we're coming to the end of our agreement. Before I can stress about that, though, Felix kisses me. As long as he's kissing me, I can hold on to the time we have left.

Chapter
TWENTY-NINE

Felix

"GIMME, GIMME." BROGAN GRINS LIKE AN IDIOT AS he, Archer, and Lucas pillage the leftover food on Dahlia's tray.

She laughs and pushes it across the table so they can each grab what they want.

"Tell me the truth," I say, lowering my head to whisper in her ear. "You get extra knowing they're going to steal half, don't you?"

"Half?" she asks, turning her head and giggling. "Brogan ate every one of my grapes."

"They were good, too," the man himself says with his mouth full of something.

"I have a couple grapes left," I say. "What'll you do for 'em?"

"Hmm." She presses her lips together and leans closer. "What do you want?"

"Dangerous question, babe." I can't resist brushing my lips over hers.

"Maybe I want a little danger."

She's taunting me and I'm here for it. We've been making out every chance we get since I got back Sunday. Which is a lot of chances. We meet between classes, after classes. Basically, if we aren't at practice or class, our lips are glued together. I've even given up my lunchtime nap.

Today's our last official day together. Neither of us has mentioned it, but I know it's on her mind.

"How late can you be for class?" I circle an arm around her waist and pull her onto my lap.

We decided to do it up big for our final night together. The guys at The White House are throwing a party we plan to hit up, but before it, we're going to dinner with my sisters, Teddy, and Lucas. We take up a huge corner booth at The Hideout.

Dahlia seems nervous tonight. We decided the easiest way to end things was to just stop hanging out and let people figure it out for themselves. She won't come to breakfast anymore, and we won't hang out at each other's houses. We're bound to run into each other on campus and at parties, but it won't take long for people to realize we aren't together anymore. And if, or rather when, someone asks us directly, we'll admit we've broken up and let the rumor mill do its thing.

It seemed better than staging some fight. Dahlia and I would never be one of those couples to fight in public and make a big scene. I can't imagine us ever fighting, really, but maybe that's because what we're doing is fake and there's no need to fight in a fake relationship.

"Are you bringing her to meet Mom and Dad this weekend?" Stella asks as we're finishing up dinner.

"Oh, I can't," Dahlia says quickly. She twists her fingers

together in her lap. "I have a tournament, plus my dad is coming down."

"The tournament is during the day, right?"

"Yeah. Friday and Saturday." Dahlia nods.

"So come meet them at dinner Saturday night," Holly suggests. "We won't eat until late because of the game."

"She's busy. She'll meet them another time," I say, knowing that won't happen, but wanting to stop my sisters from harassing her.

We're quiet on the ride from The Hideout to The White House. Once we're inside, I grab her a seltzer and myself a water.

"Thanks," she says, and we head outside.

"Everything okay?" I ask when she falls silent again. We haven't kissed in twenty minutes or so, something is definitely up.

"I just feel bad about lying to your sisters. I really like them."

"They like you too, and you're not going anywhere. You'll still see them at parties and stuff." I duck my head to meet her troubled gaze. "We're having people over at the house after the Homecoming game next weekend. You should come. We can show everyone that we're still cool."

"That's when I'm flying to LA."

"Right." I find myself smiling as I picture Dahlia designing clothes for literal rock stars. "You're such a badass. Someday when you're super famous, will you return the favor and invite me to some epic Hollywood parties?"

"Definitely," she says with a small laugh, then takes a step closer and her expression morphs from playful to serious. "Thank you."

"For what?"

"Everything." One shoulder lifts in a shrug. "The past month and a half has been incredible."

"I didn't do anything."

"But you did." She rests a hand on the center of my chest. "You changed my life."

I start to protest, but she continues, "It wasn't just the parties or everyone thinking I was your girlfriend. You changed me. People see me differently, but more importantly, I see me differently."

"You were always amazing. I didn't do that."

"Well, now I believe it."

My chest tightens. "You're welcome, hot stuff."

She laughs. "I still don't believe that, but I like hearing it just the same."

I take her hand, interlacing our fingers. Some emotion I can't quite put my finger on hovers around me, but I push it away for now. I want to enjoy tonight. And like I told her, she's not going anywhere. I'm still going to see her around. We'll go to the same parties and we're bound to run into each other. Things won't be that different.

I'm not drinking tonight, but Dahlia gets pulled into a game of beer pong with her roommates. I take a seat next to Jordan. He glances my way and smiles. "Look at you, Walters. Holding her drink and purse. Never thought I'd see the day."

I look down at my lap where Dahlia's purse rests and I lift the seltzer can his way. He's got a beer in one hand and a seltzer in the other.

"Like you're any better."

He chuckles. "Takes one to know one and all that, I guess."

I hum my agreement and then let my gaze go back to Dahlia. She wore my favorite dress tonight. It's a plain black one, almost like an oversized T-shirt. I'm ninety-nine percent sure it's one of her own, instead of the skintight, spandex numbers she borrows from Jane. And not that those aren't killer because they absolutely are, but she was wearing this one the first night I met her. It's this vision I have of her, no matter how many times we've hung out. All wide-eyed and nervous, and fucking beautiful.

I wonder if she knows that. I should probably tell her. The next time I see her that kind of thing might be weird.

"Surprised to see you out tonight," I tell him. The hockey team has a game Friday at home against one of their top rivals.

"Yeah, it's going to be an early night, but Daisy told me it was your last night as the boyfriend extraordinaire. Am I going to get to see her throw a drink in your face?" His grin is all hopeful and shit.

"Fuck you." I laugh. "And no."

"No, I'm not going to get to see it, or no, she's not going to go all scorned woman on your ass?"

"Dahlia? Please, she's too nice for that."

"Good point," he says. "It'll probably be Jane. She scares me. Hope you wore a cup."

He's right. It would be Jane. "It's not going to be like that," I say. "We're still going to see each other and hang out. We'll be friends. Just like before."

When he doesn't respond, I turn my head to look at him. "What?"

"First off, you two were never friends. You wanted to sleep with her, and she was a scared rabbit."

"And secondly?" I challenge.

"It's not going to be like before. Maybe if you'd kept your hands to yourself, but not now that you've been hooking up." He grins. "I know you are. Daisy told me. And I get it. You've always had a thing for her and pretending to be a couple while having real feelings for her can't be easy. I can see how things could get out of hand."

"Is there a point or are you just busting my balls?"

"You like her, she likes you…" He trails off then adds, "Is my point really not obvious?"

"It's not like that. I'm not looking for anything serious and neither is she. She wanted a different life. She wanted people to see her, and they do." I wave toward her.

Head held high, smiling. She's changed. I'm not taking any credit for that. She just needed to put herself out there a little more, gain a little confidence.

"She'll have no problem finding someone new." Someone that wants to be the type of guy I can't be right now.

"Oh, I know she won't. I'll bet there are fifty guys here tonight just waiting for you to screw up so they can swoop in."

I grind down on my back molars, and Jordan laughs.

"It's never going to be like it was before. Might want to think hard about that before you set her free. All I'm saying."

I can't completely shake Jordan's words the rest of the night, but I do my best. It's easier when Dahlia drinks too much and I can focus solely on keeping her upright. I stay glued to her side, holding her up, and smiling as she rambles and laughs. Everything is funny to her right now and she has zero inhibitions, including not holding back on showing me affection. Every touch feels amplified knowing that it's our last night together. Fucking Jordan got in my head.

Dahlia and I will always be cool. And maybe we'll even continue to hook up. That feels easier to swallow than this being the end all, be all for us, so I hold on to that while I walk her home. I'm more carrying her than walking her, to be honest. Getting her up the stairs to her room is a real treat. I fall onto my back beside her once I do.

She lets out a half-giggle, half-sigh as she rolls on top of me. "Felix Walters is in my bed."

"Yes. Yes, he is." I run my hands down her sides to the hem of her dress, then glide my fingers underneath and up to the band of her panties. "And he is real happy to be here."

"How happy?" She sits up and lifts her dress, flashing me her tits in some lacy pink bra.

I lift my hips to press my hard dick against her core. "That happy."

Her cheeks dot with pink. "Condoms are in the nightstand."

"Are they now?" I palm her breasts and her eyelids flutter closed.

"Mhmmm."

I sit up so I can bite her nipple through the soft material.

Her head falls back, and she arches into me. She's stunning. So fucking sexy. I liked her before, timid and unsure when I was around, but I love being the one to see her like this more—confident and asking for what she wants.

I run my hands over every inch of skin, following it with kisses.

"Felix," she murmurs as I tug her down onto the bed and roll on top of her. Her voice is husky and her skin flushed with desire. Her dress is bunched up around her neck and her chest heaves with each breath.

"I've got you." I kiss down her body and settle between her thighs. I run a finger slowly down the center of her panties, then lick the wet spot, tasting her through the material.

Her body trembles as I hook my fingers into the small band around each hip and pull them down so she's completely bare to me.

"You do have me. I'm basically putty in your hands," she says, eyes closed.

I push her legs farther apart with my shoulders and run a finger down her slit. I do the same slow motion with my tongue.

"Oh my gosh." She cries out. "You're so good at…everything."

My plan to take it slow is quickly tossed aside as she threads her fingers through my hair and gives the strands a tug.

I'd be lying if I said that some primal part of me loves that she's never done this with anyone else. I want to watch her experience all her firsts, but I'm not enough of a prick to take all of them from her knowing what we're doing might end tonight. This will have to be enough.

So I give it everything I have. Getting her off is my new favorite sport. She comes apart whimpering my name with her legs tight around my face.

"Oh wow," she says, body going limp as she finally lets go of my hair. "That was… wow."

"Wow is right. You taste so good." I run my tongue along my lips.

A sleepy smile pulls at her lips. "I'm not sure I believe you."

I dive for her, kissing her deep so she can taste herself on me. "Believe me now?" I ask when I pull back.

"I'll believe whatever you want if you keep kissing me like that."

I chuckle and move to the edge of the bed to put my shoes on. "I'd love to, but I have to get going."

She sits up. Hair rumpled and lips puffy. "Now? Tonight? You aren't staying? I thought…" Her voice trails off and all the plans she had for us tonight flash through my mind. Maybe I am an idiot for not having sex with her. My dick certainly seems to think so.

"I have to get up early for practice." I brush my thumb along her bottom lip, then lean forward and press my mouth to hers.

"This is really it, isn't it?" She brings her knees up to her chest and hugs them.

"The last month and some change were a blast. You were the best fake girlfriend I've ever had." My chest aches as I think about the truth of those words. She wasn't just the best fake girlfriend, she was the best girl I've hung out with, period.

She smiles. "You were the best fake boyfriend I've ever had."

Summoning every ounce of willpower I possess, I stand. "I left you something on your desk."

"What is it?" She tries to see around me.

"Just something so you don't forget about me."

"Impossible," she says, then her voice lowers. "We're still going to see each other and hang out sometimes. Right?"

"Yeah. Of course."

Her smile is wobbly. "Good."

I head for the door, casting one last look at her. "See you later, hot stuff."

Chapter
THIRTY

Felix

FRIDAY NIGHT, ALSO KNOWN AS TWO DAYS WITHOUT KISSING Dahlia, I go to the basketball game with Lucas. We meet up with some of the other guys. Our game is tomorrow afternoon, so curfew is early. We have enough time to watch maybe half before we have to duck out.

The stands are packed. It being parents' weekend means a lot of students have family in town.

"Hey," Brogan says as he juts his chin in our direction. He and Archer move down a seat to make room for us. "Dahlia coming too?"

"No." I focus way too hard on the court where the guys are still warming up.

"Where's she been?" Archer asks. "She wasn't at breakfast the last two mornings either."

"She had a golf tournament today, and her dad is in town, so she's probably hanging with him tonight."

"Probably?" Archer and Brogan ask in unison.

"They broke up," Lucas answers for me.

I shoot him a side glance. We haven't talked about Dahlia at all. In fact, he hasn't asked once where she's been, unlike Brogan, Archer, Teddy, and my sisters. The latter are pissed at me. I knew they liked Dahlia, but I didn't expect they'd take the news so hard. They're the only ones I've told, plus Teddy. And I guess now these three.

"I heard it from a girl in University Hall today, who heard it from some girl who has a class with Dahlia," he clarifies.

Geez. The rumor mill is even faster than I thought. "You knew and you didn't say anything?"

He shrugs. "Figured if you weren't telling anyone, then you didn't want to talk about it."

I nod. It's been weirder than I expected. I knew I'd miss hanging with her, but I didn't expect it to feel so…fuck, I don't even know. It's like nothing I've ever felt before.

"I also heard you were getting back together with Bethany," Lucas adds, and then waits for my reaction.

"Definitely false."

He looks relieved, but says, "That's not what she's telling everyone."

I shake my head. "Zero chance."

"You and Dahlia broke up?" Brogan stares at me, slack-jawed.

"Yeah. Yesterday."

"Why would you break up with Dahlia? She's great. Or did she break up with your dumb ass?"

"It was mutual. We're both busy and…" I trail off, letting him fill in the rest.

He seems super unimpressed by my lackluster response. "Sounds stupid, but what the hell do I know?"

"Is that a trick question?" I smirk as I deliver the playful jab, hoping to move on from this conversation.

He elbows me in the side, then he lowers his voice, tone sincere as he says, "I'm sorry, man."

Well, fuck. I didn't expect to be getting sympathy from him.

"Actually, no, maybe I'm not. Dahlia is single." He rubs his hands together and then laughs. There's the asshole I know.

I glower at him and he just grins back, smug as fuck.

"Touch her and die, dickwad."

At halftime, we have to head out for curfew. Lucas catches a ride with Brogan and Archer so I can swing by and check on the guys at the dorms to make sure they've all made it back. Game day will look a little different tomorrow with all our parents in town. We'll still meet up in the morning for a light workout to shake off the nerves, but then we're having a brunch, where families can come and meet the coaches and get a behind-the-scenes peek at the facilities.

My parents have already done that stuff and I'm thankful I can use that time to prep for the game instead of giving a tour of the locker room for the fourth time.

As I push through the mezzanine level on the way out of the fieldhouse, I spot Dahlia in line at the concession stand. Her long, blonde hair is pulled back into a low ponytail and she's wearing a blue Valley U T-shirt with jean shorts and Jordans.

She and Violet are talking and smiling, and I find myself walking toward her without really deciding.

Violet sees me approaching first. Her smile turns hesitant, and she glances at Dahlia for her reaction.

"Hey." My voice is light and friendly. I thought it would be awkward, but all I feel is happy to see her.

"Hi." She smiles up at me, not looking quite as comfortable in this scenario. I really hope she doesn't go back to freezing up around me. I'd miss talking to her.

There's a beat of uncertainty as we both grapple with how

to handle the situation. Do we hug? Wave? Fist bump? Fuck, I don't know.

Ultimately, I step forward to hug her and she comes into my arms, burrowing her head against my chest. I tilt my head down, inhaling her familiar scent on instinct before she pulls away.

"Is your family here?" she asks, taking a look around me.

"No, they get in tomorrow. Did your dad make it in?"

"Yeah." She hitches her thumb behind her. "He's off buying a foam finger or sweatshirt or something." Her tone is a little uneven, words coming quick. "I'm surprised you're out this late."

"Heading out now to do curfew check. What about you? How's the tournament going? What time do you tee off tomorrow?" Fuck, now I'm rambling.

"It was good."

"She's tied for first," Violet says proudly.

"Congrats."

She smiles. "Thanks. And I don't tee off until nine tomorrow. I'm sure we're going to leave pretty soon too, though. Thanks for the licorice by the way." Her cheeks are turning pink.

"You're welcome."

Violet's gaze pings between us. I wish she wasn't here so I could talk to Dahlia alone, tell her she doesn't need to be nervous around me. Not ever.

"Well, I guess I should go," I tell her when neither of us seems to know what to say next. "Good luck tomorrow."

"You too." She steps back and holds her hand up in a wave.

"Heck of a game," my dad says, putting his arm around the back of my mom's chair and smiling across the table at me.

We're at The Hideout for dinner before my parents head back. The five of us, plus Teddy.

"Thanks," I say, letting myself feel the pride in his words. I'm not sure if they saw this path for me, playing football and hoping to make a career of it, but both my mom and dad have always been supportive of my dream.

We won the game, my family was there watching and cheering me on, and there are a number of parties and people going out tonight to celebrate. I should be ecstatic, and I am, but I also find myself wondering how Dahlia's tournament went. It might even still be going. I consider texting her, but resist. I'm sure I'll see her out tonight.

"How's everything else?" My mom asks. She has a twinkle in her eye—a happy glint that tells me she knows something. But what? I'm not sure.

"Fine," I say, hesitantly. "School is school."

She keeps staring at me like she expects me to say more.

"They broke up," Stella says.

Mom's happy expression falls.

I glare at my sister. "You told them?"

"I didn't realize it was a secret," she tosses back.

"It isn't. It wasn't." I look to my mom. "I didn't tell you because it wasn't that serious."

Stella scoffs.

"I liked her a lot," Holly says, quieter, but meeting my stare.

"Yeah, me too. We're both just busy. Geez, she didn't die. You'll still see her around." I shovel in a few fries to have something to do.

My dad takes pity on me and brings the conversation back to the game. They're driving back home after dinner, so when we're finished, we head out to the parking lot.

"It was so good to see you." My mom hugs me first.

"You, too." I squeeze her harder and lift her off the ground. She laughs like she always does when I do it. From the time I turned sixteen, I've been taller than her and I remind her by picking her up every time we hug.

When I set her down, she smooths out her shirt and then reaches forward and pinches my chin. "We're so proud of you."

"Thanks, Mom."

She steps back and moves to say goodbye to my sisters.

Dad hugs me next. "You're having a great season. It's clear to see how hard you're working, but don't forget to have a little fun, too."

That's Dad. He's all about work-life balance. Work hard, play hard. I'm pretty sure I got that from him.

"No worries there," I tell him. "I'll have a beer in my hand by the time you hit the freeway."

When they're gone, Holly and Stella catch a ride with Teddy, and I get in my car. I have a ton of new texts, but I bypass them all and send one of my own.

Me: How'd the last day of the tournament go?

I wait a few minutes for her reply, but she must still be on the course or hanging with her dad. So, I open up my unread texts to figure out where the best place is to grab a beer or twelve.

Chapter
THIRTY-ONE

Dahlia

"**D**O NOT RESPOND." JANE COVERS THE SCREEN WITH her hand. "Forget about Felix for a night and let's meet some new, cute guys."

"Yes!" Daisy exclaims. She's already tipsy. Her face is flushed, and her eyes are lit with excitement. "We are celebrating. Tonight is all about you! Let me introduce you to some of Jordan's teammates."

I tuck my phone away and nod. His text has been taunting me for two hours. I won the Valley tournament today. My first collegiate win! My dad was there. Jane, too. I had a shaky start on the front nine, but then something came together. I was present and focused and that mixed with a whole lot of determination and luck, maybe a few bites of red licorice, had me shooting my lowest score ever and coming out on top.

I think the real reason my friends insisted on celebrating to-night, though, was to keep me from sitting around and thinking about my now ex-boyfriend. I feel like I've been walking around in a haze the past few days. Sad isn't the right word, though I am. More than that, I just feel a little lost.

Who knew breaking up with your fake boyfriend could hurt so much? I did, or I thought I did. But it hurts even worse than I expected.

"Shots!" Vi carries the little cups of liquor over to us. We're at an off-campus apartment where some of the hockey players live.

"Oh, I don't know. I think I'm sticking with seltzer." I drank too much on Wednesday night and woke up Thursday morning with the worst hangover of my life. I'm not loving the idea of feeling that way tomorrow, especially with my dad still in town. We're supposed to have breakfast in the morning before he flies back home.

"I'll take hers," Jane says.

While they toss back the shots, I glance around the party. Lots of people are already crammed into the living room where we're standing. Some are playing video games and others look like they just wanted a spot to sit down and make out.

I follow my friends outside on the balcony. It's less crowded out here. Jordan and his roommate Liam are talking with a few other guys I don't know. Daisy cuddles up to Jordan's side, and he wraps an arm around her waist without breaking conversation.

"Hey." One of the guys juts his chin at me. The movement reminds me of Felix. But it's the only thing about him that's similar. He has blond hair and the greenest eyes I've ever seen. "You're—"

I wince before he finishes the sentence, knowing what he's about to say and wishing I could rewind back to a few minutes ago and take that shot. I forgot what it was like to be known as the girl from the video. Felix shielded me from that. Maybe even more than I realized. But the words that come out next aren't what I was expecting.

"Dahlia, right?"

I stare back at him, a little stunned. He cocks his head to the side, and I finally nod. "Yeah. Yeah, I'm Dahlia."

He smiles, revealing a dimple above the corner of his mouth. "I think we had a class together last year. Psychology with Professor Handler?"

"Yeah." Now that he mentions it, I do remember him from that class. His hair was shorter, or maybe he always wore a hat? He sat in the back row. We never spoke. "I'm sorry. I don't remember your name."

"Steven." He sidesteps so we're closer. He's not as tall as Felix, but I still have to tip my head up to look at him. "You're one of Daisy's roommates?"

"Yeah. There's four of us. Do you know Jane and Violet?"

At their names, my friends join the conversation. I introduce them and Steven is polite, but quickly turns his attention back solely to me.

"Do you need another drink?" he asks when I finish my seltzer.

"Oh, uh…I haven't decided if I'm having another."

"We have water and some other non-alcoholic stuff inside." He jabs his thumb over his shoulder.

Jane nudges me forward. "She'd love one."

I almost fall into him. I turn a wide-eyed glare at her, before smiling at Steven. "Yeah, I could use another drink."

I follow him inside. He goes to the fridge and calls out my options. I decide on one more seltzer. After this, I'm switching to water. He hands me a can and grabs himself another beer. Leaning against the counter, he smiles at me.

"So, you live here?" I ask.

"Yeah. Want the tour?"

It doesn't look like that big of an apartment, but he's cute and seems nice, so I say yes. There are three bedrooms. He points out his roommates' bedrooms, but we only go into his. It's about the same size as mine. It's clean. Black comforter and matching pillowcases. A few jerseys hang on the wall and an old hockey stick. Framed photos sit on the desk under the window. It makes me think of Felix's room, all bare walls except for the poster his friends hung up.

When I'm done taking it all in, I look at Steven. He's standing just behind me staring at me like maybe he wants to kiss me. At least that's the look Felix would get. I wanted experiences, but now they're all wrapped up in him. I'm adept on all things Felix, but still clueless when it comes to other guys.

"I like your room." My voice is tight and my heart races.

"Thanks." His fingers brush mine and I startle. I have got to get my shit together. This is exactly the kind of guy I used to dream about paying attention to me.

"I should probably get back to my friends," I say. "We're having a girls' night. I don't want to bail on them."

"Yeah, of course. Come on."

Back outside, I find Jane and Vi playing beer pong at a little table set up on the far side of the patio. Daisy is sitting with Jordan, so I go to her. Steven goes to hang with another group, giving me some space. I think I might have blown him off. I wasn't exactly trying to, but I don't know if I'm ready to make out with someone new.

I don't have a lot of experience in the making-out department, but I don't think two guys in one week is how I roll.

An hour later, some people decide to go to the Prickly Pear. It's a dive bar. We rarely go since none of us are twenty-one yet, but my friends are drunk enough that they don't care, and I just want to have fun with them. A night of fun with my friends so I don't think about how weird it is being out without Felix.

We go straight to the little dance floor in the back, while the guys go to the bar to get drinks.

"He's so cute," Violet says, looking over my shoulder.

I steal a glance behind me to find Steven with the guys at the bar, sipping a beer and meeting my gaze for just a second.

My pulse speeds up and I whip my head back around.

"He's really nice, too," Daisy adds.

"Dating history?" Jane prompts.

Daisy thinks for a second. "He was hooking up with a girl on the volleyball team for a while last year, but that's it as far as I know."

"Hooking up or dating?" Jane scoffs. "No more guys with commitment issues."

"I could ask Jordan," Daisy offers.

"No," I say at the same time Jane nods aggressively.

"No," I repeat, and grab hold of Daisy's arm before she can go dig up dirt on Steven. "I'm not even sure what I'm looking for, so it doesn't matter if he wants to hook up with me or date me or whatever."

"That's the spirit." Vi bumps her hip against mine. "Have fun, get to know him, then decide what's what."

The guys push a bunch of tables together. More people than I thought came with us. Lots of Jordan's teammates. Gavin's, too. And where the hockey and basketball guys go, the girls flock.

After a few songs, Daisy and Vi take a break and leave me and Jane on the dance floor.

Jane takes my hands, and we keep moving to the beat. We're soon joined by a flock of others looking to shout the lyrics of the song and shake their hips. I step back and collide with a hard chest. When I turn, Steven reaches out and steadies me.

"Hey," I say, but I doubt he can hear me over the music. I turn back to Jane, and she gives me a look, silently asking if I want her to intervene. I love that about her. She always has my back. I give my head the smallest shake to let her know I'm okay, then turn back around to dance with Steven. Out of my peripheral I see her move to Liam and force him to dance with her. He gives in, though he looks a little shy about it. Jane is very convincing when she wants to be.

Steven's a good dancer, and as more and more people walk out to the little dance floor, we're pushed closer together. Eventually his hands find my waist, and I rest mine on his forearms. And I don't hate the way it feels.

Maybe I can do this. I can move on, kiss lots of boys, and forget about how much I miss my fake ex-boyfriend.

Chapter
THIRTY-TWO

Felix

THE PARKING LOT OF THE PRICKLY PEAR IS PACKED when Lucas and I arrive sometime after eleven. It's been one of those weird nights where we've bounced from party to party, none of them all that exciting, until Gavin texted and said he was at the Prickly Pear. I guess he wasn't the only one with that idea.

I spot Gavin's car as Lucas and I hop out of the sober ride and walk up to the front of the bar. That's clue number one that Dahlia's already inside.

Clue two is the calm that washes over me the second I walk through the doors of the small bar. That anxious thrum I've felt all day eases knowing I'm going to finally have a chance to talk to her. I see Violet first. She and Gavin are at the bar just inside the door. He's sitting on one of the bar stools and she's standing between his legs.

The bar at the Prickly Pear is shaped in a horseshoe. On one side there are pool tables and dart boards, and the other has tables and a dance floor.

"I'm gonna see if I can grab us next on one of the pool tables," Lucas says and heads in that direction.

Without looking at him, I nod and scan the right side where I recognize lots of Valley U students sitting at tables and congregating on the dance floor.

That's where I find her, dancing with some guy in the middle of a big group. Blonde hair hanging down her back, sexy green dress showing off a whole lot of leg. Her profile is to me, but she turns ever so slightly so I can see her face. She's smiling, and that hits me funny for reasons I don't quite understand. She's here and having a good time. Why the hell does that feel like a punch to the gut?

I step up to the bar next to Gavin.

"Hey, man. You made it. Great game today," he says.

"Thanks." I order a Jack and Coke from the bartender.

"I'm gonna go dance," Vi says and kisses Gavin before heading that way.

I get my drink and then lean a hip against the bar.

"Did your parents come down this weekend?" he asks.

"Yeah. Yours?"

"Nah, they couldn't make it."

"That's too bad."

"Eh, it's whatever." His gaze follows mine to where Dahlia is dancing. Dancing with some guy with a death wish. "Should I have warned you?"

"Nah. We're cool." I take a long drink of the Jack and Coke.

"Uh-huh." He watches me carefully. "Violet will kick my ass and then hand me over to Jane and Daisy to finish me off if you make a scene and embarrass her. They're protective of Dahlia."

I hate the way he says it like I'm someone they need to protect her from.

"I'm not going to make a scene. Everything is chill," I promise him.

"Good." He stands. "Want to let me kick your ass at darts then?"

I scoff. "As if."

I take one last look at Dahlia and then follow him to the left side of the bar. I try really hard not to stare, but I find myself watching her every chance I get. I can't even carry on a conversation, and Gavin does kick my ass at darts. Twice.

She looks…well, fuck, she looks happy and carefree, like she's having a blast with her friends. Our plan worked. She broke out of her shell and is meeting new people. I should be happy about that. I want to be happy about that.

When she goes to sit down at the long table filled with hockey players and their girlfriends, I finally catch her eye. I tip my head in a small greeting. My lips curve into a smile now that I have her attention on me.

She pushes a lock of hair behind one ear and lifts her other hand in a wave. Damn, she's beautiful. My stomach dips and my pulse spikes. Then her gaze drops, and she takes a seat with her back to me.

"That's it?" I mutter under my breath. I keep staring, waiting for her to look back up.

"Hey, can we get in on the next game?" Jordan asks, coming to stand in front of me with one of his teammates.

I nudge his shoulder to move him over an inch so I can see her again.

"Okay, then." Jordan steps out of my way. "What's up with him?"

"He's chill," Gavin says and then laughs.

"Clearly," Jordan says dryly. He swivels to track my line of sight. "I hate to say I told you so…"

I cut him a glare, and he holds up his hands defensively, then chuckles.

When I glance back at her, Dahlia stands from the table and heads toward the bar on the other side with Jane. "Be right back."

"Don't make a scene," Gavin yells behind me.

I flip him off over my head and go after her.

By the time I get there, some of the hockey guys have joined them. I approach Dahlia on the side. My fingers wrap around her arm in a soft caress. My thumb glides over her skin as she turns to face me.

"Felix," she says my name all breathy and nervous. "Hi."

"Hey." I lean closer. "I texted you."

"Oh, I…" She trails off and won't quite meet my eyes. "I'm sorry. I meant to reply and then the night kind of got away from me."

I can't say that doesn't sting, but I force a smile. "No biggie. So, how was the tournament?"

"I won." Her shoulders inch higher like she's a little embarrassed to talk about her victory.

"That's amazing." I can tell by her body language (and the side-eye Jane is giving me from her other side) that sweeping her off her feet into a spinning hug would be crossing some imaginary *ex-boyfriend* line, so I hold up my hand for her to high five. "I knew you'd do it. Congrats!"

"Thanks." She presses her palm to mine. I close my fingers around hers to hold it hostage. The guy she was dancing with earlier picks this moment to call out to her.

She pulls away from me and opens her stance to include him.

He gives me a quick glance before he asks her, "Want to be my partner in darts?"

She hesitates, but nods. "Yeah. Fair warning, though, I'm terrible."

"I'll teach you," he says.

A pretty blush climbs up her face. Fuck, I hate every second of this. I think I'm having a heart attack. My chest is tight and blood pounds in my ears. Twenty-two seems young for a heart attack, but I'm not a doctor.

"Steven, do you know Felix?" she asks, probably trying to break the tension rolling off me.

"Yeah, of course." He leans against the bar. His arm brushes against hers and stays there. "How's it going, Walters?"

I know Steven pretty well from hanging out with Jordan. He's all right, I guess. I might have even liked him once, before he put his hands on Dahlia. Now he's just some guy in my fucking way.

"Going okay," I say. Or that's what I think I say. I'm not really interested in chatting up Steven right now.

He nods and then looks back at Dahlia expectantly.

"I'll be right there," she tells him.

When he's gone, I invade her space. I need to break through the weirdness. Once upon a time, this might have been a perfectly fine interaction with her, but not anymore.

"Are we okay?" I ask.

"Yeah, of course."

"It doesn't feel okay."

"It was bound to be awkward the first few times we ran into each other, right? We'll figure out how to be friends again." This time, her smile is genuine. She really believes that. And fuck me, I finally realize the problem. I don't want things to go back to the way they were. Not if that means we dance around each other and barely talk. If this is what it means to be friends, then I don't want to be her friend. I never wanted to be her friend.

"I better go," she says. "It was good to see you."

"Yeah, you too."

She walks backward a step, still hitting me with that smile, then turns on her heel to go find Steven.

A girl at the bar slides over. Her arm touches mine and I flinch.

"Hey," she says. "Want to buy me a drink?"

I just stare at her for a second. Long enough to realize there's no world in which I want to hook up with some other chick to-night. "No. Sorry."

I head back to the guys. As much as I don't want to, I give Dahlia space the rest of the night. I play pool with Lucas, and then Brogan and Archer show up and the four of us get a pitcher and a table. I'm across the bar from her, but I'm still aware of Dahlia's every move. Steven taught her how to play darts, and I'm now considering burning down the boards in every bar across town. She went from timid and shy to throwing like a pro and probably kicking all their asses.

Steven is attentive. Not overly touchy in a sleazy way, but enough that I can tell he's really into her. Everything I know about him is that he's a decent guy, which is super annoying right now. I wish he were an asshole, or crossing some line, so I could swoop in and tell him to get lost. He's exactly the kind of guy I might have seen her with a month ago, but now the thought of anyone else touching her or kissing her has a red mist falling in front of my eyes.

At last call, I push out of the bar and take a deep breath of the cool, night air. Three hours of torture. Lucas and I pause at the end of the building where the sidewalk meets the parking lot. I hardly drank, but I'm jumpy and on edge. Electricity hums under my skin. There's no way I can go home and go to bed.

"Teddy can be here in five or there's an Uber a block away," Lucas says, staring down at his phone.

"Take the Uber," I tell him, tapping my thumb against my thigh. "I'll be right behind you."

He starts walking across the parking lot, but he stares at me as he goes. "This about your ex and her new guy?"

"Nope," I say and backtrack toward the bar doors.

It's not about her and Steven at all.

Chapter
THIRTY-THREE

Dahlia

"**S**TEVEN LIKES YOU," DAISY SINGSONGS AS WE WASH our hands in the sink inside the restroom at the Prickly Pear.

"He barely knows me," I say back, but my stomach does a little flip anyway. Do I even want him to like me? I don't know. I'm so confused. Running into Felix tonight didn't help. He seemed so…hurt or angry. But I don't understand why. He walked out on me the other night. He's the one that has always said he didn't want more.

Daisy's phone pings in her pocket. She quickly dries her hands and pulls it out.

"It's Vi," she says. "She and Gavin are leaving. I need to run out with them. I left my purse in Gavin's car. Do you want me to wait?"

"No, go ahead. Jane and I are going to grab an Uber."

"Bye." She hugs me. "Tonight was so much fun."

"It was," I agree.

"See you tomorrow."

I take an extra second in front of the mirror to finger comb my hair, then pull out my phone. I could tell myself I'm not looking to see if Felix texted, but that's a lie. I miss him. Being at the same place and barely interacting just made it all too real. This is our new normal and it kind of sucks.

Chastising myself, I shove my phone back in my purse and head out of the restroom. A hand wraps around my wrist and tugs me farther back into the dark hallway. I yelp seconds before his familiar scent envelops me.

"Felix." My heart is beating way too fast as I look up into his steely blue eyes. "What are you doing?"

"Something I've wanted to do all night." His hands come up and frame my face, and he covers my mouth with his.

I gasp in surprise, but my hesitation is short-lived because my body reacts all on its own. One more kiss. One more touch.

I wrap my arms around his neck and lift up onto my toes to deepen the kiss. He continues to caress my face so tenderly. Long fingers splayed out over my cheeks and the thumb on his right hand holds my chin in place as he sweeps his tongue into my mouth.

I missed this. Missed him.

Finding a single thread of restraint, I pull back. "Wait. Wait. What are we doing?"

"I'm kissing you and thinking about putting my hand under this tight little skirt," he says, brushing his lips over mine again.

"We broke up."

"Technically, we weren't ever really together."

"Felix." I take a tiny step back.

"Dahlia." He drawls my name out in that way that drives me crazy.

"What is this?" I motion between us.

"I don't know. I don't have all the answers, but this is the first time I've felt like myself in days." He closes in on me and rests a hand on my hip.

229

My phone buzzes in my purse. "That's probably Jane."

"Come home with me."

"I can't leave Jane."

"We can drop her off on the way."

He must read the thoughts on my face. "You don't want her to know."

I feel bad about that, but I don't think she'll approve. I'm not even sure I approve, but I want to anyway. He nods and presses his lips to mine again. "Go home. I'll be right behind you. Leave the window open."

He leaves me alone in the hallway with my heart in my throat. I pull out my phone with shaky hands.

> *Jane: You've been in the restroom a really long time. Every-thing okay?! Uber is two minutes out. Let me know if I need to stall the driver while you poop.*

> *Me: OMG, I'm not pooping.*

> *Me: omw*

Jane talks a mile a minute in the back of the Uber. She mis-reads my silence as exhaustion, which works out well. As soon as we get home, she follows me upstairs and says, "I know you've had a crazy long day, so I won't make you stay up all night talking to me, but tomorrow after your dad leaves, we are discussing the events of tonight *at length.*"

I hear a car door shut outside and my nerves ramp up.

"Okay," I say and hug her.

She starts toward her room down the hall.

"Hey," I say. "Thanks for coming to cheer me on today. You're the best."

"Duh." She laughs and then flips on the light in her bedroom. "Love you too."

I close my door and then rush to the window to open it. Felix is waiting on the roof. He climbs inside and shakes his dark hair. "It's starting to rain out there."

I'm frozen in place, staring at him. The way the black T-shirt hugs his chest and arms. The light stubble of facial hair dotting his jaw.

"What's wrong?" he asks.

"I never thought you'd be in my room again."

"If you want me to go—"

"Shut up and kiss me." I close the space between us, throwing myself at him. And in true Felix fashion, he catches me easily.

We fall to the bed in a tangle of limbs. His mouth never leaves mine, but his hands roam up my legs and over my stomach, then up to caress my face and finally tangle in my hair.

I can't seem to get close enough or kiss him hard enough.

His hand strokes my calf and then slides up past the underside of my knee. I scramble for the hem of his T-shirt and yank it up. Felix pulls back long enough to get it over his head and toss it on the floor, then his mouth is back on mine.

I run my hands over his stomach and chest, unabashedly enjoying the warmth of his skin and the way his muscles contract as he moves on top of me.

"Dahlia," he whispers my name as his hand disappears under the hem of my dress. It's bunched up around my upper thigh, so it doesn't take him long to reach my bare hip. He hooks one finger into my panties and slowly drags the material down as he continues to kiss me.

I help him get them off and then I go for his jeans. It's a struggle to get the denim pants off without breaking apart for more than a few seconds, but piece by piece, we strip down until there's nothing between us.

Felix drops a hand to my stomach. "You're so beautiful."

I soak up the compliment and the dark look in his eyes.

"About the other night," he says, stroking the skin just above my belly button.

"Yeah?"

"I shouldn't have left like that. I knew what you wanted, but I thought it would be easier if we didn't have sex. I didn't want to take that from you when we were just…whatever we were doing."

"And now?"

"I think I was screwed long before that." One side of his mouth lifts into a smile that I can feel when he presses his lips to mine.

"Me too." I rest my fingertips on his jaw.

My heart bangs against my rib cage as Felix's hands roam over my boobs, down to my stomach, my hips, my inner thigh. It's like he can't decide where he wants to focus his attention, or maybe he wants to focus it everywhere all at once. I feel it everywhere, that's for sure.

When we've kissed so long my lips hurt, he finally reaches for the nightstand and rummages around until he finds a condom.

Felix smooths my hair out of my face and meets my gaze. "You're sure you want to do this?"

"Definitely." I swallow thickly and my pulse speeds up.

He rips the foil packet open, covers himself and then blows out a breath. "Fuck, I'm nervous."

"You?" My brows lift.

"Yeah, if it sucks, I might turn you off of sex for life or something."

I sit up, resting on my elbows. "It's not going to suck. You and I are both too competitive to be bad at anything. Plus, you're stupid hot, remember? If you say my name the right way, I don't even need your big dick."

A cocky glint flashes in his eyes and he curls forward in laughter. "Fuck, I love it when you ramble."

"You do?"

He moves up, forcing me to lie flat. "Mhmm."

His head lowers and he covers one nipple with his mouth. I arch into him and rake my nails down his back. He goes from one breast to the other until I'm writhing beneath him. He shifts and the head of his dick nudges at my entrance.

"Dahlia?"

"Yeah." The word comes out in a pant.

He doesn't speak right away, and I look up to find a playful smirk on his face. "Just checking to see if you need my *big dick*."

As I laugh, he pushes inside me. All the air leaves my lungs.

"Are you okay?" He stills.

I nod and bite my lip.

He studies my face, gauging the sincerity of my words.

"I'm okay," I say. "Really."

"Breathe." His lips brush mine.

His kiss is sweet and soft. He moves carefully, letting my body relax and adjust so that he can push farther in. It takes a minute, but eventually the pain fades and in its place liquid warmth pools in my lower belly.

When I start to meet his thrusts, Felix picks up the pace. He pulls out almost completely before driving back in. Each time it causes a delicious shiver to roll down my spine. My gaze locks on his face. His expression is a mix of concentration, restraint, and pleasure. He's close but holding back, trying to make sure my first time is everything I might have imagined.

I never imagined it like this—overwhelming and all-consuming.

He shifts, moving his upper body upright while still driving into me. He stares down at where our bodies connect. His fingers on one hand have a tight grip on my hip and the other splays out on my lower stomach as his thumb rubs slow circles over my clit.

"Dahlia." My name comes out with a tortured groan. "Are you close?"

"I think so," I rasp.

He increases the pressure on the sensitive bundle of nerves and my body lights up.

"Dahlia," he says again, and this time, it's my undoing. The orgasm is like none of the others before. It keeps building until I think I'll pass out with the force of it.

When I finally start to come down from the best high of my life, I let my eyes flutter open. Felix is staring down at me with a look so sweet and yet still cocky.

He kisses my stomach, then disposes of the condom before dropping onto the bed next to me.

"That didn't suck." I let my head fall to the side to look at him.

He laughs as I roll over and curl into him. I drape an arm over his chest, and he covers my hand with his. "Definitely not."

"Can we do it again?"

He blows out a breath. "You're a little minx."

"Is that a yes?" I ask as I climb up and straddle him. I run my palms over his chest, and his hands go to my hips. I can feel him growing hard underneath me.

"Give me a minute."

"I'm pretty sure this night is going to ruin me for casual sex. It's not usually this good, right? I've sat through enough girl talk to hear terrible stories of hookups with guys who don't know the meaning of foreplay and last all of fifteen seconds."

The corners of his mouth lift and he hits me with one of those wide smiles that makes my stomach do several somersaults.

"What?" I ask when he just keeps staring at me.

"Be my girlfriend, hot stuff."

"What?" My hands still.

"I want you to be my girlfriend. For real this time." He sits up. "You're right. Nothing about this feels casual. It never did. I want to be the guy taking you home, not the asshole sitting across the bar watching you with some other guy."

"You want to be my boyfriend so we can keep hooking up?" I ask. "Felix, I don't need to be your girlfriend for that. We can keep things like they are and see where it goes."

"That's not what I meant. Fuck. I'm not saying this right." He wraps his arms around my back. "We're good together. I like you. I'm pretty sure you still like me. I want to go back to hanging out like before. I want to be the guy that takes you to the party and the one that takes you home. I liked being your boyfriend. It didn't feel fake."

"I thought after Bethany..." My words trail off. "You said you didn't want or have time for a girlfriend."

"You're not Bethany. No one is, but it's taken me some time to realize that I don't have to carry her issues with me. You showed me that."

"Me?"

He runs a hand through his dark hair and blows out a breath. "I've never really told anyone this, but Bethany cheated on me. Lots of times, in fact. It was her thing. I wouldn't pay enough attention to her, and she'd get back at me by kissing someone else or disappearing with some other guy at a party to make me jealous. It worked too, at least enough times that it became the cycle of our relationship. It's why she's still doing it because it worked in the past."

I'm speechless. Why the hell would anyone cheat on Felix? I can't imagine a better guy. Plus, he has the whole stupid-hot thing going on. He's the total package.

His jaw is set in a hard line. "After that, I thought that I couldn't be a guy that made someone else a priority while still working toward my dreams, but with you, I feel like anything is possible. You never make me feel like I have to choose."

"You shouldn't. You don't. You're a great guy, Felix, and you're going to do incredible things."

He nods, but his expression is still pained. "Be my girlfriend, hot stuff?"

I'm too stunned by everything he said for the idea to really sink in. Be Felix's girlfriend? Like for real, for real?!

He takes my hair into his fist and tugs lightly, tipping my lips up toward his. "You don't have to answer now. Just promise me you'll give it some thought."

Chapter
THIRTY-FOUR

Dahlia

"WELL, WHAT DID YOU SAY?" JANE ASKS. SHE'S moved from her position, lying on the pillow fort beside my bed to sitting, hugging a pillow to her stomach, and staring at me wide-eyed as I tell her about last night with Felix. Well, almost all of it. I left out the stuff with Bethany because it didn't feel like my story to share.

"I told him I'd think about it, then we had sex again and passed out. I had to get up early to meet my dad, so we didn't have a chance to talk this morning."

Her lips pull into a huge smile. "Oh my gosh, Dahlia! This is so exciting."

"Is it?" I ask, really needing to hear her take on the situation. "I can't help but worry that he hasn't really thought this through. He said he wants it to be like before, but before, we were pretending. I don't know. What if it's not the same? I don't know how to be a girlfriend, not a real one. Too many things are happening at once. My mind is literally spinning. Tell me what to do?"

She laughs a little at my rambling. "I can't, babe. This is way beyond my expertise. But for what it's worth, you would be a great girlfriend if that's what you decide."

I groan and fall back onto the bed. It still smells like Felix.

"When are you seeing him again?"

"I don't know." I sit back up and pull my hair over one shoulder. "He had to catch up on some school stuff today, and I have a lot to do before I leave Friday to go meet with Eddie."

"Oh right." Her wide-eyed grin is back.

"Speaking of, would you come with me?"

"Me?"

"Please? I know it's a big ask to miss a day of classes, stay in a nice hotel, and have VIP passes to an Eddie Dillon concert, but I need all the moral support I can get."

"That does sound fun, but wouldn't you rather take Vi? She actually knows something about design."

"But you know LA and you're a great hype woman. I need all the hype."

She chuckles. "Yeah, okay. I'll come."

"Yay!" I clap my hands in front of me.

"But first tell me the part where Felix grabbed you in the dark hallway and kissed you again?"

I laugh, but my body heats at the memory. "One more time and then I'm taking a nap."

"Deal." She squeals.

Felix and I text throughout the beginning of the week, but our schedules keep us from seeing one another. And, okay fine, I might be avoiding him. I need to figure out what I want before I see him because when I see him, all I'm going to want to do is kiss him.

I understand him better now that I know more about what went down with Bethany, and I see how that made him hesitant to get into another relationship, but even putting that aside, I still have this worry that he's confusing his desire to keep having sex with me to wanting me to be his girlfriend. If I hadn't been a virgin, would he still be so insistent that he doesn't want casual?

I get the feeling he knows I'm avoiding him because he hasn't shown up at my door (or my window) like he would have a couple weeks ago, but I appreciate that he's giving me space to figure out what I want. The only downside is that all the time apart has me picking through every conversation we've ever had, every interaction. I'm looking for clues that we should or shouldn't be together like I'm Sherlock freaking Holmes.

On Thursday, we planned to meet up to grab dinner after both of us were done with practice, but his runs late and then he doesn't have time before he has to go to a football alumni mixer. It's only then that I worry him giving me space is really him changing his mind or deciding I'm not worth all the effort.

I have a mini panic attack over it as I'm packing up everything for my trip. Not just over Felix. It's also knowing that I'm going to show my designs to Eddie and his team. A literal rock star.

All week I've been stressing over the situation with Felix, and I pushed away the impending freak out of seeing Eddie. But now that I'm less than twenty-four hours from arguably the biggest meeting with a potential client ever, I'm panicking over that too. The jumper I made for Penelope was an amazing opportunity. Landing Eddie could show people that I'm more than a one-trick pony. It would give me another amazing design for my portfolio.

There's a knock on my bedroom door followed by Daisy's voice, "Dahlia? Can I come in?"

I swing the door open and smile at her. "Hey."

She steps into my room. "Woah. What happened here?"

"I'm panicking," I tell her honestly. "I don't know what to pack to wear to meet Eddie Dillon. And I still need to email my professors to let them know I'm going to miss classes tomorrow. And I haven't showered." I smooth a hand over my messy bun.

"Deep breaths." She comes closer and meets my gaze.

I inhale and then nod. "Thanks."

"You're welcome." She holds out a package of red licorice with a white envelope on top. "This was on the front porch for you."

I take it from her and smile. All my worries feel dumb when I see his gift.

"Felix?"

"Yeah. It's his way of saying good luck."

"Have you talked to him yet?" she asks. It didn't take Daisy and Vi long to get the Felix gossip out of me Sunday.

I shake my head. "We've been texting every day, and we were going to hang out tonight, but it doesn't look like that's going to happen. His practice ran late."

"I'm sorry," she says.

"It's okay. I need to focus on killing this meeting with Eddie anyway."

"All right. Well, what can I do to help?"

I glance around my room. It looks like a tornado came through it.

"Help me figure out what outfits to pack?" As I ask the question, Jane and Violet appear in my doorway with takeout containers and a bottle of wine.

"As if we'd leave you alone to prepare for Eddie Dillon," Vi says.

So with my three roommates in my horribly messy room and a new bag of red licorice, I finally take a deep breath.

Chapter
THIRTY-FIVE

Felix

F RIDAY MORNING AT BREAKFAST, I DECIDE TO COME CLEAN about things with Dahlia. To be fair, I only intended to tell Lucas. But then Teddy and my sisters showed up, followed by Brogan and Archer, and it's a freaking after-school special as they all weigh in with their unsolicited advice and opinions. And questions. So many questions.

"So, you were faking it the whole time?" Lucas asks, for at least the third time. He's struggling to let the news sink in.

"Yes. No. Sort of." I sigh. "It's complicated."

Holly tosses an apple at me, hitting my left shoulder.

"Ouch. What the hell, Holl? That hurt."

"I was aiming for your head. How could you be so dumb?"

I rub at my shoulder. I'm lucky she's the less coordinated one.

"Damn. I know, okay. I'm an idiot and Dahlia's the best. Can we stop yelling at me and help me figure out how to fix it?"

"I do miss her sitting with us for breakfast," Archer says. "She always shared her leftover food with me."

Brogan nods his agreement. "And she carried those little packets of Vitalyte."

"Oh yeah. I could use a little boost right now," Lucas says. "Anybody packing?"

My teammates turn to each other and start mumbling how they wish Dahlia was here and how they could really use some electrolytes.

I look to my sisters. "Do you think I should text her again?"

"Duuuude," Beau's voice sounds from Stella's phone, lying on the table between us. She turns the screen, and her boyfriend is giving me a smug, pitying look. "Have a little self-respect or don't. It'll prepare you for the ass kicking you're gonna get in a couple weeks."

The guys all boo him, but he just chuckles. We play Beau's team at home the second weekend in November. It should be a good game. A tough one. My favorite kind to play. There's nothing like competing against the best and winning.

"You fucking wish, Ricci." I flick the phone back to my sister dismissively, but he's not wrong, my focus is anywhere but football. Practice all week has been utter dogshit. Coach thinks it's all the team events for Homecoming week messing with my head, otherwise he'd probably have replaced me with Armstrong by now.

"Do you two have to talk all day, every day?" I ask Stella.

"Yeah," she says automatically. "It's called being in love. Perhaps you've heard of the concept?"

I stick my tongue out at her like I'm a child.

"So, I should text her again then?" I haven't seen her all week and it's killing me. I told her to take some time to think about it before I realized how hard it would be to wait for her answer.

I considered sneaking through her window last night, but I don't want to push her to make a decision. And if there's any part of her that thinks I want to be with her just to keep hooking up,

I want to squash that. Sneaking into her bed late at night probably isn't the best way to reinforce that, but it was *really* hard not to do it anyway.

I don't just want to be the guy taking her home. I want to be the guy who watches her kick everyone's ass at flip cup, the guy who makes her ramble and blush, and I want to look up from the field at every game to see her cheering me on (preferably in my jersey). I want her.

I sent her a message early this morning wishing her a safe flight, and she replied with a thank you, but I haven't heard from her since. I know she's busy being a badass and everything, but I want her to know that I'm in this thing. I want a real relationship. Do I have any idea how to do that with someone as amazing as her? No, but I'm a fast-fucking learner when I want something. And I want Dahlia.

"You need to chill out," Brogan says. "Who cares if you're casual or exclusive? You're hooking up with her either way."

"And if you're hooking up, at least she'll probably come back to breakfast," Archer adds.

"God, you're all idiots." Holly tosses a balled-up napkin at him. She's really worked up this morning.

"Lucky she already threw her apple at me," I tell him.

Teddy places an arm around my sister's shoulders and pulls her into his chest, but I don't miss the amused smile on his lips.

Dammit, I want to be as annoying as Stella and Beau or Holly and Teddy. That might have freaked me out before, but it doesn't freak me out now because it's Dahlia. But I get why she might not be sold on the idea. I haven't been the ideal picture of boyfriend material.

My thoughts are interrupted by my ex approaching the end of the table. She looks directly at me, avoiding the glares of my sisters and friends. "Hey, can I talk to you?"

Stella makes an annoyed sound. I should say no, but I know

Bethany, and if there's something she wants to say to me, she'll find a way. Might as well get it over with now.

"Yeah." I stand. "I'll catch up with you guys later."

Bethany falls into step beside me. She doesn't say a word as I toss my trash and then drop off my tray.

"What's up?" I ask as we exit the dining hall. My skin itches being this close to her. I can't believe I ever thought she was the type of girl I wanted.

"I heard about you and Dahlia. I'm sorry."

I stop and cross my arms over my chest. Yeah, I'll bet.

She smiles coyly and bats her lashes. It annoys the fuck out of me. "Okay, fine. I'm not sorry. I miss you." Her hands come up to rest on my chest. "We were so good together. Don't you remember?"

I stare down at her long, pink fingernails. I feel nothing but irritation. "No."

"No?" she asks, eyes widening in surprise.

"No, we weren't good together. You were toxic, and I was too blind or preoccupied to care."

Anger flashes across her face, but she masks it quickly. "You don't mean that. We had so many good times."

"You cheated on me. More times than I can fucking count."

"I never had sex with anyone else," she says as if that's the line. "I only did what I had to do to get your attention."

"Yeah, and when you had it, you said that I was boring and—"

"I didn't mean any of it. Let me remind you how good we can be together." Her fingers walk down my stomach.

I step back, letting her hands fall away. "It's not going to happen. Not ever."

I turn from her and head outside toward my first class. I stop before walking into the room and lean against the wall. I pull up my text conversation with Dahlia. My thumb hovers over the keys, but in the end, I decide not to send her another text.

I told her that I'd give her time to think. I can do that and, in the meantime, I'm going to stop moping around and figure out how to lead my team to a win tomorrow night. Seeing Bethany reminded me of all the lies I've told myself since we broke up—that I wasn't anything more than a great football player and that I could never be the kind of guy a girl deserved because of it. I can be a great football player and a great boyfriend. I know I can, but now it's time to prove it to myself.

Plus, I don't want to be the guy trying to steal away her attention while she's doing this big, amazing thing for herself. Even if it's killing me that we've barely talked all week.

Time. She wanted time and I'm giving it to her. But when she gets back to Valley, it's game on.

Chapter
THIRTY-SIX

Dahlia

L A IS A WHIRLWIND! ON FRIDAY, JANE AND I FLY IN MID-
morning. We have the day to relax and explore. She takes
me to some of her favorite spots and then in the evening we
go to watch Eddie perform. Tonight's concert is at a small venue
where he had his first gig.

An assistant named Beverly hands us passes and shows us to
a table near the front of the stage where we can watch the concert.
Jane is subdued while I'm not-so-silently freaking out.

"How are you so chill?" I ask as I try to stop my leg from
bouncing up and down. I run my palms up and down my thighs.

"What? I'm not chill," she says brightly. "I'm so excited for
you!"

"Us. Excited for us. You get to meet Eddie Dillon, and I get
to dress him. Maybe. Hopefully."

"You will." She squeezes my hand. "You are the most talented
and deserving person I know."

"Wow." I wipe a tear from the corner of my eye and chuckle. "Way to ruin my makeup, bitch."

"I love you," she says, and rests her head on my shoulder.

"Love you, Jane." I tilt my head against hers. "Thank you for being here."

"You always show up for other people, and I'm really happy that I get to return the favor today."

My phone pings. I glance down to my lap and Jane sits straight.

Felix: You don't need it but sending you all the good luck today. Knock 'em dead.

"Felix?" Jane asks.

"How'd you know?"

"You're smiling like you only smile for him."

I run my finger along his message. "Is it weird to say I'm a little disappointed that I'm here this weekend and not watching a college football game?"

She laughs. "Yes."

"Don't get me wrong, I am so thankful for the opportunity."

"I know, babe," she says with a reassuring smile. "Does that mean you've decided to officially be hottie QB's girlfriend?"

Eddie walks onto stage. People around us clap and yell. He lifts one hand, the other is holding a bottle of water.

I tuck my phone away for now. "One life-altering thing at a time."

The concert is amazing. Beverly returns for us, and Jane and I follow her backstage, down a winding hall before she stops in front of a room and motions for us to go ahead.

My stomach has been in one giant knot since he walked onto the stage earlier, but my mouth goes dry and my face gets hot as I step in and see Eddie sitting on a brown leather couch.

Eddie Dillon is exactly how he seems in videos and pictures. Handsome, suave, larger than life. I'm not attracted to him in the same way I am Felix, but he still makes me incredibly nervous.

Eddie stands and flashes a warm smile. His hair is damp, and he smells like soap.

"Dahlia." He hugs me, a quick one arm around the neck embrace. "How are you?"

"Hi. Good." I move to the side and look to Jane. "Eddie, this is my friend, Jane."

"Jane." His brows pinch together as he extends a hand for her to shake. "Did you come with Dahlia last trip?"

"No. That was Violet," she says. "I'm one of the other roommates."

"Ah," he says, nodding.

Jane doesn't miss a beat. "You were incredible out there."

"Right," I add. "So good."

"Thanks." He turns his attention back to me. "You're here. I'm so stoked to see what you have for me."

"I gave Beverly the pants, but I have photos on my phone. I'm really happy with how the pants came out, but if you don't love them, I will totally understand. And I brought my sketchbook with a few more ideas I've been working on." I pat my purse where I have it stowed.

Jane nudges me lightly with her elbow.

"Sorry, I'm rambling," I say, feeling the heat in my face. "I'm really excited about this opportunity."

He takes a seat and leans back and hits me with one of his trademark sexy grins. It doesn't flip my stomach, like I'm sure it does most girls, but it reminds me of Felix and that settles me a little. If he were here, he'd tell me to take a breath and remind me that I'm amazing.

"I can't wait to see it all," he says, motioning to the chairs next to the couch. "Sit. Sit. Let's catch up and you can wow me with fashion tomorrow."

I relax, knowing I have another day before he sees my work. The three of us sit and chat. It doesn't take long to catch up, since Eddie and I aren't exactly BFFs, but Jane and I ask about his tour and then soak in every detail he offers up. His life is so interesting, but I get the feeling it's lonely at times too. He tells us the travel is amazing but brutal. That he often forgets what city he's in and that he hasn't seen his family in months.

"What about you?" He takes a long drink of water. "How's college life? I thought about college, but school was never really my thing."

"It's good," I say. "And classes are only a small part of it."

"Frat parties and beer bongs then?" He quirks a brow.

"A little of that," I admit.

He smiles, staring at me a little more closely. "You seem different. New haircut?"

"Umm…no. It's the same." I run a hand over the long strands hanging over one shoulder.

"It's something. Don't tell me. It'll come to me." His gaze slides to Jane and he shakes a finger. "And you. You look familiar. You're sure you didn't come to the concert this summer?"

"I get that a lot. I have one of those faces."

He smiles. Bev steps into the room. "Mark wants to see you before you leave."

"Tell him I'll be right there," Eddie says. "I have a few things I need to do."

"Of course," I say. "Thank you so much for inviting us tonight."

We say our goodbyes, and then Jane and I head back to the hotel. I'm exhausted from a week of crappy sleep, so we order room service and put on an old movie. Jane falls asleep quickly, but I'm restless. More often than I'd like to admit, my mind wanders to Felix.

We've exchanged a few texts, but nothing substantial. It's Homecoming weekend and he's been busy with a bunch of media stuff: interviews and photos, and that's in addition to the events he has to drop by with the rest of the team. Last night, they had to attend an alumni mixer for past Valley U football players. Tonight, they have to go to the bonfire where the Homecoming royalty is announced. And in all of it, Felix is front and center. He grumbles about it, but he handles the pressure of being the face of the team well. Plus, his face is a really, really good one.

Saturday morning, a car picks us up and takes us to the stadium where Eddie will be performing tonight. This place is way bigger. Bev is, once again, our tour guide. She takes us through a maze of hallways until we reach our destination.

When we finally step into a room behind her, my heart races. Racks of clothing are pushed to one side, while on the other side, people are busy doing things from mending to steaming clothes. The energy is focused but a little chaotic. I love it.

"Dahlia!" Eddie calls from the back of the room. Two women stand in front of him, circling and eyeing his outfit. When they finish, he steps forward to greet us. "You made it just in time. I was saving your pants for last, hoping you'd be here for the reveal."

"I'm so excited," I say honestly. "And I love that. Amiri?"

He glances down and pulls at the shirt. "Good eye. They sent a few items over this morning."

He turns and heads back to the women who are now eyeing me and Jane carefully. "Come on. Let me introduce you to some people."

So many people have a hand in Eddie's wardrobe it's a little overwhelming. I meet his stylists, Maria and Emily, the head of wardrobe, Victor, and all the crew who travel with him, plus several more people that I don't catch the titles or names of, but who are performing tasks ranging from fixing clothing items to labeling and organizing everything in a very specific way.

Seeing Eddie in the pants I created is totally surreal. They fit him perfectly and the smile that lights up his face makes me feel prouder than I ever have.

He's handed several shirts to try on with them. I bite the corner of my lip as I watch it all come together. He tries on a mesh tank top first that Maria immediately vetoes, then a button down. Emily brings a hand to her mouth as she studies him.

"I imagined it with a basic white T-shirt," I say. Everyone stops moving and looks at me. I feel the flush on my cheeks but keep going. I step to a rack of shirts and pull one off. "Something like this."

Eddie shrugs and holds his hand out. "I love a basic tee."

"Me too. It's classic," I say.

I'm relieved when he puts it on, and everyone seems to okay the look.

Both pieces are labeled and organized with the others. Jane and I sit back and observe as they finalize the other outfits.

A couple of times, Eddie asks my opinion. I can't get a read on his head of wardrobe, Victor. Maybe I'm overstepping, but Eddie invited me and he's asking, so I give him my thoughts when asked.

When it's all done, Victor comes over to me. He hands me an envelope. "The construction of the pants was pretty good."

"Thank you," I say like I'm not sure it was a compliment. *Pretty good?*

"If you're ever looking for a job, let me know."

I'm stunned, but manage to get out another thanks before he turns and starts barking orders to his team.

"OMG!" Jane screeches. "I think he likes you."

"I thought he was going to yell at me."

"Yeah, well, something tells me you'd have to get used to that if you worked for him." She nods toward the envelope. "What's that?"

"I'm not sure." With shaky fingers, I open it and pull out a check. A very large check. Eddie and I didn't discuss payment, but this is more than I ever would have asked for. "Woah."

Jane laughs. "I guess you're buying lunch."

Lunch ends up being catered. Eddie invites us to his dressing room to hang out while we eat. He barely gets a bite in before he's pulled to do…something. I don't know when he has time to relax, let alone eat. Again, it reminds me of Felix.

I pull out my phone to check on the game.

"What's the score?" Jane asks.

I look up from my phone. "It hasn't started yet."

"Sports fan?" Eddie asks, coming back into the room and taking a seat with his food.

"Not exactly."

"She's dating the quarterback of the football team," Jane says.

"I'm not sure that's accurate. We're hanging out."

"He asked her to be exclusive and she's freaking out." My best friend, once again, fills in for me.

I shoot her a playful glare.

Eddie snaps. "That's what it is. You're in love. I knew something was different."

My face instantly warms.

"I'm not…" I start, but then I think about it. Really think about it. I've always been attracted to him, but it isn't just that. I like spending time with him. He makes me smile and laugh. Sometimes I still feel absolutely frozen and nervous around him, but he also has a way of putting me at ease and making me feel so wanted and cared for. Besides, would I really want to be with someone who doesn't make my heart feel like it's going to leap out of my chest? I might not like how I clam up around him, but it's the equivalent of a gut check. Maybe some of it was fake, but I think most of it was more real than either of us realized. I never would have let myself fall for him, but I'm glad I did.

When I blink and look back at Eddie and Jane, they're both grinning at me.

"Well, crap. I think I'm in love with him."

Eddie laughs. His gaze slides to Jane. "And you? Wait. Don't tell me. You seem like the type that goes after the bad boys. Maybe a rock star?"

"Oh no," she says. "Rock stars are attention whores. I need all the focus on me."

His head falls back as he laughs. "I so get that."

"Jane is an amazing singer," I tell him proudly. "She's coming for your job one day."

"Oh my god. That's it." His eyes widen and his face lights up. "You're that girl from that show…Ivy. Ivy Greene. God, I loved that show. What was it called? You were so good. You still sing then?"

"Jane on a TV show?" I laugh it off, but when I glance at my friend, she looks like she's going to be sick. "Wait, what? You were on a TV show?"

My head swivels back and forth between them as an awkward silence hangs over the room.

"It was forever ago," she says, finally breaking the silence. "A lifetime ago. I quit acting when I was sixteen."

I'm speechless, and Eddie realizes he's just dropped a bombshell. "Shit. I'm sorry. You were really great. You were my first voice crush. You're not acting or singing anymore?"

"No, not really. I'm doing the college thing now."

"Right." He rubs at the back of his neck and looks between me and Jane.

Bev comes for him again and Eddie stands, still looking apologetic for outing Jane. "I'll be right back."

"Yeah, of course." I force a smile, but I'm still completely thrown by the Jane news.

Neither of us speaks until Eddie is out of the room.

"I'm so sorry," she says immediately.

"You were on a TV show?!"

"Yes. *Sing Your Heart Out.*" Her smile is pained. "And some commercials and other things."

"*Sing Your Heart Out,*" I say the name, trying to jog my memory. It sounds familiar, but I can't remember if I ever watched it.

"It was a show about a group of pop star sisters slogging through a Midwest middle school, and in the summers, traveling

the world and performing for millions of fans in their spare time."
She says it all a little dreamily and animated, like she's repeated it
a million times before. "It ran four seasons. Penelope was a guest
on the final season. Our uber-talented cousin who joined us for
part of the tour. That's where she got her big break."

"He called you Ivy."

"Ivy Greene. My agent didn't think Jane Greenfield had a
good enough ring to it."

"How is it possible I didn't know this?"

"I wanted to tell you a million times."

"So, you were some famous child actor and then you just
quit acting?"

"After the show was cancelled, I tried to get other jobs, but
after what felt like a million rejections, I decided to get my GED
and go to college."

"How has no one else recognized you?"

She shrugs. "It was a kids' show that ended almost five years
ago. I've grown like five inches since then and got boobs. Plus, I
had green hair."

"Green?" I shake my head. "Wait. I think I do remember it."
She smiles a little sheepishly.

"Why didn't you tell me? Do Daisy and Violet know?"

"No. No one knows."

"But, why not? You've done so many amazing things. You
should be proud."

"It's just that people sometimes get weird when they find out.
Especially people outside of LA. I got recognized at the Phoenix
airport once. This sweet girl, a year or two younger than us. And
when she asked what I was doing now, and I said I'd stopped acting, she looked like I'd said I decided to kick puppies and tell chil-
dren that the Easter Bunny is a sham."

I snort a laugh.

"At least when I was living here, I was just another out-of-
work childhood star, you know? LA is full of them. But when I

decided to go to Valley, it felt like a fresh start. A new me. And then I met you, Daisy, and Violet."

Childhood star?! That phrase is never going to sound normal. But I get wanting a new start.

We fall silent for a few moments. Wow. My best friend is a child star, and I'm hanging out in a rock star's dressing room. What even is my life?

"I should go and let you do your thing," she says. "This is why I didn't want to come. I was afraid someone might recognize me, and this is your weekend. I'm going to go back to the hotel and meet you back here later."

"Oh no, *Ivy*, you're sticking with me. I have so many more questions."

My interrogation is cut short when Eddie returns with Victor. Seeing the older man immediately sets my spine straight.

"Dahlia," he says gruffly. "We're down a runner tonight. How'd you like to fill in?"

"Me?" I squeak as my stomach bottoms out. I turn to look at Jane. I don't want to abandon her.

"Go. Go," she insists. "I'll be fine."

I'm whisked away, given a quick rundown of my job which is basically running costume changes during the show. There are two of us. I'm paired with a nice girl named Ria, who assures me that she won't let me screw up.

Hearing the show from back here is sort of surreal. Eddie's smooth voice is the soundtrack of a lot of behind-the-scenes' work. I have a whole new appreciation for everyone involved.

Every little break I get, I check the score of the game. When Valley wins, I feel such pride and excitement. I wish I were there. Not because I want to stand on the sidelines wearing his jersey where everyone can see, but because I want to show up for him like he has for me the past couple of months. He's always the first person to tell me I'm amazing, and I want to be that for him.

I find Jane in the crowd during a long stretch where Eddie doesn't need a wardrobe change.

"Hey!" she says, smiling when she sees me. "Are you done?"

"Not yet," I lean in so she can hear me over the noise. "Do you think we can get a flight back tonight after the show or...I don't know, drive?"

"You want to get back to Felix," she says with a knowing grin.

"I was an idiot. I should have said yes. I just hope it isn't too late."

"It's not," she assures me. "Let me see what I can find on flights, but worst case, we'll pull an all-night road trip and have you there in the morning."

"Thank you."

"No thanks needed. I'm so happy for you." She hugs me.

"Okay, I gotta get back. Ria mentioned Victor hires summer interns, so I want to impress them." I cross my fingers and hold up my hands for Jane to see.

I do my best to push Felix out of my mind for the next hour while I continue to run wardrobe with Ria, but when Jane texts me and says there aren't any more flights to Valley tonight, I'm disappointed. I know it's just one more day, but it's been twenty years of wishing for things to happen, and now I want to make my own dreams come true.

When it comes time for Eddie's last change, Ria and I take the pants I made with the basic tee to just off the stage where he runs as the band plays to keep the crowd occupied.

"How was it?" Eddie asks me, pulling off his sweaty shirt and taking the one Ria hands him.

"Amazing. Thank you for everything."

He grins, then changes into the pants. As he's buttoning them up, he asks, "And the boy? Have you talked to him yet?"

"No, not yet. He had a game and they'll be partying tonight to celebrate." After their win, I bet Felix is ready to relax after an especially grueling week. "I was hoping to catch a flight back tonight and make some grand gesture, but it's too late."

A lady wearing a headset is motioning impatiently for Eddie to get back out there.

"I'll talk to him when I get back tomorrow."

"Go now," he says. "This is my last change. Your job is done. Tell Bev to get you a car to LAX asap."

"There aren't any flights."

"I've got you," he says, then walks onstage to a crowd of screaming fans.

Chapter
THIRTY-SEVEN

Felix

O UR HOUSE WAS TOO SMALL TO HOST A PARTY Homecoming weekend. A lot of alumni come back, and the parties are huge. I'm standing in the backyard at The White House surrounded by more people than I've ever seen at a party.

"Did you see Bethany?" Lucas asks with a chuckle. "Girl is something else."

I grind my teeth. "Yeah."

"I wonder if she's going to wipe off your number before she fucks Armstrong," Brogan says and turns his head to watch her across the yard. "There is no way I'd hook up with a chick wearing some other guy's number. No freaking way."

My ex showed up to the game with my jersey number painted on her face. She tried to get my attention throughout the game, screaming and cheering for me from the front row, and then again after by showing up in the parking lot wanting to help me celebrate the win (and by celebrate, I mean sex), but when I reiterated that I wasn't interested, she decided to throw herself at the nearest guy.

She keeps looking over at me like she expects me to stomp over to her all jealous and pissed off. Why can't she get it through her head that I don't care anymore?

"Are you going to say something to her?" Archer asks.

I shake my head. I'm annoyed with Bethany, but I'm done putting any energy into thinking about her. Besides, I might be tired of her games, but Armstrong has to know the score by now. If he wants to be her plaything, he can be my guest.

"Is Dahlia coming?" Brogan asks.

"No, she's still in LA." She comes back tomorrow, but that feels like an eternity to wait. I fucking miss her. If I had any doubt about my feelings before this week, they'd be gone now. This isn't some casual hookup that I don't want to end.

"Too bad. I was hoping to recruit her for flip cup." Brogan tips back his beer and finishes it. "Anyone wanna play?"

"Why not," Lucas says.

Archer nods.

"Sure." I follow my buddies over to a table where a group is already in the middle of a game.

I fill my cup with beer while we wait for them to finish, then we divide up to play with equal teams. It's just my shitty luck that Bethany and Armstrong have the same idea. Or maybe it isn't luck at all. Bethany comes to stand next to me. I look across the table to Lucas. "Switch me?"

"Yep." He comes around without a second thought. I don't miss the scoff from Bethany.

Archer kicks things off for my team. I'm fourth in line and only half paying attention for my turn. My phone is burning a hole in my pocket. I think I feel it vibrate but know it's my mind playing tricks on me. Longest week ever. But we won the game today. I played well and proved to myself that I can keep playing great and care about someone else. Now I just need my girl to get back in town so I can prove it to her.

Archer goes, then Brogan. A chick I don't know is between us. As she chugs, I push out all the distractions and get ready.

When she finishes, I bring the cup to my mouth. The beer hits my lips at the same time a soft voice from behind me asks, "Can I play?"

That voice has my heart racing. I spin around, the game completely forgotten.

She smiles at me, and I think I forget to breathe for a few seconds. Fuck, I missed her.

"Dahlia." It's the only word I can get out.

"What the hell?" Brogan asks, then his voice lowers. "The ringer is here! Dahlia's on my team."

"We're playing a game here," Bethany calls from across the table. I'm vaguely aware that everything around us has stopped with Dahlia's interruption. Like I freaking care.

I ignore everyone and step forward to pull her into my arms. "Fuck. I'm so happy to see you. What are you doing here? I thought you had the concert tonight."

"I did," she says against my chest. "We left during the final song."

"You came back early? Why?" I pull back to look down at her face.

"It was the craziest day. Eddie loved the pants. I met his entire wardrobe team, then I got to work backstage with them during the concert."

My chest squeezes at the way her face lights up talking about it. "I knew he'd love them."

"It was all so amazing. I dressed a rock star and hung out with him and a famous actress. I got to see and do so many incredible things. I even flew home in a private jet." Her expression is one of awe and disbelief.

"Brag much?" Bethany mutters.

Dahlia keeps going, eyes still ablaze. "But I couldn't wait to get back to see you. Longest week ever."

"No kidding." I wrap my arms around her lower back. She hasn't said if she wants to be with me, but right now, I'm just so fucking glad she's here. With her here, I can show her just how serious I am about us.

"Congrats on the game. I checked the score so many times, I had Eddie's entire wardrobe team asking for updates."

"Oh, for the love of God!" Bethany screeches.

I'm ready to lay into her, but Dahlia steps in front of me. "Do you mind? I'm trying to have a moment here."

I hear Brogan laugh next to me.

"Yes, I mind," Bethany spits. "This whole desperate chick thing you have going on is pathetic."

"Call me whatever you want. I really don't care what you think of me."

"Maybe you should." Bethany props her hands on her hips. "You're making a fool of yourself. Felix will never end up with a girl like you and everyone here knows it."

"And let me guess, you're the kind of girl that he's going to end up with?" Dahlia asks.

"Someone like me, yeah. Someone who can stand next to him when he goes to the NFL. You aren't exactly what I would call red carpet ready. Let's face it, you'll never look as good with him as I did."

Dahlia laughs. "I'm not as pretty as you? That's the best you've got, really?"

Bethany's eyes narrow. Her gaze darts around the table at all the guys holding back laughter at her expense. "Whatever. You're both pathetic. I don't know why I ever wasted my time. He's hot but he's a total bore during the season. And he's not even that great in bed."

Dahlia's cheeks pinken, but she doesn't back down. "You are a vile human. I might not look as good with him, but I know that what he needs isn't someone who talks shit behind his back and sleeps with his teammates for attention. You don't care about him. I don't even think you ever took the time to get to know him. You couldn't have and said the awful things you did. Felix is kind and funny. He's considerate and dedicated and loyal. And he's the best hype man. I feel sorry for you that all you saw was a hot, successful guy to stand next to, because he's so much more than that."

The table is silent. Bethany looks pissed, but she doesn't say another word. Instead, she spins on her heel.

Before she can march off, Dahlia stops her. "Oh, and Bethany?"

Reluctantly, my ex turns back around. Her eyes are wild and angry, jaw tight.

Dahlia takes a step closer. Damn she's sexy standing up for herself and for me. I don't think anyone has ever fought so hard for me. It's straight fire. "I think the bad sex thing might be a *you* problem because he's *great* in bed."

Bethany's face is bright red as she storms off.

"Holy shit," Lucas says, admiration clear in his tone.

The table explodes in cheers and laughter.

"I'm sorry," Dahlia says when she turns back to face me. "I couldn't listen to her for one more sec—"

I frame her face and drop my lips to hers. She squeaks her surprise, but then tosses her arms around my neck and kisses me with everything she has.

"Fuck yeah," Archer says, and then everyone else cheers louder.

Dahlia laughs into my mouth and pulls back. "I take it you aren't mad I just yelled at your ex and told everyone you were good in bed."

"Are you kidding? That was awesome."

Brogan comes over to us and cuffs me on the shoulder. He looks at Dahlia as he says, "I have never seen anyone stand up to Bethany like that. Mad props, D."

"Thanks," she tells him. "Sorry about interrupting your game."

"All will be forgiven if you join my team for the next round."

"Oh no." I take Dahlia's hand and interlace our fingers. "She's busy."

"One game?" Brogan yells as I use our joined hands to tug her into me.

"Busy," I tell him and then lean down to take her mouth.

"Wait," she says against my lips.

I kiss her again. "Yeah?"

"Yes. My answer is yes. Of course, I want to be your girlfriend. If that's still what you want."

The smile on my face couldn't get any bigger. "I think you made that very clear to everyone at the party with your speech back there, hot stuff."

She laughs and a faint blush creeps onto her face. "I meant it. All of it. You're the best person I know."

I press a kiss to her lips, lingering there to soak up this feeling.

Dahlia sighs. "And wow, can you kiss."

I bark a laugh and then brush my fingers along her jaw and behind her neck. "Then stop interrupting me, babe. I'm just getting started."

Chapter
THIRTY-EIGHT

Dahlia

"I FORGOT MY KEY."

Felix is too busy kissing my neck to hear me, so I turn to face him. "I'm locked out. We have to go back and see if we can find one of the girls to let us in."

"Is your window unlocked?" he asks.

"Yeah. I think so. Why?"

A delicious smirk plays over his face as he bites his lower lip. "Oh, no."

"Oh, yes. Tracking down one of your roommates could take forever." He pulls me against him. He's hard. To be fair, we stayed at the party way longer than we should have for two people that couldn't keep their hands off each other.

I think even Brogan was happy when we walked away from the flip cup table. As it turns out, we're very into PDA as a real couple.

"What if I fall and break my neck?"

"A little faith, babe. I'd never let you fall."

I follow him over to the side fence. He helps me up first and then instructs me to pull myself up onto the roof. Is he serious? I think I've only done a handful of pullups in my entire life, and it wasn't up onto a roof in a skirt. When I don't manage to do it, he hops onto the fence behind me and rests his hands at my hips. "On three."

He counts down, and then I jump and use all my strength to try to lift my body onto the roof of the porch. Felix's hands move to my ass, and by his groan, I know he can also see right up my skirt. I'd be self-conscious if I weren't worried about falling to my death.

By some miracle (and a lot of help from Felix), I successfully get onto the roof and step back so Felix can do the same. He opens my window and motions for me to go in first. As soon as we're inside, he's kissing me again.

He walks me backward toward the bed. I fall onto the mattress, and he stares down at me with heat in his gaze. He pulls off his black T-shirt, balls it up, and tosses it on the floor.

Leaving Eddie's concert early was the best idea ever. I owe him. I can't imagine waiting even one more day for this.

"Remember that time you said you wanted to climb me like a tree?"

The laugh that breaks free sends warmth to my face. "Yes."

"Let's do that."

I scramble up and throw myself at him. He catches me and his hands go around my butt to keep me in place. Once I'm steady, legs wrapped around his waist and arms around his neck, his hands glide under my skirt and cup my ass. His touch mixed with the way the hard bulge in his pants hits my core, makes my entire body tremble.

"I think I should have gotten you naked first."

Laughing, he sets me down. I hurry to get his jeans undone and push them down over his strong, thick thighs.

"Stupid hot," I mumble as I stare at his muscular and chiseled body.

"Right back at ya," he says as he runs the pad of this thumb along my bottom lip.

"We could do the other thing I said in the video too."

His brow furrows like he's thinking back to remember exactly what I said.

"Lick every inch of your body."

His eyes darken. "Later. I need to be inside you."

I grab a handful of condoms from the nightstand and dump them on the bed. He smirks. "Here's hoping."

He rips one open and covers himself. Then instead of picking me back up so I can make good on my climbing him like a tree vow, he covers my body with his. Tenderly he nips and teases my lips as he slowly pushes inside me.

He pulls back to look into my eyes. "Are you okay?"

"Perfect," I rasp out the word as goosebumps dot my arms. "Boyfriend."

"Girlfriend." He brushes his lips over mine. My body clenches around him.

"Oh fuck," he mutters. "You're squeezing me so tight."

"Say it again."

"Girlfriend." He moves slowly out and then pushes back in. That word is magic. I'm his. I can't believe it.

My heart is beating so fast. Every thrust sends a new wave of pleasure.

"It feels so good. You're so deep. Are you bigger than average?" I don't give him time to respond. It's either say every thought in my head or combust. And I don't want this to end yet. "I like you so much."

I have just enough wherewithal to bite back the words *I think I'm actually in love with you.*

"So much," he parrots.

"Like an insane amount." He shifts up on the next thrust and hits a spot that makes me gasp. "Do that again."

Laughing, he brings his lips down to cover my mouth, effectively silencing me. I cling to his neck and press my body tighter against his as he moves in and out at a quicker pace. I feel his muscles tense as he gets close.

"Are you there?"

"Yes, I think so." Every one of Felix's touches feels like I'm going to detonate.

He slides down my body. I whine at the loss of him inside me, but when his mouth covers my pussy, I cry out. His tongue flicks over my clit and then down my slit. I gasp and writhe.

"I'm gonna come," I tell him when I can't take it a second more before exploding.

He teases me longer, testing just how close I am before moving from between my legs. His face is covered in me. He wipes his mouth with the back of his hand. "Turn over, babe."

I hesitate, not sure where this is going, but he places a kiss on my hip bone and then nudges me to roll onto my stomach.

He wraps a hand around my hair and uses it to tilt my head back.

"Girlfriend." He punctuates the word with a searing kiss, then his free hand slides beneath my stomach and lifts me onto my knees and elbows.

With my hair still wrapped around one hand, he pulls me back onto his dick.

All the air is knocked from my lungs as he fills me so completely, and I know I'll never be the same.

"Still with me?" he asks.

I can't speak, so I nod. His grip on my hair brings a little pain with the motion. "Yes. You don't have to worry. I'm good. Don't hold back. I want the full Felix Walters experience."

He leans down and bites my shoulder. "You mean the Dahlia Brady effect."

"I just want you. Whatever that is."

"Same, babe. Same." He drops a kiss to the same spot where he bit me a second ago and then continues pushing in and out of me until my limbs are like jelly and I don't think I can hold myself up.

One of his arms hooks around my stomach, holding me in place. His fingers glide down, and he rubs a slow circle over the sensitive bud.

"Felix," I pant as I shatter beneath him. And the resounding groan he lets out as he follows makes my heart skip. This sexy, strong man is mine.

He pulls out slowly. The muscles in my core fight to keep him inside me, even as my arms give out and I fall face down onto the bed. He drops next to me and pulls me into him. I don't know how I can be so tired and so ready to go again at the same time. My hair is knotted and sticking to my face and his chest.

"Ugh. My hair is everywhere."

He chuckles as he smooths it out of my face. "Sit up for a second."

"What?"

"Hand me the hair tie around your wrist and sit up. I have a solution."

Visions of my hair wrapped around Felix's hand moments ago flash through my mind, but his touch is soft when his fingers brush the long strands back out of my face again.

"O-kay," I say slowly. I sit and give him the black elastic hair tie.

I feel his fingers work through my hair. My scalp tingles. Who knew that having a guy play with my hair was such a turn-on?

"That feels so good." I close my eyes and feel my shoulders relax.

I lose track of time as he continues. Eventually, he kisses my neck and says, "All done."

I run a hand along the back of my head, then swivel around to face him. "You braided my hair?"

He grins.

I get up off the bed and go over to the mirror. Not just a braid. A French braid. "How?" I ask. "Is this some sort of kink?"

His body shakes with silent laughter. "Not that I'm aware of."

I look at him wide-eyed for an explanation.

"I have two sisters who really liked to do makeovers when we were younger," he admits with a shrug, looking a little embarrassed. "Now you know my secret talent."

"I'm impressed."

"I can do a Dutch braid, too. And I think I remember how to do a fishtail braid, but it's been a while so don't hold me to that."

"I can't even braid my own hair."

"Now you don't need to." He winks. "Want me to try another?"

I climb on top of him. "Later. I still need to make good on a few things."

Chapter
THIRTY-NINE

Felix

"OH MY GO…" My words trail off as I cover my mouth with a fist.

"You like my costume?" Dahlia asks and turns in a circle.

I don't know where to look first. The black shorts that barely cover her ass, my jersey tied up on one side, the black eye paint smudged under her eyes, or the football in one hand. The football is a weird focal point, I know, but it's just so hot seeing her small hands wrapped around the worn leather.

"You definitely wore it better." I close the distance between us and glide one hand around her back to grab her ass.

Dahlia uses the football to push on my chest, and her gaze scans my costume. "And you. You look —"

"Ridiculous," Brogan interrupts. "What are you supposed to be?"

"I'm her," I say, tipping my head toward my girl.

"And I'm him." Dahlia leans against me.

"I get it," he says, looking between us and nodding. "Cute."

Cute? Psha. I'm killing the golfer look. I have on a pink polo—the one with the little green alligator, of course, black slacks, and matching black hat. Oh, and a golf club, which is hooked over my shoulder.

"The real question is what are you?" Dahlia asks, brows lifting as she giggles into my chest.

"Ah. One sec." Brogan pulls down a pair of sunglasses from his head to cover his eyes and then holds his hands out.

White T-shirt, hideous brown vest, khakis... "I don't get it."

He holds up a finger and then grabs a nearby Archer and pulls him over. Archer has on a Red Wings hockey jersey.

"*Ferris Bueller's Day Off*!" Dahlia exclaims.

Brogan grins at her. "That's right. Pretty awesome, right?"

Dahlia looks to me. "We should have done *Can't Buy Me Love*."

"Still haven't seen it," I tell her.

"We're watching it. Soon." She links her arm through mine. "Let's go check out everyone else's costumes."

Sigma is where everyone is at tonight. There are a lot of girls in sexy animal costumes and guys in flight suits and aviator sunglasses. We stumble on Violet and Gavin. He smiles sheepishly as both Dahlia and I start laughing.

"Yeah, yeah, get your jabs in," he says.

"Anne and Captain Wentworth?" Dahlia asks.

"Hear that? I'm a captain," Gavin says and pulls at the fabric around his neck.

"Vi, I can't believe you made these. They're incredible." Dahlia steps closer to get a better look at the complicated-looking dress her friend is wearing.

"Thanks. Have you seen Jane yet?" Vi asks.

"No, and the suspense is killing me. Is she here?"

"I haven't seen her, but Daisy and Jordan are over by the keg. You won't even recognize Daisy," Vi says.

"Look for the guy in the wife beater," Gavin calls as we keep walking in search of them.

We don't make it far before we're stopped by some of my teammates wanting to have a good laugh at my costume and ogle my girl. I let them have a pass for the night. She's smoking hot. It would be hard not to notice.

Lucas dressed up as the Joker—the Jared Leto version. Stella is the cheerleader from *Stranger Things*, and I'm never going to be able to unsee Teddy dressed up as Buddy the Elf. Holly is Buddy's elf girlfriend, Jovi, of course.

"I still haven't seen Jane," Dahlia says as we get another drink. "Or Daisy and Jordan."

"They're around here somewhere," I say and wrap my arms around her hips. "And in the meantime, I know how we can kill some time."

Her eyes twinkle as she brings her hands up to my shoulders. "What a coincidence. I had a few ideas of my own."

I lean down and whisper in her ear, "Do they include my hands down the front of those tight shorts?"

Her breath hitches, and she nods. "Maybe we should walk to your place."

It's almost a mile away, but if it's the difference between making out with her and not, I'm tempted. Luckily, I know a spot at Sigma. An old teammate was a member here and told me about it, but I had to promise not to share it. Like I'd give up the details on a secret make-out spot.

"I have a better idea. Little halftime show for my hottie QB."

She giggles. "Are we going to get dirty on the back nine? Hit it into the rough? Choke down on the shaft? Get it into the hole?"

My dick twitches. These slacks are not going to do a good job of hiding it if I get a hard-on in the middle of this party. "Good god, woman."

"Golf has the best dirty phrases." Her smile is all sweetness and charm.

"Come on. I know a spot where we can bang it in or bump and run."

"I know those are football terms, but I have no idea what you just said," she says as I pull her behind me.

"Real happy to show you, hot stuff."

We go up a flight of stairs off the kitchen and then hang a left. There's a bathroom at the end of the hallway. The way it was told to me, it's the president of the frat's private wing. The rest of the bedrooms are on the other side of the house, and there are restrooms downstairs so people don't think to come up here.

I turn the handle and then bend down to bring my lips to Dahlia's and walk backward into the space.

"I have had dreams, *vivid dirty dreams*, of fucking you in this jersey."

"As long as you don't yell 'touchdown' as you come." She rushes to undo my pants.

Laughing, I mutter, "The things that come out of your mouth."

"It's your fault. You broke the barrier. I used to not be able to speak around you and now I can't stop every thought from spilling out." She shoves my pants and boxer briefs down and my dick springs free.

"Every thought, huh?" I slide my hand down the front of her shorts. "What are you thinking now?"

"I like you," she says. "*So* much. And that feels…" She trails off when my fingers slide through her slick center.

"Already so wet."

"And you're so hard." She reaches out and strokes me gently.

I'm too keyed up to let her explore for long. I lift her onto the vanity and strip her out of the tiny shorts and even tinier thong. In the week since we've been official, we've spent a lot of time naked, but fuck if seeing her like this doesn't hit me with the force of a burly linebacker every single time.

I swipe my tongue along her folds. She leans back and scoots closer to the edge to give me better access. While lapping her up, I reach down for my wallet and grab a condom. I want to eat her until she writhes against my tongue, but I also need to be inside her.

"What are you thinking now?" I ask as I cover myself and line up the head of my cock at the entrance to her pretty pussy.

She hesitates, then lets out a heavy sigh. "I'm the luckiest girl in the world."

I push in slowly, and we moan in unison. It's never felt like this. Nothing feels better than being connected to her, body and soul. She owns me. It's too soon to be as gone for her as I am, but I hardly had a choice. She came into my life like a snowstorm in the desert. Quiet and beautiful and completely unexpected.

She arches into me as I find a rhythm that has us both burning hot and fast. She comes first, squeezing my dick so hard I see stars and follow along after her.

Her breathing, quick and shallow, is the only sound above the steady thump of the music outside. I pull out, then tie off the condom and trash it.

"What are you thinking now?" I ask, taking in her rosy cheeks and limp body.

"There are no thoughts right now. You screwed them out of me."

"Mmmm." I drag my thumb along her bottom lip. "Want to know what I'm thinking?"

"It's pretty clear what you're thinking," she says as she eyes my dick. It's true, part of me is already ready for round two.

"I'm always thinking about being inside you, babe. Next time I want you in my bed so I can see my name across your back as I pound into you from behind."

She laughs lightly, hops down off the vanity on wobbly legs, and pulls on her panties and shorts. I get dressed too, but before we leave our little haven and return to the party, I hug her to me.

Her hair is pulled back in a low ponytail, and I run my hand down it and tug gently so her head tilts up. The smile on her face is a straight punch through the chest. So fucking beautiful.

"Ask me what I'm thinking."

Her expression is happy and amused. Or maybe that's just my own happiness reflected back.

"What are you thinking?" she asks.

My pulse kicks up before I even say the words. "I love you."

Her lips part and eyes widen. Her body tenses.

Oh shit. Panic hits me all at once. Maybe I misread her. She tells me she likes me so much, or likes me an insane amount, or some variation, constantly. I assumed that was her way of saying the words that feel way too early to say, without really saying them. I'm second-guessing that now as she stares back at me dumbstruck.

"If you're not there yet—"

Her hand shoots up and covers my mouth. "I love you too."

I exhale audibly.

"Of course, I do. How could I not?"

The relief I feel makes me dizzy. "It's my abs, right? Maybe my charm and wit. Or my magic fingers."

"It's all of you." She tangles her hands into my hair and kisses me.

That's the thing about Dahlia. She sees past all the superficial bullshit. I'm not just a guy with terrific arms (her words, obviously), or a successful college quarterback, or a guy most likely heading to the NFL. That stuff doesn't mean anything to her. I have no doubt she'd support me the same way if I were playing beer league softball. And as long as she's there cheering me on, the rest will work itself out.

I'm considering lifting her back onto the vanity for round two, when the door opens.

"Oh, sorry," Jordan says, quickly averting his gaze, then does a double-take and realizes it's me and Dahlia. He shakes his head at me. "How do you know about this spot?"

"How do you?" I fire back. "And what the hell are you wearing?"

"He's Shawn Mendes," Daisy says, coming in behind him.

My brows lift when I get a good look at her. Ripped, skin-tight black jeans, a mesh tank top with a black bra underneath. Big hair, big lashes. I don't know who the hell she's supposed to be until she unfolds a poster in her right hand and holds it up. In big, glittery letters it reads I heart Shawn.

"You're his groupie?" I ask.

Her smile is big and pleased at my guess. "Number one groupie."

"Jane's downstairs," Dahlia says, glancing down at her phone. "She says she'll meet us out back."

I grab my girl's hand and tug her toward the door.

"Oh, I can't wait to see," Daisy says.

"But we just got here," Jordan whines, as they follow us back downstairs and outside to the party.

It doesn't take long to find Jane. There's a crowd of people around the DJ table. As we get closer, I realize the music playing is actually Jane singing. Her blonde hair is dyed green, and she has on a sequined gold dress that catches the light as she moves around, belting out some song I've never heard before.

I spot Lucas and come to a stop next to him. "What's going on?"

"She's Ivy Greene," he says.

"Who?"

Dahlia gasps when she finally sees her friend at the center of everyone's attention.

I tilt my head toward her. "I don't get it. Who's she supposed to be?"

"Herself," Dahlia says.

Chapter
FORTY

Dahlia

I WAKE UP WITH FELIX'S ARM WRAPPED AROUND MY WAIST. I keep my eyes closed, basking in the feel of him a little longer. When his hands grip me and pull me against him, my body heats. I wriggle against his dick and instantly his hold on me tightens.

"Morning, gorgeous," he says, voice gruff.

"Morning." I turn around in his arms and bring one hand up to palm his cheek. Dark stubble dots his otherwise perfect jaw. I still can't believe it sometimes. He's here in my bed, smiling at me and looking at me like I'm someone that makes him incredibly happy.

I'm still wearing his jersey from my costume last night. We had plans that involved a bed and this jersey that we never got around to, but I'm ready now.

"Good morning," Jane chirps from the other side of him. I still, and then peer over Felix to see her lying in the pillow fort.

She changed out of her dress and into shorts and a T-shirt, but her green hair is still styled straight, and her makeup is smudged.

After waltzing into the party last night dressed as her character from the hit TV show and singing the theme song, people went nuts. Some recognized her immediately, others had to look it up, but by the time we left the party, Ivy Greene was the talk of Valley U.

My plans with Felix were interrupted when she came home last night. The three of us stayed up so late talking, I must have fallen asleep mid-conversation because I don't remember saying good night.

"Morning, Hannah Montana," Felix drawls out. He props himself up on an elbow and grins at her.

"Ha, ha," she says the words without actually laughing, but she smiles.

I sit cross-legged in bed and hug my pillow. "Last night was amazing, babe. I have never heard you sing like that. You've been holding back."

Jane smiles, looking almost embarrassed. A first, I think.

I glance at Felix. "Have you heard from Lucas this morning? He was seriously freaking out. I'm pretty sure he said he had posters of Jane in his room growing up."

"I'm afraid to check my phone," he says.

"He showed me his Instagram. He's following every single Ivy Greene fan account." Her laugh, the same old Jane laugh, settles any nerves I had about everyone finding out about her past. She's my best friend and I'm fiercely protective of her. I'm glad at least that Daisy and Vi finally know too. It was torture keeping it from them, but I wasn't planning on her making the announcement quite so dramatically. I should have known. Same old Jane.

"What should we do today?" I ask, looking from my best friend to my boyfriend.

"All of my ideas involve this bed." Felix pulls me back down next to him and his arm slides up to rest just under my boobs.

"The more hot girls, the better?" I tease.

He chuckles. "Maybe not in this instance."

Jane sits up. "Okay, okay. I can take a hint. I'm going to shower and give you two some time to…whatever, but let's do a movie day."

"Yes!" I agree. "Oh, we have to watch *Can't Buy Me Love*. Felix still hasn't seen it."

"You're going to love it." She gets to her feet and goes to the door, but before she leaves, she looks directly at Felix. "You have thirty minutes alone with my girl. I'll be back."

"Knock first," he warns and then rolls on top of me as soon as the door closes behind her.

"Better work quick, Walters." I run both hands over his biceps.

"Quick I can do. You with that smudged eye black is a weird fantasy I didn't know I was so into until now."

My hands shoot to my face. I completely forgot to wipe off the black painted under both eyes.

His body shakes as he laughs. "Super hot, babe."

"Shut up." I smack at his chest.

"No, I'm serious. It's really doing something for me. Do you still have that football around somewhere? I have the urge to tackle you."

"You're so weird."

"But I'm a weirdo with a surprise." He drops his mouth to mine and then pulls back. "Look up."

"Look up?" I repeat as I tilt my head back and glance toward the ceiling before I can think too hard about why, but even if I had run through the possibilities, seeing a giant poster of Felix's face wouldn't have been one I came up with.

I burst into laughter. "When did you put that up there?"

"Yesterday. Jane let me in before the party." He grins proudly. "You said if you had a poster of me, that's where you'd put it."

"I love it." I glance between his giant head on my ceiling and him on top of me. "I love you."

"I love you too." He presses another kiss to my lips, then glances up. "It's creepy, isn't it?"

"A little bit," I admit. I wrap my arms around his shoulders. "Now I have the fantasy and the reality. And if you make me mad, I have a nice dart board."

His gaze darkens. "No darts."

I swear I played darts with one other guy once and the man has boycotted the game for life. "You won. I'm all yours. I think you can let it go."

"Never," he says, but he's smiling.

"It wasn't ever really a competition, you know? You own my heart."

"Right back at ya, hot stuff." His eyes crinkle at the corner and his mouth twists into a playful smirk. "But I still fucking hate darts."

EPILOGUE

Felix

COLLEGE IS OVER. GRADUATION WAS A MONTH AGO. I'VE packed up my car and moved out of the house I shared with my buddies for the past three years. And I got a job. I have to relocate to Minnesota (winters are going to be a bitch), but the pay is pretty good and most of my new co-workers seem pretty nice. Except one. Out of all the teams we could have ended up on, Beau and I were both drafted to the same one.

I've been going against him for so long, it's going to be super weird wearing the same jersey. Stella is stoked. I think we really stressed her out last year every time we played each other. Including the conference championship where Beau's team beat us. It was a tough loss, but it was a great season and I have no regrets.

So, life is good. There's just one more thing I need to do before I head north.

I pull up to the Valley U golf course and grab my clubs from the trunk. It's early, but in June in Arizona, it doesn't matter what time it is—it's hot. But the heat isn't what has me sweating as I walk into the clubhouse.

Dahlia spots me immediately. Her face lights up and it calms me just a little.

"Hey," she says as she throws her arms around my neck. When she pulls back, I do my best not to look down at her boobs. I swear she wore a low-cut shirt today just to fuck with me. She takes my hand. "My dad is waiting outside."

"Great." I finally peek at her cleavage now that I know her dad is out of sight.

"Do you want to hit some balls first? Our tee time isn't for another ten minutes."

"Sure. Yeah."

"I'm so glad you wanted to come today." She swings our hands between us.

"Are you kidding? I wouldn't miss a chance to see you choking up on the shaft."

I get a playful, haughty look that makes me laugh.

"When's the last time you played?" she asks as she grabs a golf club from her bag strapped to the back of a golf cart.

"It's been a minute," I admit.

Listen, when your super hot and awesome girlfriend asks you to golf with her dad, you say yes. You say yes even if your clubs have been collecting dust in your parents' garage for the better part of a decade.

She grabs us a small bucket of balls and we walk to the driving range. Her dad takes a few steps toward us when he sees us approach. He moves his club to his gloved, left hand and extends the right. "Felix. Good to see you again."

"You too, sir."

"Great day to be on the course." Paul smiles at me. He's such a nice guy. This is the third time I've seen him, but from the moment Dahlia introduced us, he's been so welcoming and kind.

It doesn't make today any less stressful though. I've got a

diamond ring in my bag, and I need to somehow get permission to marry his daughter, while trying to remember how to swing a golf club.

Dahlia dumps the balls onto an open spot for me next to her dad, and I select a club and stretch with it to loosen up.

"Oh my gosh. That's Keira Brooks!" Dahlia's voice is filled with awe as she stares back toward the clubhouse.

"Who?" I ask.

"Keira Brooks. She is a pro golfer. She won the U.S. Open last year. She went to Valley." Dahlia spits out facts like they're going to help me piece together who she's talking about.

When I stare back at her blankly, she gives me a disbelieving eye roll. "Oh my gosh. Long brown hair, white tank, black skirt."

"Ah, yeah." I shake my head. "Never seen her before."

"She's a legend. She's killing it on tour. And that guy with her is her husband. He's a swing coach. He has this really amazing online coaching site."

"Sounds cool. You should go say hi."

"Oh no. We've never met. She was gone from Valley before I got here."

"So?"

"What would I even say?" Her dark blue eyes widen at the prospect.

"How about, 'Hi, I'm Dahlia. I'm a huge fan.'"

"No," she says, but keeps staring at her.

"Go on. I'll keep an eye on you and if it looks like you're frozen and staring at the poor girl like a star-struck groupie, I'll come save you."

"Okay." She doesn't move. "I'm gonna do it."

It's another few seconds before she finally starts walking that way.

Paul laughs softly when she's out of earshot. "I'm impressed."

"Why's that?" I move to stand closer to him but keep my gaze on Dahlia as she approaches Keira.

"We saw Keira and Lincoln last summer at a tournament. She wouldn't go near them."

"Second time's the charm, I guess."

"You've been good for her."

I'm surprised by his words. I tear my gaze away from Dahlia and look at him. "I'm trying. She's incredible and I like reminding her."

His head nods slowly and he rests his weight on the golf club.

This is my shot to ask him while she's not around, so I take a deep breath. "Actually, sir, I wanted to ask you something before she gets back."

"All right," he says.

"I bought a ring, and before I head up to Minnesota, I'd like to ask your daughter to marry me." I get it out all at once. I had a much more eloquent speech prepared, but I kinda feel like I want to throw up.

"Is there a question in there somewhere?"

Before I can answer, Dahlia comes running back. Her smile stretches out across her entire face. "Oh my gosh. She's so nice. She even invited me to golf with them."

"That's amazing. You'll have so much fun."

"I'm not leaving you two," she says, like she's offended I'd suggest otherwise.

"Felix and I can handle eighteen by ourselves. Can't we?" her dad asks.

I swallow thickly. "Yeah."

Oh shit. That sounds ominous. Is he going to interrogate me for the next few hours? Who am I kidding? Of course, he is.

"Yeah," I say again more convincingly. "We'll be great. Don't worry about us."

"Okay." She steps forward and kisses me. "Have fun." Then she looks to her dad. "Take it easy on him, Daddy."

He waves her off. I have a real bad feeling as she takes off with Keira and Lincoln, but at least one of us is going to have a good time today.

Paul slides his club into his bag, pulls off his glove and sticks it in his back pocket, and then looks at me. "I like you, Felix. I'll tell you what. You beat me today and I'll buy dinner tonight to celebrate."

"And if I lose?"

He just grins.

Fuuuuck.

By hole three, I stop keeping score. By six, I have blisters (even on my gloved-hand). And by thirteen, my shirt is so wet, I look like I dumped a beer over my head (and believe me, I thought about it).

Paul is cool and collected as I tee up on eighteen.

I wince a little as I grip the club. "New deal. I get par on this one and you at least think about it. You don't even need to buy dinner."

He chuckles. "Par, huh? You haven't gotten close to par all day."

"I'm just finding a rhythm," I lie.

"Whatever you say."

"Deal?" I ask.

He nods, then rests both hands on his club to watch me tee off. The last hole of the Valley U golf course is a par three. The green is a straight shot less than two hundred yards away, but there's a lake in the middle of it. And since my short game is atrocious, I need to get close to the pin in one if I have any hope of tapping it in for three.

Inhaling slowly, I glance down the fairway and adjust my stance. *Here goes freaking nothing.* I don't drop it in the water, so that's something. Paul hits a beauty, putting his ball within a foot of the pin.

He doesn't say a word as we drive up to the green. Or when I march toward my ball with a look of desperation on my face. I pace back and forth, checking my line and saying about a million silent prayers. I take my best shot, which goes a foot wide and two short.

Paul taps his ball in and then stands back to wait for me. "One more shot. You can do it."

His encouragement gives me a little extra pep in my step. My hands tremble as I grip the putter, but I take a deep breath and let it fly. I hold my breath as the ball circles the hole and rolls inches away. I groan and let my head fall back.

I don't hear Paul approach. He claps me on the shoulder and then chuckles when he removes his wet hand. "You've got grit, kid. You just don't quit, do you?" He laughs again. "Dahlia's mom and I would be delighted to have you as part of the family."

"You would? But I thought…"

"I was messing with you. I'm old. I gotta get my kicks where I can these days." We walk back to the cart and he unzips a side pocket on his golf bag and pulls out a red jewelry box. "This was my mother's. I know it's probably not as fancy or expensive as the one you picked out, but I know Dahlia's always liked it."

"Thank you." I open the box and stare down at the ring. It's perfect. "Thank you so much. You just happened to have this with you today?"

There's a twinkle in his eye as he says, "I had a feeling that's why you asked me to come this weekend."

I surprise us both by hugging him. Then I remember I'm soaking wet. "Sorry."

"Yeah, maybe you want to shower first and then meet us for dinner," he suggests.

"Good idea."

"Go." He tips his head. "I'll tell Dahlia you're meeting us there."

When I get to The Hideout, Dahlia's waiting for me in a booth by herself.

"Hey," I say, kissing her and then dropping into the seat across from her. "Where's your dad?"

"He said to send his apologies, but he was tired from today, so he was going to order room service at the hotel, but he gave me two hundred bucks to order whatever we want."

"Oh, that's too bad."

"Did you guys have fun today?"

"Fun might be a stretch, but not because your dad isn't great. I'm a terrible golfer," I admit.

She's obviously holding back a laugh. "I heard. I'm sorry. Thanks for being such a good sport anyway."

"It was nothing." The water glass feels great against my beaten-up hands. "Tell me about your day."

She does as we order food, then wait for it. And she's still talking about it when we finish and pay. I love that she had such a great time. Seeing her excited is even worth the blood, sweat, and tears I shed today.

We head back to her house after dinner. Both of us are quiet, soaking in our last night at Valley together. Dahlia heads to LA for a summer internship with Eddie Dillon's wardrobe team, and I'm moving north. I'll be back to visit her in the fall, of course, but it'll never be quite like this.

In her room, she plops down on the bed. "What do you want to do?"

"I have a few ideas, but first, I have two gifts for you."

"Two?"

"Yep. Close your eyes."

She does, smiling and sitting a little straighter.

I take a seat on the bed in front of her with both hands behind my back. "Okay. Open your eyes and pick a hand."

"I love this game." She pulls her bottom lip between her teeth and then lets it slide free. "Right."

Moving my right hand in front of me, I slowly open it to reveal the ring.

She gasps. "Is that…" she trails off, then starts again. "Are you…"

I find I'm a little frozen now that this moment is here. Everything I want depends on her answer.

"I love you so much. I know the next year is going to suck being apart, but I don't want to wait another day to ask you to be mine forever. Marry me?"

Her blue eyes are filled with tears. She nods, and I remove the ring and slip it onto her left ring finger.

"Oh my gosh, Felix. It's beautiful. And huge. I can't wear this around campus. What if I lose it?" She wipes her tears away and then hugs me around the neck. When I don't wrap my arms around her, she pulls back. "What's in the other hand?"

I hold out my left hand and open it. Dahlia looks from me to the box and back again. "I don't understand."

I flip it open and show her the ring her dad gave me today. More tears fall. "Is that my grandmother's?"

I take out the ring and toss the box on the bed beside us, then remove the ring I just put on and slide this one on instead. "I picked out the first one. I wanted something big and flashy to show you just how happy you make me. I'd buy you a dozen more if you lost it, babe. But something tells me this one is probably more you."

"I love them both so much," she says. "I used to sneak it out of my grandma's jewelry box and wear it." She stares down at her hand and then to the ring I'm still holding. "But that one is more beautiful than anything I ever could have imagined, and I love that you picked it for me.

I put the other ring on her right finger. "Then they're both yours. Two rings for the number of lifetimes it's going to take to show you how much I love you."

PLAYLIST

- If You Had My Love (Kav Verhouzer Remix) by Twopilots feat. De Hofnar
- Santa Monica by Everclear
- Get It Girl by Saweetie feat. Raedio
- Sure Thing by Miguel
- Champions by NLE Choppa
- Pretty Girl Magic by Moonlight Scorpio
- I Don't Fuck With You by Big Sean feat. E-40
- One Dance by Drake feat. Wizkid, Kyla
- Graduated by Two Friends feat. Bryce Vine
- Need to Know by Doja Cat
- Bejeweled by Taylor Swift
- I Am Woman by Emmy Meli
- Stupid Feelings by 220 Kid feat. Lany
- Finally (Cannot Hide It) by Amorphous feat. Kelly Rowland, CeCe Penis
- Nonsense by Sabrina Carpenter
- Bloody Mary by Lady Gaga
- Cool for the Summer – Sped Up (Nightcore) by Demi Lovato feat. Speed Radio
- Escapism by RAYE feat. 070 Shake
- Players – DJ Saige Remix by Coi Leray feat. DJ Saige
- Calm Down by Rema feat. Selena Gomez
- Cold Water by Major Lazer feat. Justin Bieber, MØ
- Uh Oh by Tate McRae
- Blank Space by Taylor Swift
- If We Ever Broke Up by Mae Stephens

Also by
REBECCA JENSHAK

Campus Wallflowers Series
Tutoring the Player
Hating the Player
Scoring the Player
Tempting the Player

Campus Nights Series
Secret Puck
Bad Crush
Broken Hearts
Wild Love

Smart Jocks Series
The Assist
The Fadeaway
The Tip-Off
The Fake
The Pass

Wildcat Hockey Series
Wildcat
Wild about You
Wild Ever After

Standalone Novels
Sweet Spot
Electric Blue Love

About the
AUTHOR

Rebecca Jenshak is a *USA Today* bestselling author of new adult and sports romance. She lives in Arizona with her family. When she isn't writing, you can find her attending local sporting events, hanging out with family and friends, or with her nose buried in a book.

Sign up for her newsletter for book sales and release news.

WWW.REBECCAJENSHAK.COM

84739558R00164